Darkness in Malaga

Paul S. Bradley

Paul S. Bradley is a pen name.
© 2018 Paul Bradley of Nerja, Spain.
The moral right of Paul Bradley to be identified as the author of this work has been asserted in accordance with the Copyright, Design and Patents Act, 1988.
All rights reserved.
No part of this publication may be reproduced or transmitted in any form or by any means, electronic or mechanical, including photocopy, recording, or any information storage and retrieval system, without permission in writing from the publisher.

This is a work of fiction. Any resemblance of characters to actual persons, living or dead, is purely coincidental.

Editor; Paul Dinas; www.pauldinasbookeditor.com
Cover Illustration; Jill Carrott; www.virtue.es
Layout; Paul Bradley
Darkness in Malaga is the first volume of the Andalusian Mystery Series
Publisher; Paul Bradley, Nerja, Spain.
First Edition; January 2018
Contact: info@paulbradley.eu
www.paulbradley.eu
All rights reserved.

ISBN: 1541132661
ISBN 13: 9781541132665

Available in eBook on Kindle and most other online bookstores. See website for details.

Dedication

To the memory of Cecilia Natalia Coria Olivares, murdered in Nerja on September 28, 2008.

Your stolen life inspired this author to write.

Acknowledgements

Sadly, my mentor for Darkness in Malaga, author, humorist and old friend Drew Launay, died before this first edition was published. I hope it is worthy of his exacting standards.

My heartfelt thanks go to him along with Simon Cole, Jill Carrott, Daisy Carrott, Michael Kellough, Elizabeth Francis, Fran Poelman and Renate Bradley.

Paul S. Bradley

Darkness in Málaga

1

"Pray that the surf is gentle tonight, brother," said Karim Idrissi gruffly in Moroccan Arabic, as he wrestled with the steering wheel of the battered Land Rover.

"And a fair southerly breeze to blow them toward Spain after the fuel runs out," responded Mohamed Idrissi, hanging on tightly to the grab rail in front of him as they bounced down the rough, steep track through dense pine trees.

The daylight was fading fast, but they dare not turn on the vehicle's headlights; the police boats patrolling the Moroccan coast would spot them instantly. Thankfully, Karim knew the way intimately; it was one of their regular beaches.

The combined weight of the trailer and its cargo they were towing pushed them even faster, forcing them to the edge of the track. Even with the four-wheel drive engaged, the vehicle struggled to avoid the trees, and Karim dare not touch the brakes on the treacherous muddy surface. He changed down to a lower gear. The Land Rover slowed, and Karim managed to hold it on course. They approached the final bend where the track leveled out, and headed toward the water's edge, forging deep ruts in the soft sand.

"How many liters of gas are we giving this lot?" asked Mohamed.

"There were only a few drops in the tank, so I added another three. That'll be enough to sail out of Moroccan territorial waters. After that, who cares?"

"How many are waiting for us on the beach?"

"Assuming they all made the three-kilometer walk from Ceuta, they'll be thirty-seven, but one woman is heavily pregnant. There could be thirty-eight by the time they reach Spain."

"Have they all paid?"

"Of course, but I didn't charge the pregnant woman extra for her child to be."

"You're becoming too soft, brother."

"We can afford to be more generous nowadays. It will improve our reputation and bring us more customers."

"But the flow of migrants to Spain through Morocco is increasing substantially; why should we be so kind when business is booming?"

"We will put our prices up for the next group."

"Good thinking, but don't include any more goodies. They'll be expecting cushions and caviar next."

The Land Rover reached the water's edge. The surf was indeed gentle. It was why they preferred launching from the Mediterranean beaches; the Atlantic was far too rough.

Karim drove into the surf and turned the vehicle around to face the track so that the trailer could be reversed into the water.

They opened their doors and clambered out.

Karim and Mohamed looked around them.

"Any sign of the beach guard?" inquired Mohamed.

"His palm has been well greased, but he'll be back in twenty minutes, so we better hurry," urged Karim.

Mohamed removed the protective cover from the boat's small motor while Karim unstrapped the seven-meter inflatable rubber dinghy from the trailer. They were continually looking for similar boats for their weekly consignment of human misery. They purchased some from the police, who as fast as they confiscated them sold them back to other smugglers to supplement their meager pay. They'd stolen this complete rig late the previous night. It was outside a café where the owner was using the restroom. They'd parked alongside, switched the trailer over to their Land Rover, and driven away without anyone noticing. Even if they had been seen, their vehicle number plates were covered in sand, and they were two faceless men dressed in long black robes, heads wrapped in Tuareg turbans. Nobody could have recognized them.

They looked around for their passengers.

One by one, they emerged from under the pine trees, plodding toward them across the soft sand in bare feet, wearing an assortment of dark clothing, including jeans, T-shirts, hijabs, turbans, robes, and baggy trousers. Most had thick jackets to ward off the night chill on their imminent but dangerous voyage.

They came silently but resolutely. As instructed, no one carried any belongings. Karim read their body language instantly. They were terrified. It was the same with every group.

A short fifteen-kilometer ride in an overloaded boat through one of the busiest shipping channels in the world would worry anyone. However, the prospect of a new life in Spain drove them onward relentlessly. This was it—the final stage of their long, perilous journeys.

Many had been traveling for years to arrive at this point. They were from all over Africa: Gabon, both the Congo Republics, Nigeria, Niger, Mali, Mauritania, Senegal, and Sierra Leone. All escaping the mess that was the dark continent—riddled with poverty, sickness, war, corruption, and starvation. They'd left their loved ones behind, struggled across deserts on foot, hitched rides on occasional trucks, been robbed, beaten—often by policemen, and some of them sexually abused. Doggedly, they picked themselves up, dusted themselves down, and continued heading toward Ceuta, the Spanish enclave east of Tangiers—their portal to Europe and paradise. Most had tried on several occasions to climb the razor-wire fences surrounding Ceuta, but it was too well protected by armed guards, sensors, and guard dogs with vicious teeth.

All this way for nothing.

Then they'd met the unscrupulous Mohamed and his brother Karim.

The brothers were extraordinary salesmen who hovered on the edges of the Ceuta border, promising an easy ride to Spain and an introduction to potential employers in exchange for anything of value. If interested passengers didn't have enough to pay the fare, they faced an undetermined future in the hills above Ceuta, risking imprisonment, slavery, or death.

Alternatively, they could steal the fare; Mohamed

would show them how to pick the pockets of unsuspecting tourists shopping in the Souk Al Had in the nearby frontier town of Fnideq.

Most accepted the brothers' offer; what else was there? Even though none of them had any idea what they would do to earn a living in Spain, couldn't speak a word of Spanish, and carried no papers, any kind of life in Europe had to be a vast improvement compared with that they had left behind. That's what they'd been told, and that's what they chose to believe. It was that dream that had kept them going when they were dehydrated, cold, hungry, and disillusioned.

Karim opened the back of the Land Rover and extracted liter bottles of drinking water. He passed them around. Each bottle taken eagerly.

"Hands up; who's missing?" Karim shouted in French.

Nervous laughter was the reply.

Most understood some French. They might not be literate but were accustomed to trading with neighbors. Hunger is a forceful taskmaster, and in order to survive their arduous and lengthy journey, they would quickly have assimilated the necessary French vocabulary for basic communication. So it would be on their arrival in Spain.

"Then let's make a start," announced Karim to the group. "We'll launch the dinghy now. I will reverse the trailer into the water. I need six of you to stand in the shallows and hold the dinghy steady while everyone climbs aboard. Nine rows of four abreast, so board four at a time from the front and sit still. The final row is adjacent to the motor where there is only room for two. Who will steer?"

"I will," said a tall young Nigerian, stepping forward, dressed in dirty jeans and T-shirt.

"Keep pointing toward the northern star," said Karim, waving his arm at the darkening sky.

"I know where it is," answered the Nigerian indignantly. "How do you think we crossed the desert? Signposts?"

"Allah be praised, we have a navigator on board," countered Karim. "Listen, my friend, the little island, Jazīrat Tūra or Parsley Island to the Spanish, is two hundred meters in front of us. It disputably belongs to Spain, but it's uninhabited. There are lethal rocks in the shallows that could tear a hole in the dinghy. You need to give it a wide berth and leave it to your left, heading northwest. Keep pointing that way, and you'll spot the lights of Gibraltar in about an hour. Try not to bump into it. Aim to the right where the beaches are flat. I should warn you that, roughly halfway there, you will cross the main shipping channel. You have no reflectors, so these huge tankers and the like cannot see you on their radar. They are well lit, so it is not difficult to keep out of their way. The bus station in La Linea de la Concepcion opens at six o'clock in the morning, and you should be there in plenty of time."

The brothers looked on as the migrants struggled through the water and onto the dinghy. Two men hoisted the heavily pregnant woman on board; she thanked them profusely in French. Five minutes later, they were all crammed into the boat. It sat low in the water but seemed stable enough.

They were ready to leave.

"Wait," shouted a breathless voice in French from the darkness behind them. "I will go with them."

All the heads in the dinghy turned to see who this last-minute arrival was, as a young man appeared out of the gloom. He was perspiring heavily, had long hair, a beard, and lighter skin than the Africans. He was also dressed smartly in new jeans, a dark-colored short-sleeve shirt, and the latest Nike sports shoes. A canvas bag was draped over his shoulder.

"Who told you we were here?" demanded Karim.

"Your brother Abdul; I met him at the Ceuta frontier. I ran all the way here."

"And who are you?" asked Karim.

"Never mind, but I need to reach France urgently. Here, take this." The man reached into his bag, extracted a billfold, and handed over a wad of euros to Karim.

Karim thumbed through them adeptly, nodded, and put the €3,000 into the pocket sewn into his robes. He'd just been paid triple the going rate. Who was he to argue?

The man climbed into the back of the dinghy, next to the Nigerian.

Karim stepped down into the water, clipped the motor to the transom, and then opened the fuel line from the orange gas tank, which was by the Nigerian's feet. He wrapped the cord around the starter and pulled. The motor spluttered into life on the third attempt.

The Nigerian grasped the tiller and twisted the accelerator. The boat moved forward slowly, the tiny motor laboring hard.

Karim and Mohamed shoved the stern with a foot each to help them on their way. They moved to the back of the Land Rover and tidied up straps on the trailer while watching the barely visible shadows of the migrants' silhouettes as they flickered against the water's phosphorescence. Eventually, the dinghy melted into the darkness, and they were gone.

Karim and his brother didn't bother to say goodbye or bon voyage.

They were people smugglers, not relatives.

They climbed back into the Land Rover and roared off up the track and into the night.

2

Detective Inspector Leon Prado scrutinized the name plaque mounted on the wall next to the full-height oak-veneered door.

Jefe Superior Provincia de Malaga: Francisco Gonzalez Ruiz, it read in white plastic letters stuck onto a black background.

He rapped on the door twice.

"Enter," commanded a stern voice from within.

Prado turned the handle, pushed the heavy door firmly, and strode into the Malaga Police chief's spacious office.

Usually, Prado would have made a pithy remark about how the other half lived, as he walked toward the visitor chair by his boss's expansive mahogany desk. The views from the massive picture window of Plaza de la Merced and Malaga old town were spectacular. Today, though, he said nothing; it wasn't that type of meeting.

"Sit down," said the chief brusquely, while

continuing to tap away on his laptop.

Prado waited patiently and watched the chief finish off whatever vital task he was doing. He was in no hurry; he knew what was coming.

Physically, the appearances of the two men couldn't have been further apart. Prado was medium height, well built, and in his early fifties, with a thick head of silver hair and round friendly face. Gonzalez was short, slight, and in his early forties, with thin black hair swept straight back from his forehead. Chiseled features, a Roman nose, and cold obsidian eyes lent him a hard, imposing disposition.

Prado was familiar with his superior officer's body-language games to intimidate and gain the upper hand with his subordinates. Usually, they didn't worry him, but today his stomach churned with anticipation about what he might hear.

With a final flourish, the boss hit the Enter key, closed the screen, and looked directly into Prado's brown eyes. Prado didn't flinch—he was used to hiding his true feelings, especially from this man—and returned the piercing gaze with equanimity.

"It's been over a fortnight since you fucked up that kidnap case," opened Gonzalez. "Between then and now, you've been off sick for over sixty percent of the time, and when you do bother to turn up, you don't contribute anything worthwhile to our heavy workload. What do you have to say about that, Detective Inspector?"

"Thirteen days to be precise, sir," Prado responded in clipped tones and not surprised at his senior officer's rant. He'd expected it days ago. The long-awaited call, though, only came yesterday. The chief's administrative assistant had politely requested Prado to attend what she'd referred to as an appraisal. However, Prado had already heard the rumors flying around the office. He was about to be sacked from his job, heading up the Malaga Serious Crime Squad. He even knew who his successor was to be and surprisingly approved.

Prado happily conceded that he was no longer up to the challenge or the long hours. They'd already cost him his marriage, and now his health was failing. Ideally, what he wanted was a transfer to something less demanding where he could relax and continue to use his indubitable investigation talents and unparalleled experience to see out his final three years to retirement.

"Is that all you have to say?" asked el jefe, glancing down at Prado's personnel file in front of him. "No groveling or lame excuse?"

"The doctor's report is also in the file, sir."

"Doctor's report, Prado? At this level, we don't take any notice of medical opinion. Depression, it says. We're all fucking depressed, but it doesn't stop us from getting up in the morning and doing our bit for the taxpayer. You're a senior policeman; you should be immune to illness. Next, you'll be expecting to enjoy the damn job."

"Something less demanding would improve my health and effectiveness, sir."

"Less demanding he says. Such as what? School-crossing controller?"

"Your job looks just about perfect, sir."

El jefe looked taken aback, then smiled, and chuckled, his grim face softening at his elder colleague's insolence. "Ha, you don't care, do you, Prado?"

"No, sir. I've been working here for thirty-two years; I've seen it all, heard all the bullshit, thrown away the T-shirt, and frankly, I've had enough. Now fire me, or give me something passably worthwhile to do. And yes, I would like to enjoy what I'm doing; otherwise what's the point, and don't tell me money."

"I could let you go now. It's within my power."

"That would hammer my pension payments."

"So it is the money. Anyway, why would I care about the size of your pension? You could always apply for work as a private eye or security guard, and the reduced costs would look good on my statistics."

"Sir, forgive me. You might be younger than me and have the support of the politicians, but you aren't insensitive. Your low budgets might appeal to some, but I know that firing me would be difficult for you personally. You would find it hard to live with your conscience. Wouldn't you, sir?"

The chief looked long and hard at Prado.

Prado returned his gaze, unflinching.

The chief shook his head and said, "I never thought that I would have to say these words to you, Inspector Prado. You were a rising star on my team. I had you earmarked for greater things, but the way you handled that kidnap was a disaster, and your performance since can only be described as pathetic. Regretfully, it falls upon me to confirm that as of the last day of April, your employment as head of the Serious Crime Squad is terminated. In the immortal words of orange-skinned reality-TV morons—you're fired."

"Thank you, sir," Prado replied, standing up.

"Sit down, Leon; I haven't finished with you yet."

Prado slumped back down in the chair, his worst

nightmare playing out before him.

Then el jefe picked up another file on the far corner of his desk and tossed it over to Prado.

Prado picked it up and looked at the words typed on the front label:

> *New role—responsibility for crimes involving foreigners throughout the province of Malaga.*

Prado opened the file and speed-read the single printed sheet inside.

However, the title had said it all.

He looked up and found the chief looking at him softly. He said, "It's tailor-made for you, Leon."

"Except for one minor thing, Fran."

"You don't speak any foreign languages."

"Correct."

"You also won't have any staff or budget, but you may liaise with appropriate departments as needed."

"So, it's a political appointment?"

"Yes, the marketing boys at the tourist office dreamed it up—said it would enhance our focus on safe tourism. The mayor thought the idea brilliant, so here you are. The stats prove that as tourism in Andalucia increases, so does crime by foreigners and against foreigners. We're just a little ahead of ourselves for a change."

"About nineteen years, sir?"

"Ha. We managerial types prefer to call it strategic planning. At the moment, there's not much to do, just the odd minor case here and there, so it certainly fits your criteria of not demanding. I can't quite see you signing up for any language courses, though, so I suggest you find yourself a voluntary translator, maybe two or three. English will be the most important, followed by German, French, Russian, and Moroccan Arabic. I wouldn't bother with Armenian or Swahili; they all speak English. You'll find plenty of volunteers to choose from at coastal medical centers, hospitals, or language schools. You'll report to me directly. Dismissed."

"Thank you, sir," replied Prado, standing up. "When do I start?"

"First of May."

"But that was last week."

"I had every confidence."

"I won't disappoint you on this."

"I know, and by the way, I've moved your office up to this floor. It will look like a promotion to your colleagues."

"That wasn't necessary, but thank you again, Fran."

Prado picked up the file and closed the chief's door on the way out.

Isabel, the chief's administrative assistant, a well-rounded but stylishly dressed woman in her late thirties with dyed blond-highlighted hair, was waiting for him outside. She had an uncanny knack of always being in the right place at the right time. She escorted him down to the far end of the corridor, opened the last door, and waved him in.

"If I can help in any way, Leon, just call me," said Isabel, patting him on the shoulder as he walked through the door into his new domain. "It's nice to have you back. We all missed your terrible jokes."

Prado looked around.

It wasn't as big as his last office, but he couldn't spot any brooms, and the view could have been worse. At least the laundry fluttering from a line on the terrace opposite didn't have any holes in it.

A new phone and laptop were on top of the reasonably spacious but cheap pinewood desk. He opened a drawer and checked the manufacturer's label. As he thought, Swedish; thankfully, somebody else had unraveled how to assemble it. He checked out his new toys.

Latest models, even a protective case for the phone. Nice touch, thought Prado. He tended to throw phones at stupid people. Isabel had already loaded both with his customary password, files, contacts, and favorite websites.

Malaga Football Club was in pole position. She's amazing, he thought.

Prado took his jacket off and tried out his new chair.

It was surprisingly comfortable. Prado prepared himself for the first crucial task in the new job. He sat back in the chair, placed his feet up on the desk, and closed his eyes.

His mind rambled.

He breathed a sigh of contentment and pondered why hadn't he settled for a less challenging career in the first place? Why had he pushed himself so hard? Whom had he been trying to impress with his success? His parents, ex-wife, the pretty girl in reception? His colleagues? The world at large? It certainly wasn't for money, or to compensate for lack of manly dimensions, so it must have been for that inner voice that nagged him onward and upward.

Maybe if he hadn't demanded so much of himself, perhaps he would still be happily married and see more of his boys? He certainly regretted being on his own.

On the other hand, was he deluding himself? Maybe it was necessary for a man to strive for the top to gain a sense of fulfillment? A life worth living. But only a few make it right up there. Not everyone can be the boss, he reasoned. Most fail halfway up the ladder, becoming disillusioned and bitter.

His eyes blinked open at this revelation.

"Am I bitter?" he said aloud.

Initially, he'd been distraught at his failure with the kidnap case. Now he'd put it in perspective; he could deal with it.

He'd deserved to be banished into obscurity and was indeed expecting just that at the meeting with his boss earlier. The fair outcome had been a pleasant surprise and had gone some way to restore faith in his superiors. He hadn't dared to think how being fired would impact his life. One thing would have been dead sure, though. He'd have taken the school-crossing position before even considering security or private practice.

Now he didn't have to worry about making that decision.

His mind wandered back to where it all began.

Prado had been born in Cordoba just under fifty-five years ago; he was the eldest of five and the only boy. His father was a postal worker, and his mother far too busy to work outside of the home.

Prado was an average student at school and had struggled to pass his baccalaureate, but he'd stuck at it and scraped through after a second attempt. His parents were keen for him to go to university, but he declined. He had no idea what he wanted to study and was against saddling his parents with yet more debt.

At that time, several years after dictator Franco's death, military service (Mili) was still compulsory for all male Spaniards who didn't attend university. Inevitably, Prado was summoned to do his two-year stint for the homeland.

He'd been posted to the Spanish Legion base on the outskirts of the spectacular mountain town of Ronda, some seventy kilometers inland from Malaga. After basic training, Prado was offered a choice of regiments. Instinctively, he chose the military police and very quickly established that it was indeed his thing.

After his stint in the army, he joined the National Police in Malaga. Thirty-two years later, he was the most senior and successful crime solver in the province.

Then the wheels came off.

Prado had shot himself in the foot.

A kidnap had gone wrong because he'd made a bad decision.

Both victim and perpetrator had not been found.

The kidnap case remained open in the unsolved crimes section.

For several days afterward, Prado had been obsessed with reading the file over and over again, revisiting all their lines of inquiry to the exclusion of all new crimes. He'd found nothing, which had depressed him. It was as if all his experience, instincts, and talents had been erased from his mind, leaving a useless blank space only good for feeling sorry for himself.

His work suffered. Long-established relationships with his colleagues floundered. It didn't take long for him to see that he'd becoming a laughing stock in the office, so he stopped going to work determined to sort himself out. He quickly realized he was a stubborn old fool. This was not something trivial that he could lightly brush under the carpet or desensitize with a few drinks. No matter how drunk or how long the binge, his failure remained firmly at the forefront of his mind as soon as the alcoholic fog cleared and the brain clawed its way back to life. Thankfully, he'd picked himself out of the gutter long before booze had taken over. He reluctantly accepted that he was no longer Prado the invincible, wasn't capable of self-healing, and needed some professional counseling.

He made sure that his therapist had no contacts with his police network. He didn't want his boss knowing how close he was to falling apart. Thankfully, it only took one session for him to come to his senses. The therapist had advised that he leave the kidnap file alone and bury the case deep in a far recess of his mind. Otherwise, he was at severe risk of driving himself to complete mental breakdown.

For the first time in his life, he listened to advice and acted upon it. Nobody was more pleased than he was when the tactic started to work almost immediately. He pulled himself together and began making forays back into the office.

Initially, people were wary of him. But when he didn't bite their hands off and started to contribute the occasional gem of advice to a complicated case, they forgave him.

And now he had a proper job.

He just had to write the job description.

As usual, he'd make it up as he went along.

Next morning he arrived at the office with a new spring in his step. Clean shaven, silver hair freshly trimmed, looking dapper in his best light-gray suit, plain lilac tie, and panama hat at a jaunty angle. It was well before nine o'clock, much to the surprise and pleasure of colleagues, but he'd always been an early bird, and his tiny apartment was only a five-minute walk from the *comisaría*.

His colleagues made him welcome unreservedly; he felt instantly back on board. However, he knew that they would watch him like a hawk, probing for any sign of weakness or, worse, another error of judgment.

At nine thirty-five, the phone rang with his first case.

A Belgian man had killed his French wife in Nerja.

3

The Vueling Airbus A320 banked gently and then leveled out onto the final stretch of its southerly approach to Malaga airport. From his window seat on the port side, Phillip Armitage could just make out the ocean-blue Mediterranean surf lapping against the shore some two hundred meters below.

Phillip was forty-three years old, tall, medium build with shaggy blond hair, and steely-blue eyes. He was desperate to move his long, athletic limbs. Ninety minutes jammed into narrow seats was not his idea of fun, but it was quicker and cheaper than the train. He sighed in relief as the plane touched down on the western runway and then taxied toward the familiar gray steel-and-glass terminal-three building.

Nearly home.

He hoped that his friend and business partner Richard would be waiting in the arrival hall. He'd be burning with curiosity to know if Phillip had sorted his head out.

Phillip had boarded the plane at Santiago de Compostela in northern Spain, where he'd just completed the longest walk of his life. The certificate to prove it was in his checked luggage. He'd managed all 780 kilometers, nearly 500 miles, of the ancient pilgrimage route of El Camino de Santiago, or in English, St. James's Way.

The pilgrimage wasn't just another commercial video project for his and Richard's burgeoning Internet guide to Spain but a period of reflection. To call it a midlife crisis was a tad dramatic, but Phillip certainly had personal baggage begging attention.

The time alone had helped him battle against his inner demons, and yes, he had overcome them. And no, he hadn't decided to quit Spain, leave Richard to his own devices, switch soccer team allegiances, or bat with the other team.

His journey of self-examination had begun in St.-Jean-Pied-du-Port, near Biarritz in France. It was the most popular of all the routes to Santiago and referred to as El Camino Frances. It had taken him thirty-four days, despite the heavy backpack, terrible weather, soaking wet clothes, and a brief dose of food poisoning.

As he walked, he'd filmed the route with his lightweight handheld video camera. Back home in Nerja, he would edit and upload the clips to their guide's section on Spanish travelogues. Viewers could then visualize what walking the Camino involved day by day and could make better-informed decisions before launching themselves on such an arduous journey.

Phillip could have gone in the summer. He would then have avoided the rain and, if so minded, slept under the stars. But that's when everyone goes. It's hot, the bugs are a nuisance, beds are hard to find, and there's little opportunity to think without interruption, which is the whole point of going. In April, when he'd flown up to Bordeaux and caught the bus to St.-Jean-Pied-du-Port, the weather was comfortable for walking, and his fellow travelers were thankfully serious pilgrims, meaning there were no idiots around to ruin it for everybody else.

Some days he walked alone. On others, if he caught up with someone and the person was inclined to be chatty, he would stay with them for a while. On one occasion he was overtaken by a group of incredibly fit Finnish women celebrating their fortieth birthdays. They all came from the same town, went to the same school, and were happily married with families, but they had wanted to reexamine their paths through life in one another's company. They were taking bets as to whose would be the first husband to call for advice, having been left in charge of domestic duties during their absence. They were fun.

Surprisingly, Phillip had discovered most of the pilgrims he'd met were not religious but were using the experience to challenge themselves physically and to explore their spirituality. The long hours struggling up steep hills, through vast fields, vineyards, and olive groves, mostly in solitude, presented a unique opportunity to reflect on the values of life and resolve any mental turmoil.

Phillip's bone of contention had been a woman.

The beautiful Juliet. A perfect English rose.

A perfect, young English rose.

Phillip had lived permanently in Spain for around

four years, but he'd been visiting for decades. The family villa had been built by his grandfather during the sixties. He'd bought the countryside plot from a farmer selling his land off piece by piece to the growing number of foreigners arriving in the area.

When relatives have a property in Spain, it's amazing how popular they become. Phillip and his sister Glenda had spent most of their childhood holidays at their grandparents', where they'd played with the Spanish farmer's kids next door. Consequently, Phillip's Spanish was fluent, but he accepted that his pronunciation was distinctly British and there was room for improvement with his grammar. Glenda had later married the farmer's eldest son Jose, and now they ran the farm together. Then their parents died within a few months of each other.

Their mother went first after a long battle with pancreatic cancer; their dad, who had steadfastly been by her side all the way through her suffering, passed away in his sleep within months. He hadn't been able to face life without his soul mate.

Phillip had inherited the villa, and Glenda their modest cash and investments to help finance her three daughters' education.

Phillip's background was military. Armitage by name and army by nature, the family motto.

He'd been born on a British base in Germany where he learned to speak and write German fluently at the local village school. He'd followed his father into the Intelligence Corps, where he could put his language talents to good use. He'd quit after some disturbing experiences in Afghanistan and set up a business in London City providing high-level online security to financial institutions.

That is when he'd met Valentina at a trade show in Berlin.

Valentina was from Moscow. Her striking looks, blond hair, and ice-blue eyes had mesmerized him. And the way she rolled those Rs—drrrove him crrrazy. They'd married within weeks.

Valentina had taught him her language using the tried-and-trusted pillow-talk method. Her informative lessons had provided Phillip with far more than a wide-ranging vocabulary. His profanities would make a Cossack blush.

Seven years later, her affair with a Russian diplomat neighbor in Weybridge near London had ended the marriage. They had divorced acrimoniously, but that didn't deter him from continuing to love her dearly. Sadly, he couldn't stop himself from comparing potential replacements against Valentina. He resolved that somehow he had to find a way to flush his ex-wife out of his heart, mind, and soul.

After his divorce, Phillip lived on a rented houseboat moored on the River Thames near Shepperton. While it was a unique location, he wasn't happy there. The combination of loneliness, too much work, and the tedious commuting into the city of London was slowly throttling his former lust for life.

He'd often thought about quitting the rat race and heading off to warmer climes. But he felt trapped by his responsibilities to employees, customers, shareholders, and the damned bank. While the profits of his company showed steady growth, the promise of massive riches around the corner failed to materialize, and none of his major competitors seemed interested in an acquisition.

His parent's property in Nerja had opened his escape route.

Extracting himself, though, had needed a year or so, what with selling his shares and finding a suitable replacement for his position of CEO. Finally, it was done. He'd even managed to hang on to a modest amount of money, despite capital gains tax, his ex-wife's lawyer's best endeavors, and the damned bank.

He'd settled quickly in Nerja and relished the company of his family next door. Initially, he'd kept busy modernizing the villa, gardens, and pool, but when the workers had left, and after a few days of admiring his modifications with a goofy grin on his face, he realized that perhaps life in the sun wasn't quite so idyllic as envisaged? Was this to be it for the next thirty odd years? Gardening and house maintenance, endless rubbers of bridge, or rounds of golf with retired expatriates discussing medications and hip replacements. The thought of it terrified him. He decided that he was far too young to disengage his brain from the modern world and looked around for something to do.

That's when he'd met Richard.

That led him to Juliet, the beautiful young English rose.

Her resemblance to Valentina was astonishing.

She was why he was on this plane with blisters as big as dinner plates.

But at least, he'd cleared the fog from his head and had developed some new rules to manage his confused emotions.

The Jetway lumbered toward the fuselage. The captain turned off the seat-belt sign while the cabin crew fussed with the front door. Phillip couldn't wait any longer; he had to stand and move his legs. Thankfully, he was in the third row so didn't have to stoop for long. As the seats emptied in front of him, he grabbed his hand baggage from the overhead bin, which contained his camera and laptop, and headed out toward baggage reclaim.

His backpack arrived promptly; he heaved it over his shoulders, wondering how the hell he'd managed to carry so much weight over such a long distance, and then went to search for Richard and his wife, Ingrid. He hoped they had made it; if not, he'd grab a cab.

Malaga arrival hall was packed with the usual throng of meeters and greeters waving an assortment of welcome placards, floral bouquets, and helium balloons.

Blocking the way ahead of Phillip was a group of well-rounded women giggling and chatting away with broad Scottish accents. They were tottering slowly and unsteadily on high-heeled shoes, dressed in bridal headgear, pink hot pants, and skimpy tops printed back and front with the message "Last week of freedom; don't ask—just grope." They were yet another of the thousands of stylish hen and stag parties that swarmed to the Costa del Sol for the fantastic climate, cheap booze, inexpensive accommodation, and determined to make the most of their final days as single persons.

Phillip smiled wryly at Richard standing calmly by the chrome exit gate.

Richard was American. A chunky, congenial man from Boston, Massachusetts, in his early sixties with a ruddy complexion, thinning gray hair, twinkling hazel eyes, and a deep throaty voice. He raised his eyebrows.

Phillip nodded yes.

Richard looked relieved and whispered something to Ingrid, a petite, graceful, woman in her late fifties, oozing confidence, with fair curly hair, gray eyes, dressed in blue jeans, loose beige blouse, and color-coordinated spectacles.

Phillip went through the barrier and exchanged man hugs and cheek kisses quickly before they moved off in the direction of the car park.

"You're sure about this?" asked Ingrid.

"Definitely," replied Phillip.

"So when you go for coffee in the morning and see Juliet, you'll be able to handle it?"

"No problem."

"Forgive me for being skeptical," said Richard. "But before you left, I recall you were in a right fudge about her. How can a mere stroll through northern Spain clear your head so clinically, or more importantly, your heart?"

"Have you ever spent over thirty days on your own, trudging forward step by step, kilometer by kilometer with only one thing on your mind?"

"Thankfully not," said Ingrid. "But I think I know what you mean. You chip a little bit away from the lump in your head every day until eventually it either kills you or you deal with it."

"That sums it up precisely," said Phillip, grabbing her hand and squeezing it gratefully as they crossed the road and waited for the car-park elevator.

Richard pressed the button to go down. They stood in silence and, when the doors opened, crushed in with a mass of others and their luggage. They descended to the floor where Richard had parked his

Mercedes, plonked Phillip's gear in the trunk, clambered in, and headed off in the direction of Nerja some seventy kilometers east on the coastal motorway.

Phillip sat in the back, enjoying the breathtaking Andalusian landscapes as Richard brought him up to date with their business activities. There was nothing of note that needed Phillip's full concentration, so he half listened and let his mind wander.

Tomorrow morning he would see Juliet, and as he had said to Ingrid, he wouldn't have a problem with that.

Would he?

4

"My office told me that you're making a documentary, Señora," said the uniformed captain of the Spanish Guardia Civil coast-guard patrol boat, standing by the door of the control room. He was a tall, heavily muscled man in his midfifties, with thinning, dyed black hair styled in an absurd comb-over.

"For CNN," replied Amanda Salisbury. "It's about the sudden resurgence of migrants crossing between Morocco and Spain." Amanda was a shapely, olive-skinned, petite woman in her early thirties, with light-brown eyes that sparkled with flecks of gold, wearing tight blue jeans and a baggy red T-shirt."

"Then welcome aboard," said the captain. "You can stash your stuff in the chart room at the back here and then join me as we leave the harbor. I should warn you, though, that although there has been a recent increase in migrants, I can't guarantee that we'll come across any today."

The captain grabbed his cap from the shelf in front of the ship's wheel and jammed it on top of his carefully lacquered hair.

"Prepare to sail," he announced over the ship's radio.

Three crew members dashed out from the galley below the bridge and onto the starboard deck. One jumped ashore and lifted the steel hawsers that moored the ship to the quay up over the mooring posts and lowered them carefully into the water. His colleagues turned on the ship's electric winches, and the cables snaked upward and onto the deck. The man ashore leaped back on board, the captain activated the side thruster, and the ship moved slowly away from the quay and out into the mainstream.

The captain turned the wheel, deactivated the thruster, and then moved the engine control forward. The ship eased out of the harbor and into the bay of Algeciras. To the left loomed the 426-meter high rock of Gibraltar, its physical dominance of the surrounding landscape a constant reminder to the Spanish that this pimple on the bottom of the Iberian Peninsula was British territory.

Once past the rock, the captain accelerated, and the ship surged forward through the calm sea toward Morocco.

A crew member delivered mugs of coffee to the captain and Amanda. She sat down and sipped, while he steered and slurped, occasionally glancing at the radar screen in front of the wheel.

"I'd heard that small boats don't show up on the radar?" she said, gathering her long raven hair into a ponytail and slipping a band over the end to secure it.

"Wooden, fiberglass, or rubber boats are tough to

identify, so most carry radar reflectors nowadays," answered the captain. "It means they can be seen well in advance by large ships. However, smugglers don't use them so it's a matter of luck if we see them on screen. Thankfully, when it's flat calm like today and there are twenty odd people on board, we have a better chance."

"Is there a regular route that the migrants take?" asked Amanda.

"Usually, the shortest possible, which is the fifteen-kilometer gap between Ceuta and La Linea de la Concepcion, but the wind often blows them way off course. With a strong easterly, they end up in the Atlantic, and when it's a westerly, as far down the coast as Almeria. In perfect conditions like today, assuming any left Morocco last night, we're likely to find them in the middle of the main shipping lane south of La Linea. That's where most collisions and the majority of drownings occur. It's where we're heading now."

"I've heard that the number of migrants is increasing. What's your take on that?"

"This year we've seen a threefold increase over last. Since January, we've rescued just under two thousand."

"How many escape your patrols?"

"I estimate about ten thousand."

"So at that rate, there'll be over twenty-five thousand migrants this year."

"Possibly more."

"Where do they go?"

"They disperse inland as best they can. We find them at bus stations, others steal bicycles or hide in the backs of trucks, and some are collected by local crooks to work as street traders. You see them everywhere selling fake or cheap junk."

"What happens to the ones you catch?"

"We detain them in the Algeciras Centro de Internamiento de Extranjeros (CIE) or Foreigner Internment Center, pending deportation or approval of their asylum application."

"How long for?"

"We're supposed to process them within sixty days, but if we can't arrange a flight or complete the paperwork, then longer."

"They used to cross via Italy and Greece; why are they now coming to Spain?"

"The Spanish route isn't new. Twenty years ago they used to arrive in droves, using little blue wooden boats. We stopped that by agreeing on a policy of collaboration with the Moroccans. Recently, the European Union has practically closed down the Libya-Italy route, so they've started coming this way again. They can either jump over the fence into Ceuta or Melilla, the two Spanish enclaves in Morocco, or they buy passage on a smuggler's boat."

"Do you think the numbers coming to Spain will continue to increase next year?"

"In theory, no. In reality, probably. Our collaboration with the Moroccans included them patrolling their beaches to prevent boats from leaving. However, their guards work long hours and are paid a pittance, so they will happily look the other way in exchange for some smugglers' cash."

"Why don't they arrest the smugglers?"

"There's a relentless tide of humanity heading this way needing transport to cross the water. As fast as they arrest smugglers, new ones replace them. It's terrible to see so many lives wasted on such a fruitless journey."

"You feel sorry for them, Captain?"

"I despair for their dire circumstances. They all have parents worrying about them back home, hoping that their perilous journey leads to some improvement in their wretched lives. In some ways, I admire them, especially the women and children. It takes huge amounts of determination and courage to leave everything you know behind without any idea what will happen, where they will end up, or that death is a strong possibility. Can you imagine what powerful forces drive them to do that?"

"They've lived with starvation, sickness, war, and corruption for centuries. What choice do they have when there's no chance for better prospects by staying?"

"They could try to improve their own country."

"And so they should, but with no education, opportunity, or money, it's difficult to reject the smuggler's tempting sales pitch. Do you have kids?"

"Three sons, all with university degrees, but could they find work relevant to their studies in Spain? No, youth unemployment is so high that they've had to go to England and work in hotels. They detest the awful climate and being away from home, but what else can they do?"

"That's exactly what the Africans are thinking."

"You're right. What are we doing to our world?"

"Not learning from the mistakes of the past."

"Situation normal, all fucked up. Look at the radar; I think we've found you some migrants. Prepare your camera; we'll be there directly."

"Can I chat with them?"

"Do you speak French or English?"

"Both."

"Impressive—I can barely manage schoolboy English. Yes, you can talk to them, but it's best to wear a protective suit, just in case of illness on their part or yours. There's one in the chart room; it should fit you."

Amanda withdrew to the chart room and slipped into the white nylon suit she found hanging in a sealed plastic bag on the back of the door. It was way too big for her, but it would do. She heard the engines slow as she closed the face mask.

Amanda was born thirty-four years ago in Annapolis, Maryland, on the United States Eastern Seaboard, where her father had been an instructor at the US Naval Academy. When she was seven, her father had been posted to the US-cofunded Spanish naval base at Rota in Cadiz Province. It's near El Puerto de Santa Maria from where Columbus sailed in 1492. She'd attended the local school and had grown up speaking Spanish with her friends and English at home.

Her mother's parents were Moroccan immigrants who had opened a French restaurant in Washington, DC. They had insisted that Amanda carried on the family linguistic traditions. Amanda also spoke fluent accent-free Maghrebi or Western Arabic as spoken in Morocco, Algeria, Tunisia, and Libya. Like most North and sub-Saharan Africans, her French was perfect.

Amanda turned on her camera and went out onto the starboard deck.

Thirty meters ahead, an inflatable rubber dinghy,

some seven meters long and just under a meter and a half wide, was drifting on the calm surface, with its small outboard motor silent. It was crammed full of mostly young African men dressed in a wide variety of grubby clothing and turbans. The few women wore headscarves, wraparound skirts, loose tops and thick jackets. None carried belongings or wore a life jacket. They were sitting on any available boat surface or on one another. Some dangled their legs over the side.

Amanda started counting them, and that's when she noticed.

"How long have they been out there?" she asked the captain.

"They probably sailed at dusk last night, so nearly ten hours," he said.

"I don't see any signs of food and water; they must be near the point of dehydration."

"They're used to it. Crossing a desert is a lot worse."

"Yes, but deserts don't have supertankers to run them down, or great white sharks swimming underneath on their way to the Malta breeding grounds."

"No, you're right; just scorpions, poisonous snakes, and deadly terrorists."

"So what you're telling me is that they are accustomed to danger and fear and that this little journey wouldn't have worried them."

"Oh no. They'd have been terrified all right, especially as most can't swim. What I'm saying is that migrants are accustomed to living on the edge. It's part of what sustains their efforts to complete their journeys."

"Then they have my respect."

Amanda resumed her counting.

Thirty-eight—sitting silently with sullen expressions. Several men were openly glowering at their captors—their illegal passage to Spain officially over and dreams of a new life shattered. Few of them would be eligible for a visa or had any work skills to offer, other than basic laboring. All the money they had stolen, borrowed, or saved for this long, dangerous journey had been wasted. The risks they had taken had been for nothing. The women wept quietly.

The captain pressed a button on the control panel in front of the brass steering wheel. A prerecorded message announced over the ship's loudspeakers in Spanish, English, French, and Arabic that the Guardia Civil was impounding their boat. All passengers were to be taken to a detention center in Algeciras for an interview, and if accepted, they could apply for asylum. Any sick persons, pregnant women, or those with disabilities should raise their hands. They would transfer to the coast-guard ship. The remainder would stay on their dinghy for the tow into harbor.

Amanda filmed the approach to the immigrant's dinghy, which appeared to be floating well and in reasonable condition. In the background loomed the Rock of Gibraltar; further away, steam wafted upward from the oil refinery in Algeciras. A pod of dolphins swam by only meters in front of them, leaving a V-shaped wake behind them. All stopped what they were doing to admire them, providing some brief respite from the pain of capture.

Only one woman had her hand up.

Her fellow passengers eased her to the front. She was heavily pregnant.

The crew on the patrol boat lowered a small rubber dinghy over the side and into the water. It was laden with yellow life jackets. Two officers, also in white suits and face masks, clambered on top of them, started the motor, and sped across the few meters to the migrants. They talked with the pregnant woman for a few minutes, and then one officer picked up a two-way radio and spoke to the captain.

"They've been on board since dusk last night," Amanda overheard the voice from the radio. "They left the Moroccan coast from a beach just outside Ceuta, but the motor packed up hours ago. Somehow, they made it through the shipping channel, untouched. Shall I bring the pregnant lady?"

"Go ahead but watch for any idiots with weapons as you transfer them over," instructed the captain. "We don't want them taking over our boat."

Amanda filmed as the officers passed around the life jackets and then zoomed in on the pregnant woman as she prepared to transfer into the smaller dinghy.

She was about to clamber across when there was a wailing cry from the back of the remaining migrants.

Amanda's stomach churned as she heard the dreaded, "Allahu Akbar," reverberate across the water.

All turned to see who had made the noise. A young man with long hair and lighter skin than the others was thrusting his way through and over his fellow passengers. He elbowed some in the face in his desperation to launch himself at the officer helping the pregnant woman.

He reached the side of the boat and screamed something unintelligible at the officer and then squatted and girded himself to leap across the narrow gap between the two dinghies. At the last moment, he dug into his jeans pocket and extracted a small knife. He snapped it open and jumped.

Everyone gasped; several Africans grabbed him.

Their violent movement unbalanced their dinghy, which nearly capsized, causing half of its passengers to fall into the water including the attacker. The dinghy hovered on the verge of no return for several seconds and then fell back to its original position with a loud splash.

The few who could swim helped the many who couldn't back to the side of their dinghy. Several migrants, enraged by the attacker, swam toward him, grabbed his head, and shoved it violently under the surface. The long-haired attacker wriggled like a lobster dangling over a boiling water pot, seawater foaming madly from his kicking legs.

They held him under until he stopped moving. One man removed his shoulder bag, and then they let him go, watching in silence as he sank slowly into the depths. When he'd disappeared, they turned, paddled back to the dinghy, and clung onto the edge. One by one, they climbed back on board and sat where they could.

Amanda watched the man who'd taken the shoulder bag and kept her camera running as he searched inside. He removed money and a passport and then threw the bag in the water and watched while it sank.

In the madness of the attack, the pregnant woman had fallen from the migrant's dinghy into that of the Guardia Civil. She'd landed heavily, her swollen abdomen banging hard against an officer's head. He sat unmoving and halfdazed, rubbing his neck—the woman on his lap, unmoving. The other officer quickly grabbed the tiller, twisted the accelerator, and headed back toward the patrol boat.

The crew winched up the dinghy from the water, lifted the woman out, and laid her on the deck.

Amanda was shocked by her appearance. From a distance, she'd looked like a mature woman, but from up close, she couldn't have been much more than fifteen or sixteen years old. Amanda approached her and asked in French if she could help.

The girl screamed and doubled up into a fetal position, blood hemorrhaging from between her legs and staining the thin material of her shabby skirt.

The captain stood beside Amanda, looking down at the poor woman with a sad expression.

"She's about to lose her baby," he said quietly.

"Do you have any painkillers?" asked Amanda, watching the mixture of the African girl's blood and birth waters flowing toward the edge of the bleached wooden deck.

"Only morphine, but I can't give her that," answered the captain.

The woman groaned and through gritted teeth said in French, "Help me." She tried to pull herself up, but her skirt was too tight.

Amanda loosened the thin material and shoved it up her thighs.

The woman adopted a squatting position and said breathlessly, "My baby is coming soon; hold my hands. I don't know how long my strength will last."

Amanda held out her hands.

The woman grasped them with thin bony fingers. Her face in agony, tears streaming down her face as another contraction hit hard.

Amanda was impressed with her determination.

The woman screeched, then bore down, and then again, struggling to control her breathing as the contractions increased their tempo and intensity.

This is going too quickly, thought Amanda as the woman's grip on her hands grew tighter. The woman clenched her teeth, took one huge breath, and squeezed as hard as she could. What seemed minutes later, she opened her eyes, looked directly at Amanda and grinned with relief.

"Take it in your hands," she instructed.

Amanda reached between the woman's legs and felt the baby's head fully exposed. "One more should do it," said Amanda.

The woman grimaced and pushed.

The tiny baby plopped into Amanda's hands with a squelch, followed by a massive spray of blood.

The woman screamed in agony and then slumped onto the deck, unconscious.

The blood and mucus were staining Amanda's white protective suit.

She didn't notice.

"Knife, scissors, anything to cut the cord and quick," instructed Amanda, cradling the still child in her arms.

"It's OK. I have the ship's first-aid box here," said the captain.

The captain reached down and snipped as near to the baby's navel as he dared with a small pair of scissors. He passed Amanda a blanket. Instinctively, she checked the child. Ten fingers, ten toes, and everything in place. It was a little girl.

But the baby lay unmoving. Amanda's first reaction

was that it had been still born.

Her emotions ran wild. Her first birth ever and it had come to naught. She thought desperately no having a clue what to do next, but some inner voice told her to clear the mucus out of the child's mouth. She took off her protective gloves, gently probed her little finger into the child's mouth, and then pinched its nose.

After a few seconds, the baby snorted, gulping in deep breaths. Her little face scrunched up, and then it came. She took a deep breath and cried with a volume and intensity that is uniquely reserved for the newborn.

What a beautiful moment, marveled Amanda relishing the screaming baby wrestling in her arms. She felt privileged to have played a small part in her delivery. Tears rolled down her cheeks.

The captain grasped the mother's wrist and checked her pulse.

"It's faint but regular," he said. "Let's take you all to a cabin and try the baby on her breast."

The captain wrapped the mother in a blanket and then picked her up as if she was a feather and led the way to a cabin behind the bridge.

Amanda followed the captain into a large room fitted with bench seats. The captain laid the mother on one and stood back. Amanda exposed the woman's breast and put the child on her chest. The baby stopped crying and latched on immediately.

"Can you bring me some hot water?" Amanda asked the captain. "We need to wash the baby and her mother."

"Of course," the captain replied as he went out and closed the door behind him.

Amanda nodded and turned back to the baby, who seemed none the worse for wear after her traumatic and rapid arrival into this world.

The captain returned with a bucket of hot water, some soap, and a selection of towels.

"Thanks," said Amanda.

"The mother needs urgent attention," whispered the captain. "We're going to speed into Algeciras as fast as we can. Another boat will arrive shortly to tow in the remaining migrants."

"What happens when we land?"

"They'll be taken to the hospital. When the mother recovers, she and the baby will be transferred to the detention center for processing."

"And if she doesn't?"

"Try and think positively."

"How long before we arrive in Algeciras?" asked Amanda.

"Half an hour or so?"

"Does it mean that we are still in Spanish territorial waters?"

"Why?"

"If the mother doesn't survive, this baby will need a nationality. She has no papers, and we have no idea from where she originates. If this child is to have any future life, it's going to need a passport and a nurturer to accept responsibility for her. If we are inside Spain's maritime borders, the government is obliged to grant her citizenship."

"I see; I'll check our precise position at the moment she was born and let you know."

"Thanks."

Several minutes later, the baby stopped sucking and fell asleep. Amanda removed the towel and gently washed off the remaining mucus. When finished, she removed the baby from her mother's chest, wrapped her in a fresh towel, and tucked her under one arm. She then undressed the mother and washed her as best she could before covering her with a towel and checking her wrist. Her pulse was still weak but now intermittent.

Amanda worried about the afterbirth. Her vague recollection of biology classes at school nagged at her, saying that it should be expelled as soon as possible. She thought about easing it out with the umbilical cord, but that concerned her. Perhaps the placenta was blocking any further loss of blood.

She did nothing but rocked the baby gently.

It sighed and slept.

Amanda heard the ship's engines speed up to full power, felt it turning, and then settle into a straight run back to port.

The captain returned with hot coffee.

"An ambulance will be waiting on the quay," he said.

"If the mother does recover, what happens to her and the child in the detention center?"

"They'll be processed by the asylum panel."

"Can I do anything to facilitate their application?"

"Such as what?"

"Offer the mother a job?"

"Are you a Spanish citizen?"

"No. American, but I'm a tax resident."

"Then it's unlikely."

"Could I go to the hospital with them?"

"Sorry, Señora, no. We have a process to go through; it does not permit outside involvement and definitely not media."

"Could I give her some money?"

"No, once we land, she will be given new clothes and be fed properly until the panel decides what to do with them."

"Can I visit her?"

"No, no visitors."

"Can I write to her?"

"Yes, but she probably can't read."

"Well, I'm going to put my card with the mother and baby and a note on the back, offering my assistance."

"Fine, good luck, but you're wasting your time."

"You're sure I can do nothing?"

"Señora, believe me, my wife and I have tried with other children but without success."

"Very well, but I'm determined to do something. I'll speak to an immigration lawyer to find out if I can take them both in."

"As you wish. Give me one of your cards. I'll send you the GPS coordinates for her birth location and contact details for the asylum panel."

"Thank you, Captain. Here's my card. What's your name?"

"Gutierrez, Antonio Gutierrez."

"I'm much obliged, Antonio," said Amanda, taking his hand and shaking it.

"It's the least I can do," replied the captain. "Now excuse me, but I have to prepare for docking."

Twenty minutes later the ship moored in Algeciras harbor.

An ambulance was waiting on the quay.

As soon as a gangway was secured, a nurse and doctor dressed in green scrubs ran on board with a stretcher.

They checked the still unconscious mother.

"She's bleeding internally," said the doctor. "We'll have to hurry."

They lifted the woman gently onto the stretcher and took an end each.

"Can you bring the child to the ambulance, Señora?" asked the nurse.

Amanda followed the stretcher up the gangplank, gently rocking the baby still cradled in her arms. The additional movement disturbed her slumbers. She half opened her eyes, looked directly into Amanda's, and gurgled—the makings of a tiny smile on her lips before resuming her sleep.

Amanda watched as they loaded the mother into the rear of the ambulance and secured her. The doctor tested the mother's blood and plugged in a drip and a transfusion.

"I'll take the child now," said the nurse, a kindly dark-haired woman. "Is it a girl?"

"Yes."

"What's your name?"

"Amanda," she replied, passing over the baby reluctantly, tears in her eyes.

"Then we'll call her after you until the mother is well enough to name her."

"Thank you. Is the mother likely to survive?"

"Too soon to tell yet."

"Can I call the hospital to find out?"

"You could, but I don't know yet which building we're going to. Here's my number." The nurse extracted a card from her breast pocket and handed it over. "Phone me later tonight and don't worry—I'll keep an eye on them."

With that, the nurse closed the ambulance door.

It drove off, siren blaring and lights flashing.

Amanda watched it go. All thoughts of the documentary gone from her mind.

5

Phillip drove his BMW Cabriolet down to the second floor of Nerja's parking garage under the relatively new central square, Plaza España. He found a spot in his usual area near the ramp, opened the door, and eased his long limbs out of the car. He peered around the gloomy garage.

Satisfied that his precious leather upholstery would be safe from passing pigeons, he decided to leave the roof down; his plan didn't include being in town for long. He grabbed his sports bag from the back seat and headed off in the direction of his favorite beach, Playa El Salon.

At the southern end of the garage, he climbed the two up ramps and emerged from the dark interior into the bright early morning sunshine. The contrast dazzled him, so he flipped his sunglasses down from his forehead and continued toward the town hall.

He tried to begin most days with a swim in the Mediterranean. It was one of those to-do items on his bucket list when he'd come to live in Spain permanently. Nerja was blessed with several pretty beaches, but he'd settled on Playa El Salon as his regular exercise venue. The long, steep slope down and back deterred most tourists, leaving uncrowded waters. The idea was to make up for years of physical neglect and stress during his former life. Hopefully, he wasn't too late.

Phillip walked under the town-hall archway and across the Balcon de Europa in the direction of the passageway that led down to Playa El Salon.

The Balcon, as the locals call it, exists thanks to a visit by King Alfonso XII in 1884 after a massive earthquake had destroyed most of the area. He'd stood among the ruins and issued a decree that this central area of the town was to be rebuilt and referred to as El Balcon de Europa. More recently, the council installed a life-size bronze statue of the monarch leaning against the safety railings as a memento of his regal creativity. Tourists loved taking selfies, standing next to him.

Phillip turned into the passageway between Unicaja bank and Marissal Hostel and began his descent down the slope to the beach. He passed the Irish pub and, as he turned the corner, paused with one foot on the low wall to absorb the striking scenery below.

Playa El Salon is an enchanting cove several hundred meters long with limestone rocks at both ends and a stark cliff to the rear that protects against the occasional northerly breeze. Perched on top of the cliff are holiday apartments and the romantic terrace of Restaurant Marbella, a popular venue for wedding receptions. A squabble of seagulls swooped and hovered over the sands, their persistent cawing reverberated hauntingly over the beach.

There's a short palm-tree-lined promenade at the bottom of the slope in front of a row of whitewashed fishermen's cottages. At the top of the beach lay half a dozen colorful fishing boats, in various states of readiness. In July, the largest one is adorned with flowers and rowed around to Playa Torrecilla to collect an effigy of the Virgin Mary for her annual trip around the bay to celebrate the Fiesta of Virgen del Carmen. The populace admires her flotillas' progress from the Balcon, enjoying beer and tapas as she's delivered to Playa Calahonda below.

Adjacent to the cottages stands a forlorn concrete sea horse decorated with white pebbles. It marks the former site of a vibrant beach bar run by a British family from Sheffield in Northern England. Phillip recalled many happy hours there as a young man enjoying a few beers and watching Formula One with the owner. His sister had worked in the kitchen for a while; her delicious paellas had been much appreciated.

The bar's sad replacement is a temporary kiosk serving warm beer in plastic cups. Customers have to battle for the few rickety chairs, and wobbly tables huddled tightly together under a couple of weather-beaten parasols.

Out by the water's edge, Phillip spotted a slender, heavily tanned senior man with white hair and an immaculately trimmed kaiser mustache. He was wearing ill-fitting bright-pink bathing shorts, bending over at the water's edge and dangling something in the surf.

The man was Didi. One of Phillip's many German friends in Nerja. They'd met a couple of years ago in

Phillip's regular café on the Balcon when Phillip had helped him out with a discrepancy on the electricity bill for his villa. Didi's language skills were limited to German and basic English. Phillip watched him swing the mysterious object up toward his face, catch it adeptly in his other hand, and inspect it myopically. Didi shook his head in disappointment and then plunged whatever it was back into the surf.

Didi lived near Nerja with his husband for most of the year. He was a retired hairdresser from Bremen in Northern Germany but locally had become renowned for dangling his thermometer in the surf on a rope to test the water temperature. He justified his eccentricity on the need to know precise information before answering his big question. To bathe or not to bathe his delicate frame? Apparently in Bremen, dipping a toe in the shallows was considered way too slapdash.

Didi tried to swim on El Salon most mornings, but only if the temperature was at least twenty-three degrees centigrade or more. He would often stand at the water's edge for hours, waiting for the sea to warm up—patiently testing away until the mercury attained his minimum entry level. If it didn't, he went home, disappointed.

Phillip joined him at the water's edge.

"Guten morgen, Didi," Phillip said in German.

"Hallo, Phillip."

Phillip removed his outer clothing, revealing blue swimming shorts, utterly oblivious to Didi's blatant admiration of his athletic physique. He placed everything tidily in his bag and dived straight in. The water was exhilarating, and he relished its cleansing saltiness as it washed away his morning cobwebs.

He swam fast for three hundred meters to a yellow line of markers that delineated the exclusion zone for Jet Skis and motorboats and clung onto one of the buoys. While he bobbed gently up and down, recovering his breath, he looked back toward Nerja.

Blinds were being raised and curtains drawn in some of the rooms of the Hotel Balcon de Europa. Guests were collecting towels from the balcony railings and folding them tidily in preparation for another hard day's roasting on the sun lounger.

In the distance behind the hotel, the craggy peaks of the Sierra Tejeda and Almijara reflected a delicate shade of pink from the early-morning sun.

A modest improvement over Walton Bridge, Phillip thought to himself and chuckled, recalling the view from his last abode in England, the houseboat at Shepperton.

He swam leisurely back to the beach and then chatted amicably with Didi while he paced around, waiting for the warm sunshine to dry him off. Meanwhile, Didi continued his water-testing activities and, after a few minutes, happily announced that the temperature was precisely twenty-three degrees.

At that, Didi swung the thermometer rope round in the air and let it go at precisely the right moment. It landed gently but accurately on his floral towel. He turned and tiptoed gingerly down into the water until it came up to his waist. He launched himself into three breaststrokes, turned around, swam three back, and struggled out of the water.

He was breathing hard.

"Warm genug?" Phillip enquired.

"Perfekt danke. Wir sehen uns oben."

Didi retrieved his gear along with the treasured

testing instrument and then strode almost purposefully off to the showers. Phillip did a few stretches and exercises and then sat down on his towel, faced the sea, and crossed his legs to meditate for a few minutes.

Before he closed his eyes, he looked out to the yellow buoy and recalled his earlier years here when Juliet used to swim out there regularly with him. For some reason, she loved Playa El Salon but when pressed would never explain why. She preferred hanging onto his shoulder than the slimy yellow plastic. They would bob up and down together, talking about silly stuff. Favorite musicians—hers was Justin Bieber, and his Take That. He yearned to kiss her but did nothing. She pecked him on the cheek and said thanks for being there for her. Then they raced back to shore. He let her win. Didi used to hold her towel to protect her modesty as she changed into dry clothes. They both adored her and referred to her as their beautiful English rose. Then she fell in love with her first boyfriend, and that was the end of that.

Phillip gazed out to the horizon and let the warm sun wash over him as he composed himself. He closed his eyes.

He was about to walk up the hill, take a seat at his regular café, and be served by Juliet.

This time, however, he would not behave like a lovesick fool.

He reminded himself of the conclusions he'd drawn from his pilgrimage: Juliet is a beautiful young girl who has a boyfriend called Hassan, a pleasant fellow from Morocco. She likes me but as a paternal figure not in a romantic way. It is pure coincidence that she is the spitting image of my ex-wife. And no, she is not my daughter, despite the fact that if I'd had a baby girl with my ex—the result would probably have resembled Juliet. I am no longer confused about wanting to date her or buy her a dollhouse. I will not proffer unasked advice. I am just an older man friend who respects her and helps her out from time to time, but from now only when she asks. As from today, I will not waste hours sitting at the café discreetly ogling her, hoping desperately that she might come and talk to me. She has ceased being an obsession. Out of respect for my business partner Richard, I must concentrate on my work. These are the new rules. I must obey them.

Phillip opened his eyes, took several deep breaths, and asked himself out loud, "Am I ready for this?"

A seagull flying overhead at the very moment cawed loudly.

It didn't sound like laughter.

Phillip took it as a good omen, stood, picked up his bag, and went to the showers.

He washed off the salt and sand, dressed, packed his damp things leisurely back into his bag, and then ambled up the hill for breakfast.

The salty, sulfury, green smell of the sea wafted up after him.

As he reached the bend, he paused to admire the impressive panorama.

A few fluffy white clouds speckled an azure sky, contrasting against the deeper bluey turquoise of the calm Mediterranean. In the distant haze, a supertanker was heading west toward the Straits of Gibraltar. A little nearer a couple of trawlers circled a swirling shoal of sea bream while seabirds wheeled above.

Two hundred kilometers further south was Africa,

where, on the occasional haze-free day, the Rif Mountains of Northern Morocco were visible.

Phillip continued his uphill walk, turned onto the Balcon just as the clock on the tower of the imposing El Salvador, Nerja's seventeenth-century Baroque-Mudejar church, struck nine o'clock.

He headed for the café, his heart racing and not from the walk up the hill.

This was it. The moment of truth.

6

Amanda said her good-byes to the captain and headed toward her car parked at the end of the quay. Halfway there her head reengaged itself with her documentary and remembered that she hadn't talked to any of the migrants. She really needed their input to produce an authentic, moving film.

She turned back and went to talk again with the captain.

He'd been watching her from the bridge.

"I imagine that your emergency midwifery services distracted you from your real work?" he said as she climbed up the steps to stand beside him.

"Perceptive of you, Antonio," answered Amanda. "And you're right. I still need to talk with the migrants. I need to know more about their journeys. Also, I want to tell the hospital or the immigration center about the baby's mother. Then there's this man who they drowned. Who was he? What did he hope to achieve? Without answers to these questions, my video won't be powerful enough to educate European politicians about the horrors they are ignoring. Neither will it deter yet more migrants coming all this way for nothing."

"Ouch, strong words, Amanda; you know how to hit my sore spots. Usually, there would be nothing I could do to help you. Once the migrants leave my ship, they are in the hands of the immigration services and out of police jurisdiction. However, there may be a way to make inquiries about the drowned man, but I will need to consult with my superiors first. Having said that, I'm not sure how I could justify taking you in with me, especially as you are a member of the press."

"Interpreter. I could translate for you."

"Mmm. Food for thought."

"Perhaps if you mention that the drowned man may have been part of a terrorist network, it might boost the success of your request. Also, I filmed all the action and would be happy to hand over the footage in return for visitation rights."

"Until they have landed, I can do nothing."

"I can wait."

"They will be hours yet; they can't tow these dinghies faster than a snail's pace when they are overloaded. Anyway, my bosses move slowly. They'll need a day or two to decide. I'll call you as soon as I know something."

"Thanks, Antonio, and please don't forget those GPS coordinates."

"Have a little faith in us civil servants, Amanda. We might be slow, but in the end, we find a way."

"In that case, I'll say my goodbyes and wait with bated breath to hear from you."

They shook hands, and Amanda crossed back over the gangplank and this time made it to her car.

She drove her silver Prius out of Algeciras harbor with a heavy heart. The emotional highs and lows of the day had drained her usual resilience to human tragedy.

As she queued in the heavy rush-hour traffic heading toward the motorway, she tried to remain focused on her film. What should be the central theme and title? Usually, she'd relish these creative tasks, but today she couldn't think straight. As soon as she was out on the open road, she let her mind wander over the day's events.

Her eyes watered.

There had been two firsts.

A man had been killed in front of her.

Her film would not be about him. Viewers were already overexposed and desensitized to the mindless violence of terrorists and their like; they wouldn't appreciate yet more of the same.

But the baby.

Seeing a baby being born had been a miracle in the circumstances. However, for her, it had been a bittersweet moment.

On the one hand, she'd marveled at the power of nature and the strength of the young African girl. On the other, she'd despaired at the hopelessness of their situation. Miles away from home, alone and vulnerable. Unclear citizenship status. Who was the father? Was it a loving relationship, or had she been raped like so many before her? What did she hope that emigration to Spain might bring to her life? Did she even know where she was?

Amanda was proud to have helped with the birth.

To have a baby named after her, even if temporarily, made her tingle with pleasure, but in reality, the event reminded her of her own situation.

Thirty-four years old, still single, no children, and not a decent man in sight.

Holding the baby had penetrated deep into that particular cerebral recess. The one she used to bury her yearnings for a child by pretending her career was more important. Yes, she was successful, earned good money, and owned her apartment in Malaga center outright. But where was all this going? More money? More success?

"Are material things all I need to be fulfilled?" she asked herself out loud. "If being such a smart woman is so fucking wonderful, why do I have this gaping hole in my soul?"

Once again, her eyes welled with tears.

"Come on, you stupid bitch. Stop this nonsense," Amanda shouted out loud, pulled over to the side of the road, and wept desperately, banging the steering wheel with a clenched fist. "Bugger it," she said eventually, then rejoined the motorway, and switched on the car communications system. She pulled up her playlist, raised the volume, and had an exclusive car Karaoke with Adele all the way back to Malaga. Her harmony reminded her of a wailing cat.

Malaga has a population approaching six hundred thousand and is the capital city of the province of its name. It's one of the eight provinces that make up Spain's most extensive autonomous community, Andalucia.

It's a historic port city with Phoenician origins. The central skyline is dominated by the remains of two ancient Moorish hilltop citadels, Alcabaza and Gibralfaro. At the foot of the hill is the towering Renaissance Catholic cathedral nicknamed La Manquita (one-armed lady), because one of its two towers was inexplicably never completed.

The old town dates back to the seventeenth century. The town council has done an excellent job in ensuring that building and refurbishment projects retain original features. Over the last decade, it's become highly popular with visitors all year round. The Christmas lights are incredible; also, the passion and intensity of the Easter processions compete seriously with those in Andalucia's capital, Sevilla. One of Malaga's famous sons, Antonio Banderas, helps carry one of the enormous thrones.

In addition to the Picasso, there are several other significant museums: the Thyssen, the Russian from St. Petersburg, and the latest addition to the modernized harbor is the first Centre Pompidou outside of France.

An hour later, Amanda's tears had dried up. The sun was setting behind her, illuminating the sky with a kaleidoscopic array of color as she turned into the garage under her apartment block opposite Malaga's historic Mercado Central Acarazanas. The impressive wrought-iron and glass marketplace had been built in 1879 and refurbished in 2008. Today it was a thriving food hall combined with superb tapas bars.

Amanda unloaded her camera gear from the trunk, walked over to the elevator, and went up to the seventh and uppermost floor. She inserted her key in the lock, turned it, went inside, kicked the door closed behind her, and went through to the kitchen where she dumped her stuff on the black-granite worktop of the island.

She poured herself a glass of Verdejo white wine from the Rueda wine region in northern Spain, slid open the full-height glazed doors, and went out onto the terrace with her phone.

The views were spectacular as the fading sun reflected the last of its rays on the market roof. She sat down at the terrace table and sipped her wine while checking her e-mails and social media.

She brought herself up to date with everyone. It was just the usual trivia. She didn't know why she bothered with it but didn't want to stand accused of being unsociable. She spent little enough time with real people as it was.

Her parents were always pleased to hear from her. They'd retired now and had bought a small farm outside Carmona, a town with Celtic and Roman origins some thirty kilometers to the east of Sevilla. Her mother's first question was, have you met anyone today? She was just as keen to be a grandparent as Amanda was to be a mother.

She went into the kitchen, made herself an avocado salad, with walnuts, garlic and olive oil and carried it through to her study, where she kept her editing equipment. She ate the salad while the camera transferred the days filming to her hard drive.

She finished the salad, put the plate to one side, and began by entering the video title.

Stolen Lives.

It was about the only thing that she'd been able to decide on in the car, but that was the extent of it. No matter how long Amanda tried to be creative, the ideas refused to materialize. Worrying about little Amanda dominated her gray cells.

She had to know.

She dug the nurse's card out of her purse and called the number.

"Hola," answered a woman's voice after the third ring.

"Is that Nurse Mendez?" enquired Amanda.

"Yes. Amanda?"

"That's right. How…"

"I'm sorry. The mother died; she'd lost too much blood."

"Oh no, that's terrible, and er, the baby?" asked Amanda, a sickening feeling growing in her stomach.

"Little Amanda is fine. Amazing pair of lungs."

"That is a relief. Where is she?"

"She's in the baby unit in the main Algeciras hospital, where she'll stay for a few days and then be offered up for adoption. We have a long waiting list of approved parents for these eventualities."

"That is good news. Just in case the new parents are interested, I have some film of her mother if they want a clip to show her when she's older."

"That will be up to her new parents. Most prefer a clean break from the past, so don't expect much."

"Oh, that is disappointing."

"I understand; you felt some bond with the child and don't want to let go."

"That's exactly right."

"Happens to me all the time, and I've been at it for twenty years. Listen, you were a great help out there today. Many couldn't have coped with the blood and everything."

"You guys are the real heroes facing this human agony every day. It reminded me of how ignorant I am about real life, and that's upset my usual thinking patterns. So much so that I've been sitting here all evening staring at my monitor, struggling to edit my work, but nothing is happening. Authors would call it writer's block, but talking to you has reinspired me. Now I know what to do. Thanks again, Nurse. Adios."

Amanda worked until just before midnight, sketching out her concept.

I'm going to call the mother, Leila, she thought. I'll assume that she's from the Republic of Niger, ran away from her slave master, joined a caravan across the Sahara desert, and was abused by the men. Eventually, as she worked her way across Mali and Morocco, her young body matured, and she fell pregnant probably to a Moroccan, by the lighter color of the baby's skin.

Her film was about Leila's incredible journey to freedom, only to fail at the last hurdle, but at least her baby was about to find a new life in a civilized country.

She loaded the last clip, added an optional voice-over, and closed her machine for the night.

She stood up, stretched, yawned, and headed for the bathroom.

She showered, slipped into her striped sleep shirt, and collapsed into bed.

As her head touched the pillow, she thought about her plans for tomorrow.

It would be a far more mundane day.

She would complete the editing of the *Stolen Lives* video but hold off on sending it to New York until she'd heard back from the captain about getting access to the detention center in Algeciras. The video would be so much more powerful with some quotes from the migrants in the captured dinghy. Other than that she had to prepare for her next documentary, which she'd be filming the day after.

Wednesday, May 15.

Nerja's San Isidro Festival.

7

Calm down, Phillip commanded the negative voices in his head as he approached the café. We're only going for breakfast and to meet some friends—nothing more, nothing less.

Café-Bar Don Comer stood next to Nerja's church. It was extremely popular, not just with tourists but also with locals and particularly the business people based in and around the Balcon.

Manolo, the proprietor, and his wife Pepa both spoke excellent English and had provided an eight-seater table reserved exclusively for their regular customers. They guaranteed a place and quick service no matter how busy they were.

Phillip and Richard had adopted it as their morning meeting place. The coffee was excellent; it was convenient for the parking garage and bank and was a brief walk from Richard's house. Phillip took his seat. He didn't need to order. The staff would see him sitting down and knew what he wanted.

Richard was already there, chatting with Didi and one of the other foreign regulars—Klik, a Danish chiropractor. They exchanged greetings.

Richard finished his conversation with Klik, who stood up, waved at everyone in general, and left to resume his daily wrestling with out-of-kilter body frames at his clinic across the Balcon.

Richard turned to Phillip and said in German, "Didi wants to sell their villa."

"You didn't mention it on the beach," said Phillip.

"I don't like to mix pleasure and business," said Didi.

"Why do you want to sell?" asked Richard.

"Gunter and I aren't getting any younger, and although our villa is lovely, it's remote, and we are worried about ambulances or taxis getting down the track to us. We want to downsize to an apartment in the town center," answered Didi.

"Do you want to sell directly or use an estate agent?" asked Richard.

"We'll be leaving for Bremen the day after San Isidro, so best to use an agent. Can you suggest any good ones?"

"Of course," replied Richard, opening his small shoulder bag. "I'll write down the best three and the person to talk to." Richard scribbled the information on a page of his notebook and tore it out. "Here," he said, passing the list to Didi. "Please mention our name when you contact them."

"Thanks; I will," replied Didi, who folded the paper precisely in half and slipped the list into his shirt pocket.

"Are you entering the dressage competition at San Isidro again this year," asked Phillip.

"No, last year was my final effort, but Gunter and I will be watching avidly. At least this year, I'll be free to take loads of photos. Gunter can't tell one end of a camera from the other. Perhaps we'll see you there?"

"I'll try, but I'm with my nieces, so am unsure of my timings. Either way, I hope you enjoy it."

"It'll be mixed emotions," said Didi sadly. "Half of me still wants to be up there, and the rest of me remembers the aches and pains from last year. He took a final sip of his coffee, left some coins on the table, and left.

Richard Daniels had lived in Nerja for over twenty years. He'd been shrewd enough to sell his marketing agency in Boston, Massachusetts, to a large group from New York and had retired early.

According to a few friends, the Costa del Sol was blessed with a year-round balmy climate, a dense concentration of championship golf courses, and a relatively inexpensive cost of living. It sounded just like the perfect escape. He'd packed his bags and set out to test the waters in Malaga. On first inspection, the beautiful, ancient city was vibrant and fascinating, the many parks and gardens were beautifully designed and maintained, but Richard was looking for a more tranquil environment. The manager at his hotel advised him to try Marbella to the west, but he thought it brash, overdeveloped, and overpopulated with people who had more money than sense. Richard then went east of Malaga, discovered Nerja, and was instantly enamored with the place.

After several nights in the Hotel Balcon de Europa, he rented an apartment overlooking Playa Calahonda.

The next day found him at the nearest golf club at

Caleta de Velez known as Baviera Golf, a challenging eighteen-hole course designed by Jose-Maria Cañizares. The pro shop must have thought that it was Christmas as he melted his credit card on all the latest equipment and snazzy clothing. He spent the afternoon on their practice range, ironing out the bugs in his rusty swing.

Sadly, the concept of his idyllic retirement faded fast. Three months of duck hooks, banana slices, lost balls, and missed putts were more than sufficient to quell his enthusiasm for a sporting life. He ditched the tartan shorts and went to look for something to do.

It was several misleading translations in a restaurant that set his marketing man's juices flowing.

Instead of Pescado a la Plancha being translated as Grilled Fish, the menu read Ironed Fish. He could imagine the foreigners laughing and enquiring about the sharpness of the creases. Even more so when Mato con Miel, which should be Cottage Cheese with Honey, turned out to be Killed Honey, or Salchichas con Judias became Sausages with Jews and not Sausages and Beans. When Richard explained the errors to the owner, the man immediately blushed with embarrassment and looked nervously about himself, as if expecting an angry comment from a passing rabbi. He appointed Richard on the spot to mend his menus.

It was soon apparent to Richard that Spanish businessmen had little idea how to market themselves professionally to foreigners. With this contract under his belt, Richard founded the Electric Page marketing agency and went to work.

At that time, in the late nineties, the Germans were

laundering their black deutsche marks in preparation for the launch of the euro in January 2002. They were buying Spanish property in the sun like crazy, many getting ripped off in the process. Richard instinctively knew that a real-estate magazine in German was needed and, after conversations with potential advertisers, was convinced that he was onto something. The problem was he spoke no German.

As it so often does, providence presented its way forward, and within days he'd met Ingrid, a delightful German woman at a cocktail party. She owned a small publishing business in Nerja, and one of her publications was exactly what Richard was looking for.

He bought it from her.

Ingrid's previous partner had died a couple of years ago. Intrigued by this congenial American, she offered to help him expand the magazine, despite her limited English.

Somehow, they managed to find a way to work together. Within six months Richard was speaking adequate German, had redesigned the magazine entirely, and increased the advertising revenues substantially.

A year later, he married Ingrid in Gibraltar, where the paperwork for international wedding licenses was much less burdensome than Spain's unwieldy bureaucracy. Afterward, he quit his rented apartment and moved into her large house in Nerja's old town.

The arrival of the euro in Spain changed the economy instantly. The price of a cup of coffee doubled overnight, and low-cost property disappeared forever. Inevitably, supplies of dodgy German cash slowed to a trickle, and along with it, the property advertisers. Reluctantly, they closed the magazine down in the midnoughties.

Richard pottered about for a decade or so, doing various marketing projects, but was then approached by one of his former magazine advertisers. They were a Spanish supermarket chain keen to find new ways to promote themselves on the Internet to the rapidly growing number of foreigners before they arrived at their holiday rental villa. They commissioned Richard to set up a website, initially in English and then gradually adding other languages. Richard was to personally visit their main wine, cheese, and Iberian ham suppliers, video their facilities, sample the products, and write about them in a lighthearted manner.

Richard thought about it for a while before suggesting to them that he create an Internet guide to Spain and include the wonders of Spanish life and culture in both German and English. It was bound to attract more browsers than a stand-alone supermarket site.

He proposed to call it Nuestra España.

They loved the idea and agreed to be the primary sponsors.

All Richard needed now was someone to build the website and create the content.

He met Phillip at a function in Nerja's language school right around that time. They'd adjourned to Esquina Paulina, just down from the language school on Calle Cristo, where they'd gotten to know each other over the odd bottle of *vino tinto* from Ribera del Duero.

They hit it off and agreed to work together. Phillip would translate and use his technical skills to film, edit the videos, and be the webmaster. Richard would provide the articles and sell advertising.

Together, they traveled extensively around Spain, visiting the many historic cities, farms, wine bodegas, ham curers, and cheese makers. It was hard work.

Slowly they developed the site and built a nationwide network of advertising agencies, freelance writers, translators, and creative talent. The content expanded substantially while their need to travel so much diminished. Now, some three years later, Nuestra España had grown into the leading source of information about Spain in English, German, and Russian.

"Hi, Phillip, nice to see you back," a familiar female voice said as a hand gently stroked his shoulder, just as it always did. The same hand then started unloading his order from a tray. A double espresso coffee and traditional Spanish breakfast consisting of a toasted *mollete* or soft roll, smeared with garlic, drizzled with extravirgin olive oil, and topped with grated tomatoes.

Phillip took a deep breath and turned toward Juliet.

She was still as lovely as ever. Any heart would skip a beat.

Phillip's heart skipped two as she smiled warmly, obviously pleased to see him.

Juliet Harding was twenty-one and had worked at Don Comer for nearly three years. She was from somewhere near Birmingham, England. You could still faintly hear the Brummie in her rounded vowels and hard *g* at the end of "ing." She'd arrived in Nerja via a circuitous route after backpacking around Europe. She'd been making her way progressively by bus from Barcelona to Malaga, traveling along the Mediterranean coastline, but had to call her journey to a halt in Nerja because funds were running low. Manolo, the owner of the café, gave her a chance, despite the fact she spoke only a little Spanish. But over time and with lessons, she'd mastered the basics, liked the work, and stayed.

Her pretty face, long blond hair, and shapely figure along with a warm, friendly disposition toward customers was a great asset to Manolo's business. It proved popular with young Spaniards and catered to the many British tourists happy to speak with another compatriot. The café business soared.

Many of the male customers were enamored of her and pestered her for a date. She ignored them all.

Phillip never asked her out, yet she fussed over him every visit.

"You missed me then?" said Phillip.

"Place wasn't the same without you," replied Juliet playfully. "I had to listen to Richard's awful jokes, and to make matters worse, he always forgets the punch line. Thankfully, I'd heard most of them. Any plans for San Isidro this year?"

"I'll be on the oxcart with my sister and her tribe. You going with Hassan again?"

"Not bloody likely; he's gone back to Morocco—we've finished," she snapped.

"I'm sorry; I didn't know."

"How could you?" she said softly. "You were away. Deserted me in my hour of need."

"Selfish, aren't I?"

"It's no big deal. Hassan was summoned back to Nador by his family. They needed him to help run the family hotel. I was angry at first. How dare he leave me? That sort of thing. But I'm OK with it now."

"Does that mean you are alone for San Isidro?"

"Not exactly." She smiled happily. "But I could still fit you in later if you fancy it. I was hoping for another go at dancing the Sevillana with you."

"I thought your feet hadn't recovered from last year."

"No problem. I've invested in steel toe caps."

"How could I refuse such a charming invitation? Shall we confirm timings on the day?"

"Service," shouted someone.

Phillip and Juliet both turned to see a stocky man with a shaved head sporting a Real Madrid tattoo on the back of his neck, standing behind the bar and pointing at Juliet. It was Manolo. He gesticulated to Juliet to serve the two new customers in the process of sitting down at an adjoining table.

"No rest for the wicked," said Juliet, grinning, as she moved over to the new arrivals.

Phillip watched her move away.

He was tempted, but only for a second.

But then the new rules kicked in just as he'd hoped.

He turned back to Richard, took a long sip of his coffee, then picked up his mollete and took a bite. The combination of flavors was mouthwatering.

"I thought you handled that very well," said Richard. "Not your usual blubbering self."

"I thought I was going to lose it when she stroked my shoulder, but my new system seems to function."

"Good. Now that I have you back and firing on all cylinders, perhaps we can do some work?"

The two chatted about various outstanding projects, had another coffee, and exchanged more banter with Juliet. They paid up and walked toward

Plaza España, where they shook hands at the ramp down to the car park. Richard continued across the square on his way home. Phillip walked down into the murky concrete depths, analyzing his emotions.

He thought he'd acted the part quite well with Juliet. The proverbial Mr. Cool and relaxed. If the pilgrimage had enabled him to do that, then at least it was a start, but the truth was his feelings for Juliet hadn't changed one iota—he'd just learned to manage them better.

He'd have to live with that.

8

Belgian man kills French wife? Prado thought to himself, astounded.

Nerja's history of any type of crime was insignificant. Mainly bag thefts, pickpockets, local youths baiting drunken, usually British tourists outside nightclubs, or the occasional tiff between minor drug gangs. A couple of years ago, he'd spent a few weeks in the quaint town based in the Guardia Civil barracks, hunting for some supposed Russian mafia.

Local banks had been reporting the appearance of an unusual amount of €500 notes from their retail customers, particularly one women's clothing shop on Calle Pintada. Prado set up some surveillance, identified two attractive but gaudy women, and followed them to a large villa on the outskirts of town. They watched the villa for a while and monitored communications with the help of the Russian consulate. When the consulate identified the arrival of a Mr. Big wanted back in the motherland, Prado and his team raided and arrested everyone. They found several pistols and €4 million, mainly in denominations of the garish pink-colored €500 note. Prado had called the notes Bin Ladens. He knew they were out there but had never seen one. Mainly because criminals had them stashed under mattresses or, in this case, in plastic trash bags.

The Russians denied any knowledge of ownership or origins of the cash. Prado laughed in their face when Mr. Big said through an interpreter that they had found the money in the garage when renting the premises. Prado did them all a huge favor: he confiscated the pink bundles and presented them to the Bank of Spain as unwanted property. The bank, being on the verge of bankruptcy at the time, was most grateful. The Russians' expressions were epic.

Now he had an unexplained death in Nerja.

His instincts doubted the likelihood of any dark motives.

Prado had never bothered with cars. He didn't see what all the fuss was about. Which model to drive, or whether it had the latest in go-faster stripes or fancy wheels never concerned him. As long as it was reliable, could manage a reasonable speed, and be fitted with air conditioning, he was happy. He grabbed whatever was available from the carpool in the garage under the comisaría and headed east through El Palo, enjoying the beach and sea views as he threaded his way on the old coast road and out onto the autovia at Rincon de la Victoria.

It took him just under an hour to drive to the Guardia Civil barracks on Calle San Miguel in Nerja.

The security gates slid open, admitting him into the

congested car park. He blocked everyone in, left the car door open, and threw the keys at the desk sergeant on his way to the interview room.

Prado noticed a new sign on the interview-room door in three languages. He recognized the top one as being English and read it to himself,

> *The official language of the Guardia Civil are Spanish. For them that necessitate it, a qualified interpretater might be instrumental.*

He understood the first sentence, but the remainder was beyond him. He opened the door and went inside. The only window was an opaque skylight; it was shut. A ceiling fan whirred noisily but moved too slowly to generate any worthwhile ventilation.

It was hot, airless, and musty.

Sparse furnishings completed the dreary decor. In the middle of the room stood a battered wood-laminate desk. On its top lay a grubby laptop.

In the corner was a shabby beige filing cabinet topped with a wilting spider plant in a cracked ceramic pot.

A framed certificate was hanging on the rear wall.

It was askew.

On one side of the desk was a black plastic chair occupied by the senior Guardia Civil officer he'd worked with on the Russian case.

They exchanged nods.

On the opposite side of the desk were four unmatched chairs arranged tightly next to one another. One was occupied by a junior Guardia Civil officer, the other by the Belgian, a large bald man in his late sixties. He was dressed smartly in dark-blue trousers and a short-sleeved white shirt; he was perspiring heavily. He and the junior Guardia Civil officer were shouting at each other in a strange mixture of Spanish and English. It was quickly evident to Prado that Spanglish was not going to be the most effective communication method to solve this mysterious death.

Prado put his hat on the desk and sat down next to the Belgian.

"I'll take over now," instructed Prado.

The junior officer frowned at the inspector's intrusion, but he knew who Prado was and why he was here. He deferred to his superior and sat back in his chair, drumming his fingers lightly on the desk.

Prado glared at him.

He stopped drumming instantly.

Prado turned to the Belgian and asked in his limited English, "I am Inspector Prado; you have friend can Spanish speak?"

The Belgian replied, relieved, "Yes."

"You can mobile him to come?"

The Belgian nodded.

"Give him his phone," Prado requested in Spanish.

The officer behind the desk opened a drawer, extracted a phone and the Belgian's passport, and slid them toward Prado. Prado looked at both, retained the passport, and then shoved the phone over to the Belgian.

The Belgian's hand shook as he picked up his phone from the desk, but he managed to find his contact and press the call button. A man's voice answered in what sounded to Prado like German. They spoke briefly. The Belgian nodded and momentarily looked a tad happier.

"My friend Phillip Armitage is coming now," announced the Belgian in English. "He will ask for you at the gate." He then put his head in his hands and wept quietly.

Prado understood the gist of the Belgian's English and instructed the Guardia Civil officer to inform his colleagues. The officer left to carry out Prado's instructions and returned minutes later with several bottles of ice-cold mineral water and handed them around while they waited for the Belgian's interpreter.

A tall, athletic man with shaggy blond hair, wearing a dark-blue polo shirt and beige jeans, approached the robust steel security gate protecting the Guardia Civil barracks. He rang the bell.

"Si?" questioned the sergeant's tinny voice through the small loudspeaker.

"Inspector Prado, por favor," said the man, staring directly into the lens of the video camera through calm, steely blue eyes.

"Tiene cita?" inquired the voice.

"Si."

"Nombre?"

"Phillip Armitage."

"Vale. Momento."

Phillip waited patiently on the busy narrow pavement while the inspector was located and could confirm their meeting.

He knew that would take several minutes.

Meanwhile, the typical Spanish street scene provided Phillip with plenty of entertainment.

The late spring weather created a glorious backdrop for this daily live theater. Tiny flecks of white marble clouds randomly decorating a ubiquitous blue sky, comfortable temperature, minimal humidity, and a gentle breeze that tugged at Phillip's hair.

Competing aromas of ground coffee and toasted bread wafted from the café next door to the barracks but were immediately overwhelmed by the obnoxious exhaust fumes from the passing traffic.

A disabled lottery-ticket vendor had parked his wheelchair outside the supermarket entrance opposite. He announced in a loud croaky voice that he had the winning number for that night's Loteria Nacional draw. A queue formed in front of him, waving bundles of cash and blocking the pavement, forcing pedestrians into the road. Car horns blared.

In Calle America, the street to the side of the Guardia Civil, a diminutive senior female, confident and comfortable with her ample proportions, was haphazardly wielding a mop in front of her town house. Her purple dyed hair was set in curlers, and she wore the briefest of pink nightshirts, happy to display her spindly white legs gnarled with varicose veins as she twirled around daintily in bright-orange sports shoes. She chatted with her neighbor while liberally squirting *aguafuerte* or bleach over her stretch of concrete. Her raucous cackles could be heard above the din. Occasionally, she dipped the mop into a water bucket and splashed the pungent cocktail liberally over another day's detritus from the inconsiderate—cigarette butts, chewing gum, and dog excrement.

Passersby kept well out of range.

On the corner nearest the barracks, a young scruffily dressed man of Eastern European appearance was thrusting clear plastic packs of garlic and onions under the noses of passersby. His stock stood behind him packed tightly into a canvas shopping cart.

"One euro," he said quietly. He sold out in minutes.

Opposite the barracks, a sub-Saharan African man, elegantly dressed in a long colorful robe, held up his merchandise and shouted, "Looky, looky," every time someone walked in front of him. He was touting imitation Rolex watches and could say "genuine" or "very cheap" in at least nine languages.

A Guardia Civil officer in an ill-fitting uniform and cap patrolled indolently back and forth among the police vehicles parked tightly behind the high metal fence. His holstered pistol was fixed firmly to his black leather belt. He glanced at the street vendors disinterestedly. His responsibility was road traffic, minor crime, and to monitor Spain's borders, coastline, and highways. Unlicensed trading was the concern of the local police.

Beyond the patrol cars stood the barracks themselves, an aging three-story whitewashed stucco building with slatted green window shutters. The ground floor housed the interview rooms, cells, and offices. The upper levels were basic accommodation for the officers and their families.

A stone archway led to an inner courtyard. Carved into the curved upper stonework were the immortal words that appeared on every barracks throughout Spain—Todo por la Patria (everything for the homeland).

"Pasar," the tinny voice announced, and the gate slid open, squeaking intermittently as it rolled along its guide rail.

Phillip left the bustling scene behind him, went

through the gate, and strode across the car park toward the glazed entrance to the Guardia Civil.

He stretched out his hand to open the door under the arch but was beaten to it from the inside.

A smartly dressed, heavyset, medium-height man with brown eyes, a round, clean-shaven face, and silver-gray hair stepped out through the door.

"Sr. Armitage?" enquired the man?

"Si," answered Phillip.

"Bueno. Soy Inspector Prado. Pasar por favor."

Prado led Phillip into the center of the inner courtyard. It was deserted.

Prado paused.

Phillip stopped and looked at him curiously.

"Do you mind if I ask you a few questions before we go and talk to your friend?" asked Prado in Spanish.

"Please go ahead, Inspector."

"Did Sr. Faucher explain that his wife was dead?"

"Yes, something about an accident with the car."

"How long have you known Sr. Faucher?"

"About two years."

"Had he and his wife been married long?"

"They celebrated their fortieth wedding anniversary last year."

"Would you say that they were happy?"

"Sometimes, Inspector, you meet married couples who were made to be together. Marcel and Sophie were a charming, happy, and loving pair, with amazing children and grandchildren. They had plenty of money, a wonderful lifestyle, and treasured their time here in Nerja."

"Did he keep the car here permanently or drive it down?"

"He drove it down every year. They enjoyed meandering through your lovely country. Every trip they would try a different hotel. Marcel was proud that they had stayed in over forty Paradores."

"Impressive. Did he maintain the car?"

"Here, no, but in Brussels, regularly. He's a well-organized, conscientious man."

"Did he use the car much while here?"

"The occasional trip. They liked the market in Malaga. Sophie is, sorry was, a fantastic cook."

"Thank you, Sr. Armitage. Your Spanish is excellent. Was it German that you and Sr. Faucher were speaking?"

"Yes, we met at a dinner party where the hostess was German. I guess we just carried on doing so."

"Do you speak any other languages?"

"My Russian is passable, but don't ask me to give a lecture on the theory of relativity."

"I couldn't even do that in Spanish. Shall we go and talk with your friend. He's distraught, so please be gentle with him."

Prado led Phillip over to the interview room. Prado noticed him chuckle at the sign.

"That bad?" asked Prado.

"Terrible. If you give me your e-mail, I'll send you the correct text in all three languages."

"You speak French too?"

"Some, but I have a French colleague who'll double-check it, and her name is not Google."

Prado smiled and opened the door.

The Belgian still had his head in his hands but looked up with tearful eyes on hearing the door open. On seeing Phillip, he struggled to his feet, and they hugged each other for several moments."

"Ask him for his full name and to relate what happened please," said Prado quietly in Spanish.

The Belgian sat up straight in his chair and did his best to compose himself. He spoke in German, and Phillip translated simultaneously into Spanish.

"I am Marcel Faucher from Brussels," he spoke quietly and nervously. "My wife, Sophie—she is French from Strasbourg—and I were going to the market in Malaga. Sophie wanted some special fish. You remember her fish pate, Phillip?"

"Divine, Marcel."

The door squeaked open to reveal a tiny, aging cleaning woman in high-visibility lime-green overalls, standing beside a well-equipped cart. She extracted a mop, entered, and when Marcel didn't raise his feet to allow her access to under his chair, prodded insistently at his ankles.

"Is this necessary?" Prado asked quietly.

"We won't see her for another month, so yes," replied the senior Guardia Civil officer acidly.

Prado indicated that Marcel should move his feet and carry on with his explanation.

Phillip wasn't sure if he should laugh or cry.

Marcel soldiered on. The distraction helped him to continue with his explanation.

"I hadn't driven the car since we arrived just before Christmas, and it was immediately apparent that something was wrong with the engine. It wasn't firing correctly, some damp in the piston chambers I presumed. I persevered, and suddenly the engine caught.

"I had my foot down on the accelerator at the time, and I had already released the handbrake. The car almost jumped backward out of my garage, I had no control of it, so I just turned off the motor and jammed on the foot brake, and somehow I managed to stop it before it hit the underground car-park wall behind me.

"Sophie was standing in her usual position at the rear of the car, so I could see her out of the passenger-door wing mirror. She warns me if I'm getting too close to the car-park wall. The car moved so fast that she stood no chance. Phillip, it was the wing mirror." Marcel stopped talking, overcome with emotion. Phillip rested his arm on Marcel's shoulder and patted him gently. Eventually, Marcel took a deep breath and continued, "The wing mirror on the passenger door ripped out her liver. She bled to death in minutes. Her final words were, 'Sorry, my love. I was standing in the wrong place.'

"Now I have to tell our children. Phillip, I can't go on without her. Help me, please?"

Phillip patted Marcel's shoulder and translated for the inspector.

"Do you have photos of the scene?" enquired Prado of the two Guardia Civil officers.

The officer behind the desk rummaged in the drawer and passed them over.

Prado flicked through them and nodded.

"This was obviously a terrible accident," said Prado, handing Marcel's passport to Phillip. "Sr. Faucher has suffered more than enough. There will be no charges. After he's signed a written statement for the coroner, he may go."

Phillip translated for Marcel, who nodded and took a pen out of his shirt pocket.

The Guardia Civil officer went out to the next room, came back a few minutes later with a piece of printed paper, and gave it to Prado.

Prado read through it, nodded, and added his signature. He passed the document over to Phillip, who checked the text, approved it, and handed it to Marcel. Marcel signed, returned the pen to his pocket, and then struggled out of the chair. Phillip helped him out of the tiny office.

"Take this," said Prado, proffering his card to Phillip as he passed. "Any problems with the consulate or our bureaucrats with the body, let me know. Thanks for coming."

"My pleasure," answered Phillip. "I'll e-mail you those translations."

"Thanks," replied Prado. "Next time you're in Malaga, give me a call; you may like to help me with other investigations."

"Really?" said Phillip.

"My department needs people with your talent."

"Well, that would be interesting, provided that it doesn't conflict with my business."

"It shouldn't be too demanding; Nerja isn't much of a crime hotspot."

"Then, yes, I'd be happy to help out."

"Then we should meet and talk it through. There's an excellent café near my office. In the meantime, I hope all goes well with your friend. What a terrible way to lose one's wife. He'll find it difficult to recover. I'd advise some counseling."

"Thank you, Inspector. Very kind," replied Phillip.

Prado watched them go in two minds. On the one side, he was saddened by the Belgian's horrific experience, but on the positive side, he'd quickly solved his first case and believed that he'd identified his first voluntary translator.

9

Whoosh.

Bang.

The Nerja church clock struck ten o'clock as the official town firework igniter, dressed in his usual uniform of a battered straw hat, torn baggy trousers, and grubby T-shirt, sent the first of a dozen rockets aloft into a clear blue sky. The explosions echoed around the countryside, summoning the surrounding populace to prepare for the San Isidro Romeria and head to the town center.

While the bells tolled, the smoldering rocket sticks headed earthward with accelerating velocity. With luck to land harmlessly in the hot climate.

One year the awning of the then Calahonda beach restaurant went up in flames, and another, the mayor's silk underwear drying on her terrace.

The word Romeria evolves from processions of pilgrims going to Rome. Sprigs of the aromatic herb Romero or rosemary were stuck in travelers hats to ward off evil spirits and robbers.

Romerias are famous all over Spain, none more so

than the largest, held every May in Sevilla Province. Over a million pilgrims trail through the Doñana National Park to El Rocio, a village purposely built just for this one week. There are several hundred houses, a cathedral, and a couple of hotels. The roads are made of sand so that horses can be tethered right outside property owners' doors.

From the edge of Doñana, it takes the pilgrims several days to reach the village. Campfire smoke, grilled meat flavors, music, and song waft over the lengthy procession as it parks up for the night. It is a remarkably spiritual occasion. The modest consumption of the favored fiesta beverage—chilled dry sherry—assists where it can.

Nerja's San Isidro Romeria procession is minuscule by comparison but still attracts some ten thousand participants and onlookers. It starts at the church about midday and ends four kilometers away at the gardens of Nerja Caves.

Phillip walked up the ramp from Nerja's central underground car park and threaded his way through the boisterous crowds under the town-hall archway. He was dressed in his Romeria attire: a white linen shirt with a red bandanna knotted around his neck, a gray cordoba hat tilted forward to shade the face, and black jeans held up by a black leather belt to which he'd attached his phone pack. A natty secure widget for his phone, keys, cash, and cards.

Most men wore similar clothing, whether participant or onlooker.

Women wore brightly colored, tightly fitting long Spanish dresses, which for San Isidro were traditionally patterned with polka dots. No matter what shape, age, or dimensions, these dresses transformed the wearer into gorgeous, elegant women who carried themselves graciously. They were a pleasure to behold. Most men were doing a lot of beholding.

Phillip turned right out of the archway and threaded his way through the assembling masses, past the church into Plaza Cavana, where the oxcarts were forming a line.

On his way through the crowd, he chatted, shook hands, hugged, or embraced several friends, keeping an eye out for his brother-in-law, Jose. He eventually spotted him in deep conversation with his fellow herdsmen sitting at a table outside La Fragata café. They were enjoying a moment's respite from prodding their beasts of burden before the procession began in earnest. Most of them had already had quite a journey into town. It would have taken Jose well over an hour to lumber the four kilometers down the Frigiliana Road from their farm.

Jose ordered a coffee for Phillip and more water for himself while explaining exactly where the cart was parked in Calle Diputacion, in case they became separated in the crowd. They finished their drinks and headed off to join his sister and the girls.

They had just past the BBVA bank when a female voice shouted, "Phillip?"

He stopped, looked in the direction of the noise and spotted a woman coming out of an apartment-block entrance. It was Juliet.

"I'll catch you up," he said to Jose and crossed the packed street toward her. She looked amazing. The tightly fitting full-length black-and-red Spanish dress with white polka dots and frills hugged her shapely curves perfectly. Her silky blond hair cascaded over her shoulders with a red rose pinned just above her right ear.

However, Phillip immediately noticed that she seemed extremely miserable, as if she'd been crying.

They exchanged cheek kisses.

His heart skipped three beats, but then the rules nagged him tediously. As much as he tried, he couldn't push them away.

Probably just as well, he thought.

"You scrub up quite well?" he said.

"Thanks, not so bad yourself," replied Juliet, smiling wanly.

"Forgive me, but you're not your usual bubbly self. Are you OK?"

"It's just something on my mind."

"Want to talk about it?"

"I'd like to but later maybe. Are you still going on the oxcart with your sister?"

"Yes. You?"

"No, I'm walking up ahead. I'm meeting my new friend in the gardens, but I'll be free later? Could we meet somewhere?"

"Caves Bar?"

"Good idea. I'll try to be there," said Juliet. "But, Phillip, I'm not exactly sure about how long my friend might be staying, so don't worry if I don't make it. We'll have a chat another time."

"If you're there fine; if not, as you say, another time. But whether it's me or somebody else, you need to share whatever's troubling you sooner rather than later."

Juliet nodded and said, "Don't I know it. Listen I have to go; hope to see you later, and," she reached out an arm, pulled him to her cheek, kissed him, and added, "thanks for being a friend." Then with her eyes watering, she turned and melted into the crowd.

Phillip continued down Diputacion.

"Tio, Phillip," screamed three young girls.

He peered through the masses and spotted Jose's cart. His three nieces were jumping up and down in the back waving at him. His sister Glenda was standing in between the two oxen as they took turns at lapping from the plastic water bowl she proffered up for them.

She smiled serenely at her elder brother.

He put an arm around her shoulder and kissed her on both cheeks.

She'd pinned up her long, blond curly hair and clipped a bright-red rose above her right ear. She looked pretty, happy, and radiant in a shapely blue-and-white polka-dot dress.

"Are you sure you're up for this?" she asked, as he followed her to the back of the cart and hung the water bowl on a hook.

"I can't think of anything worse," he replied mischievously, grinning at the three sad faces looking down at him.

With that, he heaved himself up the short ladder and sat down on the bench opposite his nieces underneath a shady polka-dot awning.

Anna, the eldest, at nine, Louisa at six, and the youngest, Tina, at four leaped on him simultaneously, kissing his cheeks and hugging him, all demanding that he play with them first.

Then the parade marshal blew a whistle.

The procession would start in five minutes; all should return to their carts and ensure all children were sitting down safely.

Jose returned from the shop opposite with a plastic bag full of chorizo, serrano ham, and Manchego cheese. He passed it up to the girls.

Jose took his place by the oxen. Stick at the ready.

Glenda climbed up onto the cart and sat next to Phillip.

One by one the carts in front of them lumbered off.

Then it was their turn.

Nerja Caves, here we come, thought Phillip.

Will Juliet be there at four o'clock?

10

It had taken Amanda over an hour to reach Maro, the village some four kilometers to the east of Nerja that was home to Nerja Caves and the gardens where San Isidro celebrations took place.

In 1959, some local boys were out, watching bats disappear into a crevice in the foothills above Maro. They decided to enlarge the entrance to see where the bats were going and fell into a hole. After their initial screams of horror had subsided, their curiosity overcame their fears, and they bravely ventured further to discover an enormous cavern littered with human skeletons and ceramics. They ran back home excitedly to inform their parents.

Further exploration by experts revealed an enormous underground complex of impressive rock formations, columns, stalagmites, and stalactites.

Nerja Caves rapidly became one of the most popular tourist attractions in Spain and today continues to draw hundreds of thousands of visitors each year.

Amanda parked her Prius opposite the Hotel Playamar at the east end of the village.

It was outside a builder's yard identified by a large sign. The yard was protected by a high white wall with tall metal gates and secured by a sturdy padlock. She squeezed in between a sleek black Porsche Cayenne and a white Renault Kangoo van. A moped with a twisted mudguard leaned against the yard wall.

She was early for her meeting with the director of the Nerja Caves foundation but was unconcerned. She'd found a great parking space where her car would be safe for the day, but more importantly, it was only a short walk over the footbridge into the caves' gardens.

She locked the Prius and went into the hotel cafeteria for breakfast. It was busy with Festival goers dressed for the occasion. She sat down at an empty table next to three men. She couldn't help notice how obese one of them was, but was too preoccupied with her thoughts to pay them any more attention.

As she smeared grated tomatoes onto her toasted roll, she pondered over the introduction to her video. She'd considered using shots of the San Isidro effigy being carried out of Nerja church and being loaded onto the oxcart. However, that would entail taking a ladder to see over the crowds, and that was way too complicated, logistically. To date, she hadn't done anything to learn about how camera drones could improve her filming, but she was at least thinking about them.

She'd researched San Isidro yesterday seeking inspiration for a theme for her film.

San Isidro was born Isidro de Merlo y Quintana

sometime in the twelfth century. Apparently, he'd performed miracles with never-ending sacks of corn and bottomless pots of stew. He was beatified nearly five hundred years later in May 1619 for his piety in sharing food with the poor, hence the loaves of bread on his processional oxcart.

Amanda suspected that only a few seasoned festival goers would be celebrating the day for religious reasons and be aware of the saint's achievements. Religion throughout Spain and most of Europe was fading rapidly out of most people's lives, yet Spanish religious festivals were more popular than ever. Why was this, she wondered?

She'd decided that this would be the main point of her video.

Piety or party?

Amanda settled her check at the café, returned to the Prius, opened the rear door, and surveyed her camera equipment. A specially made organizer held her expensive gear in place while she traveled. She extracted what she needed and placed everything carefully into a large backpack.

A handheld, lightweight video camera with built-in microphone, plus a loose mike for interviews. Spare batteries, memory chips, and lens cloths. A retractable tripod, supplementary lighting, laptop, cables, two bottles of frozen iced tea, and several nutrition bars.

She never bothered with makeup, just a dash of lipstick, which she used to moisten her lips before struggling into the backpack and heading off in the direction of the footbridge.

The pack seemed enormous compared to her petite stature, but she was fit, strong, and hardly noticed the weight.

She noticed how pretty the Maro street was, so retraced her steps, dug the camera out of the bag, and filmed for a few seconds before crossing the footbridge over the autovia toward the caves.

She checked her watch. Eleven o'clock.

She didn't intend an in-depth documentary about the caves. There were plenty of those around. What she preferred were clips of the key features and permission to use extracts from last summer's concert.

A young dark-haired girl, wearing jeans and a Nerja Caves T-shirt with a red cave-art goat logo on the front showed her into the director's office. She shrugged off her backpack, placed it next to the visitor's chair and then shook hands with the director, Sr. Angel Gutierrez. He was a tall, gray-haired, stooped, middle-aged man, reeking of tobacco smoke. Amanda noticed a pipe smoldering in an ashtray by the window. They exchanged pleasantries, and then the director showed Amanda over to an easel on which was mounted a map of the caves system.

"Since our boys fell down the hole," Gutierrez began, "huge amount of research by the finest minds in anthropology, geology, and archeology has been undertaken. So far we have discovered three separate sections. What you are about to see is the tourist sector, and that is the smallest. The other two go way back under the mountain. We suspect there's more, but to fund a professional team to explore that possibility would cost far more than the money we raise through our entrance fees."

"That's fascinating, Sr. Gutierrez."

"Thank you. So if your video can raise our profile and increase our visitor numbers, it would go a long way to funding more research. Where did you say it will be shown?"

"I work with CNN and other American broadcasters and am expanding to other English-speaking countries. They use my videos to illustrate elements of Spanish culture and history."

"Excellent. Do you want to film everything?"

"As much as I can, yes. Why?"

"Because we have superb professionally taken footage of all the key elements and last year's concert. I am happy to let you use what we have provided you credit the foundation. I have it all on my computer. Would you like to see?"

"Yes, please."

The director turned his laptop toward her and set the film running. He picked up his pipe and went outside while she watched.

It was an impressive film and included 3D animations of what life underground might have been like during Neanderthal times. She couldn't wait to see the actual caves themselves.

Half an hour later, the film came to an end, and the director returned.

"Well?" he enquired.

"Amazing. I'd like to use some elements of it if I could."

"OK. Then I'll leave this film to burn onto a DVD while we tour the actual caves."

"Thank you. You obviously went to a lot of expense to make the film. The lighting is so much better than I could do alone. However, as we go round, I'm sure I'll see something that I want to shoot. Will that be OK?"

"Of course."

She collected her backpack as they left his office and walked the few hundred meters up to the entrance of the cave. The security guard waved them through to the stairs, where they descended into the damp, cool air.

At the bottom of the stairs was a narrow passage into the caves themselves after which it opened out onto a massive gallery. Angel paused and began to talk passionately about the history of the caves.

"After the rediscovery, it took a while for the experts in Madrid to realize the significance of what we had here. Eventually, some bright spark in Franco's regime, who had guts enough to speak up, recognized it could be a potential gold mine. Only then did things start to happen. The caves opened for business in 1960.

"It's been an outstanding success and has dramatically changed Nerja as a result, but it is so much more than a tourist attraction.

"While the caves were formed millions of years ago, they are a continual work in progress, as water continues to drip through the limestone, adding further deposits to the stalagmites and stalactites.

"Analysis of the artifacts and cave art has proved a mixed history: Neolithic burial ground, hyena hideaway, fridge for farm produce, animal shelter, and home to humans. They were inhabited by various tribes between 25,000 and 3600 BC.

"Recent testing of the seal sketches has proved that they were drawn with reddish pigments, indicating that are forty-three thousand years old. This has generated much speculation among renowned anthropologists that *Homo sapiens* and Neanderthal man may have cohabited in these very caves."

"Do the seal sketches suggest that it was colder then?" asked Amanda.

"Indeed, plus the water levels of the Mediterranean were substantially higher.

"More significantly, that column at the back of the gallery is of such gigantic proportions that it holds a place in the *Guinness Book of Records* for being the widest in the world."

"Incredible."

"The gallery also has exceptional natural acoustics. As you saw from the video, artists such as Placido Domingo, Dame Kiri Te Kanawa, and Yehudi Menuhin have all performed here."

"I can see why they wanted to," gasped Amanda, spellbound by the gigantic limestone columns soaring from floor to ceiling and sparkling with different-colored quartz and minerals reflecting the special lighting effects.

Amanda prepared her camera and took several minutes of film as they wandered around the roped-off footpath that guided the tourists around a circuit to the back of the caves. Half an hour later, they returned to Angel's office.

Angel extracted the DVD from his computer and gave it to her.

"Thank you, Angel; this is perfect."

"Anytime, Amanda. Please send me the link to your finished product. Who knows, if we like it, we might ask you to do more work."

"Cool. Will do."

She sorted her belongings and headed out into the caves gardens to hunt for a location to film the arrival of San Isidro and the procession.

11

The San Isidro effigy passed through the massive entrance doors of Nerja church on a portable throne resting on the sturdy shoulders of six Costaleros. The men, representing local religious brotherhoods, swayed in unison as they shuffled down the church steps and over to the lead oxcart elegantly decorated with palm fronds and dangling loaves of bread.

The effigy was a wooden statue, a meter and a half tall, with a golden halo mounted over his head, wearing a long brown cloak, green clothing, and beige boots. A wooden carving of a pair of oxen yoked together, pulling a plow, were at his feet. The throne was placed reverently onto the cart while colorfully dressed women danced, swirled, and twirled in front of the church, to shouts from the crowd, "Viva, San Isidro, Viva (Long Live, San Isidro)."

Once the effigy was secured onto the cart, a single uniformed horseman carrying San Isidro's intricately woven green-and-purple banner led the procession off along the Balcon, up Calle Pintada, and along the coastal road in the direction of the caves.

After the oxcarts came finely groomed horses of every color, then mules, donkeys, and a tiny Shetland pony. Some of the exquisitely dressed riders were accompanied by beautifully dressed girlfriends perched on the horses' hindquarters behind the saddle. They looked most decorous and were photographed intensively by the onlookers as the procession crawled by them.

Following the riders were an array of stylish carriages. They varied from four-seaters drawn by three elegant matching pairs of horses to single-seaters pulled by dobbin the bedraggled mule, a stubborn gray beast that needed constant prodding with a whip. The crowd laughed as the poor creature regularly stopped to nibble the grass at the side of the road, much to the annoyance of its owner.

Up next were sleek tractors towing decorated trailers that displayed shields representing their particular club or association. Many were equipped with generators to power fridges and the latest audio systems blaring with popular Latin music. On one rig a chef stood dressed in kitchen whites, flamboyantly carving a leg of *serrano ham*. Each piece cut was added ceremoniously to a nearby plate with accompanying shouts of "Ole."

People typically drank beer, *vino fino*—a crisp dry sherry from Jerez de la Frontera, and a summer punch of red wine, ice, and lemonade known as Tinto Verano. The alcohol flowed pleasantly, but not excessively; this was a family occasion. Dancers, mainly women, followed the trailers and when the procession paused to give the oxen a rest, which was often in the midday heat, the women would dance together, receiving much appreciation from the spectators.

Finally the charabancs—a mixed array of new, old, and wrecked vehicles clad with an occasional palm frond, the odd polka dot painted on cardboard, and masses of soccer club scarves. Here were the town's youngsters enjoying themselves. Their music, if it could be called that, was so loud that the speakers were vibrating, but they were having fun, and their behavior, although boisterous, was inoffensive.

Cute children ran about everywhere wearing mini versions of whatever festival clothing their parents had on and endearing themselves to everyone by drenching them with water pistols. Few complained; they would soon dry off in the sun.

Jose led the oxen on foot while Glenda hopped on and off the cart to keep him well provided for with water and a cloth to keep his shoes clean. It was almost impossible to tread carefully—the joys of processions with live animals. It was even worse further back, where over a hundred horses had added to the oxen's outpourings.

As they lumbered along the coastal road, Phillip chatted and joked with his three nieces. He was impressed how they could switch from English to Spanish and back without effort.

As they approached the last stages of the procession, they had to cross Barranco de la Coladilla de Cazadores, a deep gorge with a historic aqueduct, which used to convey water to the old sugar mill whose ruins still dominated the area. At last, they reached the steep hill up to the cave where they all clambered off the cart to lighten the load for the oxen.

At the top, Jose maneuvered the cart into a parking zone to the left of the entrance. The girls all pointed to a woman sitting on top of a wall filming them and made rude faces at her before Glenda scolded them. The woman lowered her camera briefly, smiled, and waved before returning to her task.

Jose and Phillip didn't notice; they were busy tethering the beasts under shady pine trees. They left them with plenty of hay and water, unloaded the picnic stuff, and walked back down to the entrance of the garden. They were just in time to watch the statue of San Isidro lifted off his cart and carried once more by the Costaleros up to his tiny hermitage at the top of the gardens where he would repose for the remainder of the day.

Some visitors would pay homage to him and take a sprig of rosemary from nearby bushes to stick it in their hat as a good-luck symbol for another year.

The gardens surrounding the building that now housed the entrance to the hole where the boys had fallen into have been expanded over the years into several terraces carved out of the hillside. Pine trees provided shade, hedges delineated pathways, and a botanical garden displaying many plant varieties and color.

To the north of the gardens is an enormous national park, known as Parque Natural Sierras de Tejeda, Almijara y Alhama, covering over forty thousand hectares of craggy mountains and dense woodland. It was a hideout for anti-Franco guerillas during Spain's Civil War, 1936–1939. The enormous variety of flora and fauna, including golden eagles, wild boar, and mountain goats, has made it extremely popular with hikers.

One of the advantages of Phillip's family being among the first to arrive at the caves was to have the pick of prime tables. They found one that overlooked a raised platform on the lower terrace that would be perfect to watch the later exhibitions. Flamenco displays by all ages, music groups of varying styles, and traditional Spanish guitarists would entertain the crowds until the late night hours. They opened their cool boxes and a bottle of chilled Fino and enjoyed their picnic as the terrace filled up around them.

Between the tables and stage was an open area for public dancing, where when sufficiently refreshed, many would dance the Sevillana. It's a traditional folk dance learned by all Andalusian children almost before they can walk. No matter how hard foreigners practice it, they can never match the fluid, elegant movements of the Spanish.

After lunch, Phillip danced the Sevillana with each of his nieces, who were grateful for only one bruised foot each. They congratulated him on his modest improvement from the previous year. He then escorted them to the dressage display, where they said hello to Didi and Gunter, then around the side stalls, where he managed to escape with only minor purchases of gaudy hats and sickly pink candy floss.

Just before four o'clock, Phillip returned the girls to their parents and headed off to the caves bar to meet Juliet. It took Phillip a good ten minutes to reach the restaurant through the dense crowd of festival revelers. He walked into the crowded bar and had a good look round. There was no sign of Juliet. He bought a glass of Cava, perched on the last remaining stool at the bar, and waited patiently.

Fifteen minutes later, Juliet still hadn't shown up. He finished his drink and went to rejoin his family down on the lower terrace.

12

Amanda spotted a high wall to the side of the entrance to the caves gardens. It was broad enough to sit on top. If she could only find a way to climb up there, it would be the perfect position to take the best shots.

She looked around for a ladder or something to help her up there.

There was a selection of market stalls just inside the entrance with colorful displays of hats, typical festival clothing, and other accessories.

She took out her camera and tripod and started assembling them. As usual, it didn't take long.

"Making a video, are we, beautiful?" enquired one of the stallholders.

Amanda gave him her best smile and replied, "Yes, it's for CNN and others."

"CNN? Impressive. You could film our stall if you like."

"Of course, if you could help me clamber on top of that wall and then down in an hour or so, I'll happily include you."

A few minutes later, he returned with a step ladder, smiled, and said. "My son will assist."

The wall turned out to be higher and broader than Amanda had envisaged. She had to stretch to place her equipment on its top, but there was no way that she could climb up herself. She turned and shrugged at the son who offered to give her a leg up.

It was a tight squeeze together on top of the ladder platform, but he cupped his hands, she placed her right knee on them, and he heaved her up. He gave her his telephone number to call when she needed to come down and then disappeared back to their stall with the ladder. She straddled the wall and started organizing what she needed.

The procession was running late, but after all these years in Spain, she was used to it. She sipped some iced tea, nibbled on a nutrition bar, and waited patiently.

Ten minutes later, police motorcycles with lights flashing appeared. They were crawling so slowly up the hill that their riders found it difficult to stay upright and wove from side to side.

Behind the police escort was the leader of the procession on his horse, carrying the San Isidro banner, followed by the oxcart transporting the effigy. The animals were breathing hard after climbing the long hill. They stopped just below her where six strong men unloaded the saint and swayed off up through the gardens in the direction of the top terrace. They would ensconce him in the small hermitage built there especially for him. Some visitors would pay homage during the festival; most would not.

Amanda turned on her camera and started filming.

It was twenty past two o'clock.

A little later, she couldn't help respond to three beautiful little blond-curly-haired girls sticking out their tongues at her. She filmed them briefly and then waved and smiled as their mother scolded them and mouthed sorry in Spanish.

An hour later, the procession had passed and had parked up in the caves car park. There wasn't room for all the charabancs; some had to park up beyond the tethered animals to the side of the country track that led up to the national park. She panned over to the oxen and horses munching fodder under the shady pine trees on the start of a country track. Their passengers had dispersed among the various attractions around the gardens.

The horse dressage was taking place in a sandy arena to the right of the track. The animals prancing elegantly through their routines kicked up a lot of dust. It billowed in gentle gusts toward the carts and animals.

Amanda liked the haunting effect that it created and pointed her lens in that direction. She couldn't see much through her viewfinder as the screen was too small. She did notice some people climb in a white van, reverse out of the row of parked charabancs, and drive slowly toward her. It was bumping over the tree roots that had invaded the surface of the track and had to thread its way around several people, including the three cheeky little girls from earlier. This time they were walking hand in hand with a tall blond-haired man who she presumed to be their father.

She zoomed in on the van, kept it focused as it approached, panned with it as it turned the corner, and then held the shot as it headed down the hill and out of sight.

As far as she was concerned, that was it. If people were leaving already, then it was time to go and interview some of the visitors and film the various attractions.

She turned to try and catch the attention of the son to return with the ladder, but he was busy selling hats and T-shirts. She called him, but he didn't answer, so she sent a text requesting his assistance with the ladder. While waiting, she packed all her kit into the backpack, gingerly stood up, and stretched.

She was bombarded with lighthearted offers to help her down. Several men came toward her, offering their broad muscular shoulders. But then her hero arrived.

The son barged his way through with the ladder.

"Excuse me, gentlemen," he shouted. "My girlfriend wants to come down."

They good-humoredly let him through, and Amanda was able to return to earth.

He kindly helped her with the backpack. She thanked him warmly, smiled to herself, and headed down to the lower terrace to film the attractions and talk to people.

Three hours later, she was done.

She headed back to her car, loaded her gear into the trunk, and returned to Malaga.

Back home about an hour later, she dropped everything on her kitchen island and prepared a light supper of goat's cheese and pineapple chunks. She emptied her backpack and took everything through to her studio. While the film downloaded onto her hard drive, she popped back into the kitchen to enjoy the light snack before returning to start work.

She picked out the most exciting clips of the procession and saved them to her editing software for later. Eventually, she came to the shot with the dust billowing over the tethered animals and several parked charabancs. She recalled the white van leaving and took a closer look at the moments before it reversed out and drove off.

What she saw puzzled her.

She reran the film in slow motion.

A beautiful looking blond girl with a red rose in her hair, wearing a black, red dress with white polka dots, appeared to be arguing with two men on the far side of the van. The men had their faces partly hidden by their cordoba hats. They'd also tied up their red festival bandannas above their noses against the dust swirling around them from the horse dressage arena. The girl had a terrified expression and appeared to cower away from the men.

Then one of the men moved in close to the girl, his head jerking in a threatening manner forcing her toward the van.

Then the man put his hand on top of her head and pushed downward.

The girl disappeared into the van.

13

As Phillip walked down the slope to El Salon beach for his morning swim, he saw a group of children in costumes gathered round Didi, paddling in the surf avidly watching his every move. They were apparently asking him questions, but Didi couldn't understand them and looked decidedly uncomfortable. As Phillip approached, the youngsters looked toward him. Phillip recognized them; they lived in the fisherman's cottages at the top of the beach.

"Hey, Mister," the eldest boy asked in Spanish. "What's he doing?"

"He's testing the water temperature to make sure it's just how he likes it before he goes in," answered Phillip.

"What's that thing he keeps dipping in the water?" asked another child.

"It's called a thermometer," answered Phillip.

Didi stroked his mustache furiously as he looked back and forth incomprehensively between Phillip and the children.

"What are you telling them?" he demanded of Phillip.

"Relax, Didi; they're just curious. I'm explaining about the thermometer."

"Cheeky buggers—tell them to leave me alone."

"I don't think they'll take any notice; they live in the cottages—to them this beach is their playground. You're the intruder. Why don't you show them the thermometer; they've probably never seen one?"

"Oh, if I must."

"OK, niños, he wants to show you how the thermometer works," called Phillip.

The four kids ran eagerly over to Didi, who reluctantly let them touch his precious gadget. Phillip slipped off his outer clothing and joined them at the water's edge. He bent down and showed the little ones how it worked. They were fascinated, and each took a turn at testing it.

Phillip held his hand against it and showed them how much higher the red liquid went up the scale. They tried it on each other to a chorus of giggles.

After a while, Didi joined in the fun and, a few minutes later, declared that the sun had done its work and water was now officially warm enough for his swim.

Phillip laughed as the kids ceremoniously accompanied Didi on his three-stroke out and back routine and then ran off back up the beach, mimicking his mustache stroking as they went.

"How was the rest of San Isidro, yesterday," asked Phillip.

"I really enjoyed it," replied Didi. "It was good to take photos for a change instead of wrestling with reluctant horse-flesh."

"When are you off to Bremen?"

"As soon as I reach home, no time for coffee, I'm afraid."

"Then have a great summer."

"Thanks; we'll be back in the autumn or sooner if a buyer materializes for our villa."

Didi went off to the showers; Phillip dived in and sped out to his usual buoy.

After his swim, Phillip took his seat at the Don Comer regulars' table. Bruce, a young Australian guy, was there, sipping his coffee. He was the editor of a local English magazine.

"Morning, Bruce," said Phillip.

"Gudday," said Bruce, glaring impatiently toward the café. "Service is damn slow this morning." He looked at his watch. "I'll have to go soon."

"Seconds later Manolo appeared with their respective orders. He was sweating profusely and looked extremely harassed. "Sorry, gents, short staffed this morning. Juliet hasn't shown up and won't answer her phone. I've had to call in one of my part timers, but she hasn't arrived yet."

"That's worrying, Manolo," said Phillip. "Yesterday morning Juliet had tears in her eyes. In the afternoon, she failed to turn up for a drink, and now she's not at work. After breakfast, I'll go and check her apartment."

"I'd come with you," said Manolo. "But I can't leave the café. Let me know if she's all right."

Phillip gulped down his roll and coffee, left payment on the table, and headed anxiously toward Calle Diputacion.

On the way, he called Juliet's number.

It diverted straight to voice mail.

Now he started panicking.

All those confused emotions about her came rushing back.

He arrived outside her apartment block and rang the bell.

No response.

He pressed several buttons, mumbled Amazon delivery when one answered, and was buzzed into the lobby.

He'd been to her apartment once before when she'd needed help configuring her Wi-Fi router, so headed straight for the stairs.

Mounted on the wall to the right of the stairs was a rack of mailboxes. They were stuffed with propaganda despite the large sign forbidding them. Next to the mailboxes was a cork notice board. Multicolored pins had been arranged into a question mark above a printed note in a large font, summoning the occupants to the annual general meeting of the residents' committee, three weeks previously.

He jogged up the stairs and knocked on her door.

There was no response.

He phoned Juliet again, but like last time, it was forwarded to voice mail. He put his ear to the woodwork and listened intently. All was quiet.

Where the hell is she? he thought.

He turned the door handle.

It was unlocked.

He opened it a fraction.

"Juliet," he called quietly through the gap.

Nothing.

"Juliet," he called again, this time loudly.

Silence.

He pushed the door wide open, gasped, and put his hands to his mouth.

14

Amanda watched in horror as the girl disappeared into the van. "What do I see here?" she said out loud as the man scrambled in after the girl. The other guy came round the back, climbed in, reversed out, and drove off.

It had to proceed slowly over raised tree roots and negotiate its way around the blond man holding hands with the cheeky daughters.

Amanda froze the frame when the van was at its nearest point to her camera.

She noticed that there was a partition between the driver's seats and the back of the van, so she couldn't see any sign of the blond girl. The driver was still wearing his bandanna and cordoba hat, so she couldn't see much of his face. A few different-color polka dots had been stuck on the side of the van, but there was nothing to identify its ownership.

Except that she had a crystal-clear shot of the number plate and the make; a Renault Kangoo.

She wondered if she'd filmed the van arriving with the procession. She went back to the beginning and fast framed her way through again but couldn't see it anywhere. She hadn't filmed every single vehicle, though, and had stopped twice to change batteries.

The girl hadn't appeared to struggle, thought Amanda, or scream. Perhaps it was a couple having a disagreement? Whatever—it's not my business.

Amanda went back to her editing, added some voice-over, and saved the movie. She'd look at it one more time with fresh eyes early in the morning.

She stood, stretched, went through to the kitchen and rewarded herself with a glass of chilled Verdejo, took it out onto her terrace, sat down on her lounger, and reflected on the day.

Overall she was pleased with her film. She'd integrated all the caves and festival elements and illustrated her *piety* and *party* theme quite well, she thought. Tomorrow, she would make a trailer, send it to her contacts, and wait to see who would bite.

She finished her wine, cleaned her teeth, and went to bed.

But the blond girl disappearing into that van nagged at her, preventing slumber.

She imagined all kinds of scenarios about what might have happened to her, none of them positive.

In the end, she gave in and decided that in the morning she'd burn a DVD of that part of the film. Then after her morning appointment with the cruise ship advertising agency, she'd take it to her nearest comisaría de policía. Maybe they could make something of it.

Finally, she fell asleep.

The meeting had gone badly at the agency. They'd changed much of the content for the summer cultural program, so Amanda had to retranslate several pages of text on the spot. It was well after ten o'clock when she walked into the comisaría de policía on Calle Ramos Marin. She hadn't had time for a coffee or her usual breakfast.

Her stomach rumbled as she waited in line at the reception desk.

It was impossible not to overhear what the people ahead of her were saying to the desk sergeant.

He was not a sympathetic man, curtly dismissing most complainants with a "That's a civil matter," or "No, we don't send out patrol cars to look for missing parrots."

Amanda was having second thoughts as the line shuffled slowly forward.

Am I wasting their time? she asked herself.

Then it was her turn.

"Yes, Señora," said the sergeant, a burly man in his late fifties who had probably heard every single variety of complaint or report in his many years behind this desk.

"I witnessed what I think was an abduction yesterday at San Isidro in Nerja and wish to show a film I made of it to a detective, please," she said boldly.

The sergeant scrutinized her sternly and then asked, "And why has madam waited until today to make such a report; the abducted person could be in Timbuktu by now."

"The incident happened some distance away. It was too small to see on my camera screen, and it wasn't until late last night when I ran it through my editing software on a larger screen that I noticed what was going on. Would you like to see it first? Or are you going to make me drive all the way to the police in Nerja?"

The sergeant scowled, picked up the internal phone in front of him, prodded a few numbers, waited calmly for a reply, and then spoke for several seconds before hanging up.

"Someone will be down to see you; take a seat over there. Next."

"My roommate refuses to share the washing up," heard Amanda as she walked toward the row of cheap plastic chairs along the wall to the left of the lobby entrance. The sergeant's response was uncouth.

Amanda dug her phone out of her purse and checked her e-mails.

She'd hardly started when she became aware of someone sitting down next to her.

"Any ideas how we can look at this film?" asked a quiet male voice.

Amanda looked up at a well-built middle-aged man with a smiling round face topped with silver hair. "I can show you on my laptop," she replied.

"Detective Inspector Prado of the Foreigners' Crime Department," said the man. "I'm here because the sergeant assumed that you were a foreigner. Not that your accent is noticeable, but there is a hint of a slight tang. American perhaps?"

"Very observant of you inspector. I'm Amanda Salisbury and am an American citizen, but I've lived in Spain for most of my life."

"That would explain it. We'll go up to my office. Come with me, please?"

Well, at least he's polite, thought Amanda.

Pretty girl, thought Prado. Smart with it.

They went over to the elevator, up to the fourth floor, along a corridor, and into the detective's office. Prado showed Amanda to his visitor chair. She took her laptop out of her backpack, fired it up and set the video playing.

Prado watched over her shoulder.

"You see the white van at the back of the picture," Amanda explained. "There's a blond girl there on the far side of the van. Look at her expression."

Amanda froze the screen with a grainy image of the blond girl and asked, "Don't you think she appears frightened?"

"I agree," commented Prado. "Show me the complete clip; we can always go back through in more detail after."

They watched the two-minute film together, ending with a still shot of the van's registration plate.

Prado brought up the national vehicle registry on his laptop, tapped in the number, and waited a few seconds for a result.

"Interesting," he said, looking up from the screen. "There's no such vehicle. A sure sign that dastardly deeds are in progress here. Let's have another run through the video."

Amanda clicked back to the video, reset it, and pressed the play button.

"Freeze that, please," said Prado moments later, as he watched the van crawl past a shaggy haired blond man walking with his three children. "I know that guy. Perhaps he heard or saw something. I'll call him."

Prado went round to his side of the desk, sat in his chair, swiped through his contacts, and pressed call.

"Phillip Armitage," Amanda heard a man answer, speaking with a British accent.

"Hola, Phillip," said Prado. "Leon Prado."

"Inspector, a pleasant surprise; how can I help?"

"First, let me say thank you for e-mailing those door sign translations last week, but that's not why I'm calling. Regretfully, it's a more serious matter. I'm in my office with a lady who was filming a documentary at San Isidro in Nerja yesterday. She's showing me a video of a blond girl being forced into a white van. Seconds afterward it drives slowly past you and your three daughters."

"Can I stop you there, Inspector?" interrupted Phillip. "Actually, they're my nieces, I'm not married. However, this blond girl could well be a friend of mine who's disappeared. She didn't turn up to meet me at San Isidro yesterday and hasn't arrived at work today. Even more worrying is that I've just come out of her apartment. The door was unlocked, and it has been ransacked."

"Just a minute, Phillip," said Prado, holding his phone away from his mouth. "Sra. Salisbury, are you free to come to Nerja? We need to show your video to the man with the three girls. The blond woman being forced into the van could be a friend of his."

Amanda looked at her watch. Her next appointment was late afternoon.

"I'll have to follow you in my car," she said. "I need to be back here after lunch."

"Fine, let me obtain the address details, and I'll meet you at the crime scene. Phillip," he said, speaking into his phone again, "Can you stay at the apartment until a local officer arrives? I'll be there in an hour or so with the video. What's the address?"

"Diputacion, Two Hundred Sixty-Six, Flat Four A," informed Phillip.

"See you there," said Prado.

Amanda returned the laptop to her bag and followed Prado out of the door.

They agreed to reconvene at the scene in Nerja.

Amanda walked to her Prius parked at a meter just around the corner from the comisaría, lowered herself in, and headed toward the Tunel de Alcazaba, along the eastern promenade and out onto the coastal motorway. She drove quickly but within the speed limits.

She passed Rincon de la Victoria and approached Velez-Malaga, the principal town of the Eastern Costa del Sol. It's the main distribution center for the thousands of tons of fruits and vegetables produced in the area and shipped mainly to the supermarkets of northern Europe. Millions of euros have been invested in the local transport infrastructure by the European Union to reduce the journey time between field and shelf, including a questionable loss-making streetcar system. It formed part of the project to develop Spain into the breadbasket of Europe.

Velez is also home to some incredible historical gems dating back to Phoenician times. Roman remains and Moorish towers are abundant in the old part of town. Every time Amanda went there, she wondered why the town council was wasting an incredible tourism opportunity by not exploiting their potential. Perhaps that could be her next project to stir them into action.

The region surrounding Velez-Malaga, which includes Nerja, is known as La Axarquia, probably of Arabic origins, implying land to the east. It is often referred to as Spanish Tuscany or Little Switzerland because of its dramatic landscapes, abundant agriculture, and excellent cuisine.

Craggy mountains over two thousand meters high are dotted with pine and olive trees. They form a massive bowl-shaped protectorate that defines the region and keeps the cold north winds at bay. The resulting microclimate provides balmy winters and mild summers with fresh sea breezes.

Amanda turned off the motorway at the Frigiliana junction and headed down into Nerja. She parked her car under Plaza España and walked to Diputacion. A local police car with flashing lights stood outside an apartment block about halfway along. She presented herself to the officer standing at the entrance and was told to go up.

As she approached the fourth floor, she could hear the inspector talking to someone.

She recognized the man from the video. Prado introduced them and they shook hands. He was much taller than he appeared in the film and had incredible blue eyes. She smiled demurely and blinked her eyelids.

An attractive man, she thought to herself while digging her laptop out from her shoulder bag. She booted it up, rested it on the banister, clicked on the video, and hit the play button.

Phillip stood next to her and watched the men push the blond girl into the van. Amanda could feel his body heat as he brushed inadvertently against her bare arm. She jumped at his unexpected touch.

"Sorry," he whispered, looking sadly at the video.

"It's her," said Phillip. "Her name is Juliet Harding."

They moved over to the open doorway of the apartment.

Amanda was horrified by what she saw.

In the living room, the sofa was upside down; the material had been slashed with a knife. Kitchen cupboards were open. Through the open door into the bedroom, they could see the wardrobe had been tipped over onto the double bed. A dusty but empty backpack lay on the floor by the bed.

Drawers had been removed from their chests, and their contents, mainly clothing, were scattered over the prostrate wardrobe.

"How long have you known Juliet?" asked Prado.

"Since not long after she arrived in Nerja, coming up to three years," replied Phillip.

"What do you know about her? Boyfriends, etc.?"

"I have no information about her previous life in Birmingham; she never talked about it. As for Nerja, she split from her Moroccan boyfriend Hassan Labrat recently, and yesterday morning she intimated that she was meeting a new friend at the caves gardens but gave no details."

"Does Juliet speak Spanish?" asked Amanda.

"Enough to do her work. She's a waitress at Café-Bar Don Comer on the Balcon by the church. I see her there most days when I meet my business colleague after my morning swim."

"How was she when you saw her yesterday?" asked Prado.

"The café was closed for San Isidro, but I saw her outside her apartment building as I was going to join the procession. She was upset by something and agreed that we should talk about it. We tentatively made a date to meet at four o'clock in the caves bar, but she never showed. To be fair, she did say that she might not make it. It depended on her friend's timing apparently."

"Does she have a computer?"

"Yes, a laptop and a smartphone. I have her number if you want to check her call records."

"Can you text it to me, please?"

Phillip extracted his phone from his pocket and forwarded the number to Prado.

They heard a knock on the door and turned.

"Ah, Anna, you made it, excellent," said Prado. "This is Dr. Anna Galvez, our forensics officer. Could you two wait for me at Don Comer while Anna struts her stuff? I want to talk to Juliet's boss, and I'll have some more questions for you both."

Amanda followed Phillip down the stairs and out past the officer guarding the door. The pavement was busy, so they walked quickly along the middle of the street past delivery trucks unloading pallets of drinks and foodstuffs for the many bars and restaurants in the area.

"I didn't see you filming yesterday; where were you?" asked Phillip as they approached Plaza Cavana.

"As you can see, there's not much to me," said Amanda, grinning.

"Nice things come in small parcels," said Phillip, smiling warmly.

"So does arsenic. I was sitting on top of the wall by the gate into the caves parking. Your nieces managed to see me, though. They stuck their tongues out at me, and by the way, they're gorgeous."

"Little monkeys—sorry about that."

"Their mother apologized, your sister I assume, by the similarity in your looks?"

"Yes, Glenda. What was the theme for the video?"

Amanda explained her San Isidro concept as they covered the rest of the three hundred and fifty meters to Don Comer. When they arrived, nobody was sitting at the regulars' table, so they went inside to the bar, sat on the comfortable stools, and waited for Manolo to appear.

It didn't take long.

"Well?" he asked, rushing behind the bar and drying his hands on a cloth. "Any sign of her?"

"None I'm afraid, and her apartment has been ransacked," said Phillip.

"Ransacked?" questioned Manolo.

Phillip turned to Amanda and said, "May I present Amanda Salisbury. She was making a film of San Isidro. When she returned home and saw her work on a larger monitor, she spotted Juliet being abducted by two men in a white van."

"Abducted, that is terrible?" said Manolo with tears in his eyes. "Do the police know?"

"They're at her apartment as we speak. The inspector wants to ask you a few questions. He's coming shortly."

"I better warn Pepa; she's in the office. Back in a second."

"Coffee?" Phillip asked.

"Double espresso, please, and I'm starving," answered Amanda. "Do they serve molletes?"

"With garlic, olive oil, and grated tomatoes?"

"What else is there for a Spanish breakfast?" asked Amanda.

"It's my favorite as well."

Manolo returned and noted down their order. They went outside and sat down at the regulars' table.

"I don't know how to say this," said Amanda, "but in some ways, I'm relieved that it was your friend in the video. The more I kept looking at the film, the less sure I was that she was in trouble. I worried that I was wasting police time."

"Well, thanks for bringing it in, because now we know for certain that she's disappeared."

"Let's hope the inspector can find her quickly?" said Amanda. "Do you know her well?"

"We're close friends, but as I told the inspector, I know nothing about her previous life in England."

"Perhaps something's come back to bite her in the butt?"

"Could well be; she was upset about something. Just not like her. And by the way, your Spanish is perfect," Phillip continued. "I'd never have known that you were American, or is it Canadian?"

"American, but I've been in Spain since I was seven. Your Spanish isn't bad either—still sound like a Brit, though."

Manolo interrupted them to deliver their coffees and Amanda's mollete. She tucked in straightaway.

"What do you do other than film San Isidro?" enquired Phillip.

"I make video documentaries about anything to do with Spain and sell clips of them to mainly American broadcasters. What about you?"

"Have you heard of Nuestra España?"

"Of course, I often steal stuff from it for my scriptwriting. The history articles are excellent. Wait. It's your website, right?"

"With my business partner Richard, yes. He's also American. From Boston, Massachusetts. Maybe we can help each other?"

"Would you have time to build me a website as good as yours?"

"Don't see why not."

"Then we should talk about it as soon as possible."

"Why don't I call you to arrange a lunch or something?"

"Cool; then let's exchange numbers."

Prado arrived just as they were sending messages to each other.

"That didn't take as long as I thought," he announced, sitting down next to Amanda. "The apartment has been stripped of everything personal. No photos, computer, phone, paperwork, or passport. They left just her clothes, and Anna reckons that some of those have also been taken. She's found some prints and DNA. Hopefully, we'll have some results back on those later this morning.

"Meanwhile, we've been busy. Juliet's picture has been circulated to all border controls and patrol cars throughout Andalucia. No van has been reported stolen, and Juliet's abduction has been reported to the British consul. However, he says that they need more information such as passport details before they can do anything.

"It's also possible that she may have gone back to the UK, so we're checking airlines, trains, and buses. Other than that, there's not much we can do. Did you talk to Manolo?"

"Yes, he's waiting for you inside with his wife," replied Phillip. "He may well have a copy of Juliet's passport in his safe. I understand that he organized her foreigner's number and work contract."

"Good," Prado observed. "I'll go talk to them now. Can you wait? I won't be long, but I need to ask you both something?"

They both nodded.

Prado went into the café.

Phillip said nothing; he felt dreadful. His emotions were in turmoil.

Amanda sensed that he was struggling with some inner torment.

"Is there anything I can do to help?" she said, resting her hand on his forearm.

"Sorry, but I'm desperately concerned for Juliet."

"Are you close?"

"I sort of adopted her, but my feelings became confused in the process."

"She's a beautiful woman; that's understandable. Here's Prado."

They turned and saw him talking on his phone as he walked toward them. He was carrying a piece of paper. He sat down next to Amanda, finished his call, folded the paper, and said, "You were right about the passport, Phillip." He waved the paper at him and then inserted it into his jacket pocket before continuing, "OK, things are moving fast. There's been no sign of Juliet, but we've found the van and received some results back from forensics although not particularly helpful."

"Where was the van?" asked Amanda.

"It had been parked illegally around the back of the railway station in Malaga and towed at nine twenty this morning. The engine was cold. It's now in the police pound in West Malaga; Anna is on her way to check it out and obtain any relevant security-camera footage.

"In the apartment, Anna identified which prints belong to Juliet and has found five more from different people. If we can cross-reference those to any found in the van, then we'll know it was the same people who trashed the apartment or not. We've run the prints and so far have no matches, but we're still waiting on Interpol. By the way, we'll need yours, Phillip, for elimination purposes. Can you pop into the Guardia Civil barracks here in Nerja and have them done as soon as you can?"

"Fine."

"One more thing," Prado continued. "Manolo tells me that Juliet and Hassan were having some heavy arguments before he left for Nador, so we're going to have to interview him. My office is in contact with the Moroccan police to obtain his address and permission to talk with him.

"Now, what I wanted to discuss with you both is this. I've only recently been appointed to this new department. We focus on crimes involving foreigners, either as victims, witnesses, or suspects. For this, I need some voluntary translators not only to help with the languages but also to elucidate on cultural differences. For example, we might be one European Union, but we Spanish live and think incomparably from most other member states.

"I'd like to use this investigation as a test bed to learn how we can best solve the growing number of cases in this crime category. For that, I need voluntary linguists and people from other cultures. Phillip is English but speaks German and Russian as well as Spanish and understands the cultural variances of each and has declared his willingness to work with me. How about you, Amanda? Do you speak other languages?"

"My mother is of Moroccan descent, so I can speak

Moroccan Arabic and French."

"Would you care to join us in this new venture?"

"It sounds fascinating; I'd love to help out when I'm free from my usual duties."

"Excellent, excellent," said Prado. "In that case would you both be able to accompany me to Nador tomorrow. We'll fly over to Melilla and then cross the border, coming back the same day. I know it's heavy-handed for interviewing one suspect, but I want to use the trip to acquaint myself with you better and explore if we can work together?"

"I'll have to rearrange some appointments," answered Amanda. "But that shouldn't cause too many problems, so yes, I'd be happy to."

"Same with me," said Phillip.

"Excellent. Then the first thing we should do is set up a WhatsApp group. We can all post updates, assumptions, and ideas about the case as we go about our daily business. Shall we exchange numbers?"

Prado invited them both to the group, and they accepted.

"I'll post what time we should meet at the airport," said Prado. "And listen, thank you both for giving something back to your adopted country. Rest assured, that while we may not be able to pay you, we will reimburse any expenses you incur on our behalf. OK, that's it for now. I'll see you tomorrow."

Prado went inside to pay the bill and waved as he headed off in the direction of his car parked on Diputacion.

"Another coffee?" invited Phillip.

"One per day is my limit. Otherwise, I'm bouncing off the walls all night," replied Amanda. "I'll take some water, though."

Phillip raised his hand, and Manolo's wife, Pepa, came to take their order.

Pepa was a friendly woman with a warm smile and big heart. She was woefully thin with spindly short gray hair and a nose to beat all noses, but she was well presented and elegant in the bottle-green uniform of the café. She sat down next to Phillip and asked, "Are you guys helping the cops with Juliet's abduction?"

"Yes," said Phillip. "There are likely to be several languages involved."

"Who do you think has taken Juliet?"

"Too soon to say yet," said Amanda.

"What did Prado ask you?" said Phillip.

"He wanted to know about Hassan, any relatives of Juliet and also what we were doing at the time of her abduction."

"What did you tell him?" asked Amanda.

"I told him about the huge row Hassan and Juliet had just before he left for Nador."

"I hadn't heard about that," said Phillip.

"You were gallivanting up north at the time. It was here in the café. Hassan was shouting so loudly that I had to ask him to leave," said Pepa.

"What were they arguing about?" asked Amanda.

"He wanted her to go with him to Nador, but she wasn't interested," said Pepa.

"I can understand that," said Amanda. "It would be difficult for her to adjust to living his way of life in Nador."

"Juliet's point exactly," said Pepa.

"Is it possible that Hassan might have taken her?" asked Amanda.

"His parting words were, 'I'll be back for you,'" said Pepa.

"So that's why Prado wants to talk to him," said Phillip.

"Did you want to order anything?" asked Pepa.

"I'll have another coffee, Amanda will take a water sin gas," Phillip requested.

"Have you been to Melilla or Nador before?" asked Amanda.

"No. You?"

"Never."

"I'm looking forward to it."

"Me too."

Pepa served their drinks, leaned on the back of a chair, and said, "There's something else that worries me about Juliet. In all the time I've known her, she's never mentioned her life in England. I've asked her about it on several occasions, but she just changes the subject. After a while, I gave up, and I think she appreciated that. However, on the eve of San Isidro, she received a call that upset her dreadfully. She was at the bar when it came, answered it curtly, turned white, and ran into the restroom. I went in to check on her and could hear her vomiting and then sobbing her heart out. When she came out, she swore viciously, and I've never heard her do that before."

"What did she say," asked Phillip.

"Fucking families," answered Pepa.

15

Phillip escorted Amanda back to her car under Plaza España, exchanged cheek kisses, and went their separate ways. Phillip went down to the second floor, turned the BMW's roof down, and headed up the Frigiliana Road to his villa.

After a light supper on his terrace that evening, Phillip went into his study with a glass of Verdejo. Before sitting in his comfortable Eames leather soft-pad chair at his Herman Miller workstation. He'd purloined them from his office in London as a farewell present to himself.

He cast his eyes proudly over his beloved gadget collection before turning on his Mac. He was an avid fan of anything "techie," particularly Apple computers, and kept every machine he had ever owned on wall-mounted shelves as a museum to his former career and rat-race contributions.

There were also some rare models he'd picked up on eBay, including the original Apple M0001, a remarkable machine bearing in mind it only had 128K of RAM. He also had the original Sinclair Spectrum ZX eight-bit computer given to him by his father one Christmas. They used to play Pac-Man on it together; it still worked perfectly.

He sat down and made some general web searches for Nador and Melilla. He wanted to know more about where he was going tomorrow.

The Spanish enclave of Melilla covers 12.3 square kilometers of the northeastern coast of Morocco. It has a population of seventy-eight thousand people, mixed between Spanish, Berber, Jew, and Hindu. Every religion has a church, and they all live peacefully together in what's evolved into a beautiful city. There's tree-lined avenues, art-deco architecture that competes with Barcelona and the only piece of Gothic architecture in all Africa is St. James's church. It's a free port, inexpensive to live, and the fusion of different cuisines makes for superb food.

Melilla has been an impregnable stronghold since Phoenician times around 1500 BC when humanity still assumed that the world was flat and people fell off the edge at the Rock of Gibraltar some four hundred kilometers to the west. It's a natural harbor protected by cliffs initially developed as a staging post for their trading ships.

The massive walls and original structures were expanded by successive occupants. Greeks, Romans, Byzantines, Vandals, and Hispanic Visigoths followed by Berber warlords and Arab dynasties. Each contributed their unique touches. During this time Melilla and the surrounding area was independent of any nation state; it belonged to whoever controlled the fortress.

Spain became a nation united under the Catholic

monarchs in 1492. In 1497 they dispatched troops to capture Melilla from the Berbers, worried that the Moors might use it as a stronghold to amass an army and reinvade Spain. It has been in Spanish hands since then.

In the mid-nineteenth century when nation-states were defining precise borders between themselves, the Spanish negotiated with the then Berber emir who controlled the surrounding land. They came to an unusual accord on how to determine where the border should be. A cannon would be fired from the center of Melilla castle. Wherever the cannon balls landed would be the frontier—hence it's semicircular shape.

The Spanish Civil War started in 1936 with an uprising in Melilla. Many military officers led by Franco took exception to the social reforms being imposed by the then democratically elected republican government and their chaotic management of the country. It took three years of bloody conflict followed by thirty-six years of brutal dictatorship to repress any chance of Spain becoming a Communist country.

The only remaining statue of Franco in all Spain stands in Melilla. It marks the gratitude many in Melilla continue to hold toward the long passed dictator.

Today, dealing with the relentless flow of illegal migrants from sub-Saharan Africa all dreaming of a better life in Europe is Melilla's primary challenge. They hide up in the Rif Mountains during the day and come down at night for yet another futile attempt to cross the frontier into Europe. To stem this swelling tide of desperate humanity, Melilla has built, out of its own funds, an enormous razor-wire fence all the way around their border with sensors and dogs. If any do climb over the top, they're usually sent straight back.

There's a small town at the Melilla-Morocco frontier known as Beni Ansar with a population of some 56,000. Nador itself is much more significant with 160,000-odd inhabitants. It lies at a fifteen-minute drive east along a straight road from the border. Phillip had a look at Google Earth and saw that Nador seafront was a long elegant palm-tree-lined boulevard running along the shore of an enormous lagoon, which the Spanish refer to as La Mar Chica (mermaid). It's protected by a sandbank through which there is only one passage to the open sea. It's renowned for its natural beauty, flora, and fauna.

Now he'd visualized tomorrow's destination, he was curious what the Internet could tell him about his beautiful traveling companion, fellow translator and potential coworker.

He searched Amanda Salisbury, Spain.

The top result took him to a section of video documentaries about Spain on the CNN website.

He browsed through them. The most popular was the *Festival San Fermin in Pamplona*. Phillip clicked the play button.

Amanda appeared, wearing the traditional festival clothing: running shoes, white blouse, and pants, red neck scarf, and belt. She had a chest camera fitted between her breasts.

She introduced the beautiful city in northern Spain, showed the giant figures in the procession, and the topless girls bathing themselves in bulls' blood before switching to an interview with an experienced bull runner.

Fernando was a man in his forties who had survived over twenty-five attempts at running in front of the bulls as they traversed the sand-covered streets that led to the bullring.

He described his fears and the tricks that he'd learned and insisted that it was not that dangerous, provided you were relatively fit, sober, and aware of what could go wrong. He explained that most deaths happened to drunken testosterone-fueled idiots pushing the boundaries to impress their stupid friends. Occasionally, they fell and tripped over other runners, which jammed up the street and prevented the bulls from making forward progress. It terrified the poor beasts, and they lashed out with horns and feet to protect themselves.

Nowadays, marshals rode along with the bulls on horseback to try and prevent these numbskulls from spoiling the run for everybody else. Fernando finished by inviting Amanda to run along with him.

Amazingly, Amanda agreed.

Phillip's heart raced at the prospect of watching her.

What followed was a hair-raising film of mainly Fernando's muscular backside as he ran in front of and alongside the bulls. There was a scary moment when one mean-looking black bull swerved in front of Fernando, but he managed to avoid a collision, overtook the beast at the first opportunity, and settled into a more secure position some five meters in front of the leading animal.

Amanda kept pace easily with Fernando. Her rapid panting on the soundtrack mixed with the deafening encouragement by the dense crowds emphasized the thrill of the chase.

Phillip found himself on the edge of his seat until they reached the safety of the bullring and the animals were herded away.

Amanda thanked Fernando breathlessly, and the film ended.

There were more clips of Amanda participating in classic Spanish festivals.

She was covered in tomatoes at the Tomatina in Buñol in eastern Spain. She wore the chest camera again, climbing to the top of a human tower or Casteller in Barcelona, dressed in a red silk shirt, white pants, and a black cummerbund.

"What an extraordinary woman?" Phillip said out loud. "She might be petite, but she sure packs a powerful punch."

He checked the viewing stats of her CNN films and was surprised at the low numbers. He assumed that this was down to the fact that were buried deep in the CNN website. They would be more visible on Nuestra España. He e-mailed Richard the video links and then called him on Skype a few minutes later.

"Have you seen the bull running?" he asked.

"Ye, gods. What a woman. Who is she?" Richard enquired.

"Amanda Salisbury. She's the one who filmed Juliet being taken at San Isidro. I met her this morning with Inspector Prado. We're working with him together on Juliet's case, and tomorrow we're all off to Morocco to interview Hassan."

"Well, look at you, Mr. Gadabout. I'd like to meet this Amanda. She should be working with us."

"I agree, our advertisers would love her films."

"Won't they just. Can you persuade her?"

"We've agreed to have dinner."

"Just the diversion you need."

"That's what I thought, assuming I'm not too long in the tooth."

"Nonsense—women go for the mature, man-of-the-world type."

"Fingers crossed. I'm going to call her now to fix a date."

"That's my boy."

They cut the link. Phillip closed down his machine, topped up his wine, and called Amanda.

"Hola, Phillip," she answered. "Any news on Juliet? I've just been watching a news item about her abduction."

"Hi, Amanda, none as yet. I'd forgotten that Prado was arranging TV coverage; I'll watch it when we're done. I'm calling to make a date to discuss websites and stuff. When are you free?"

"Not until the weekend, I'm afraid. Is that all right?"

"Of course, I can wait two more days. Hopefully, we'll have resolved this Juliet thing by then."

"As you say, hopefully. Where shall we meet?"

"How about halfway? Torre del Mar, for example, there's a great seafood restaurant there. Do you like fish?"

"Are egg yolks yellow?"

"Then how about Restaurante El Yate? It's delightful."

"Good choice; I know it. See you there Saturday at nineish."

"I'll bring my tablet so we can play at websites after dessert."

"I normally prefer coffee," said Amanda, laughing,

and ended the call.

Phillip went into the lounge, turned on the TV, and switched channels to Antenna Three. He had to suffer five minutes of adverts until the next news broadcast started. Juliet's case was item number five after the Malaga Soccer team losing to Sevilla, the Catalonia nonsense, Brexit, and Trump's daily antics.

It was a bit surreal watching a good friend on TV.

It was a touching item, and he hoped it would stimulate some useful calls.

He turned the TV off, sat back on his sofa, sipping his wine, and examined his feelings for Juliet. While he remained desperate to find her, he realized that he was thinking more rationally about her. His heart no longer raced, and the confusion in his head was clearing.

Were his postpilgrimage rules working?

Or was the arrival of Amanda on the scene diluting his obsession?

He put his empty wine glass in the dishwasher, set it running, and went to bed.

16

Prado, Amanda, and Phillip convened just after nine thirty the next morning at Starbucks just along from the departure gate in Malaga airport's terminal three. Prado had posted their itinerary on WhatsApp and e-mailed their boarding passes the previous evening. They had made their way independently through security.

Amanda was already in the queue for coffee, dressed in loose black pants and a light-gray long-sleeve blouse, her glossy locks tied up in a french plait. She wore no makeup or jewelry but carried a shoulder bag with her camera.

Phillip and Prado arrived almost together. She took their requests, and they went to find a table. Phillip wore his usual chinos and a polo shirt and carried a shoulder bag containing his laptop—his phone, as usual, was attached to his belt. Prado was in a smart beige suit, panama hat, and carried a brown leather briefcase.

"No hijib?" asked Phillip as Amanda arrived with the tray and distributed coffees and hot butter croissants.

"It's hijab, and no; just because my mother is a Muslim doesn't make me a believer. What about you?"

"Headscarves aren't quite my thing."

"You know what I mean," she said.

"No, I'm not religious. How about you, Inspector?"

"Only when I have to be for family events. You know, the usual Spanish obligations we have in our extended families—baptisms, first communions, weddings, etc. But otherwise, I don't have the time or the inclination. I guess it goes with the job. Not too many of my customers ask forgiveness before smashing a granny over the head for her gold teeth. Listen, before we go to the gate, I want to bring you up to date with the investigation and share our thoughts about the abductors' methods.

"We found strands of Juliet's hair in the van, plus prints on the steering wheel and the rear sliding door. They'd made no attempt to clean up after them, which I thought was terrific news until none of them matched with any known European criminals. We've extended the search globally, but that will take a few days.

"The prints on the van's sliding door were also found in Juliet's apartment, which leads us to suspect that the driver stayed with the vehicle while the other guy broke in. They probably parked somewhere discreetly, for example, on the waste ground down near Rio Chillar.

"They also purchased paper, scissors, and tape to

make polka dots for the van; the remnants were left in the back in the original bag with the receipt from a stationery shop on Calle Jaen. The transaction took place that morning at eleven twenty, and they paid in cash. We're making inquiries there to see if anyone remembers anything or has them on camera. We desperately need a facial description to circulate. Without that, we stand little chance of finding them."

"When do you think they ransacked the apartment?" asked Amanda.

"They would want to be rid of Juliet as quickly as possible after taking her, so we're assuming sometime before. Probably around one-thirty to two o'clock when the procession and crowds had dispersed."

"How did they break in?" asked Phillip.

"The lock is a flimsy affair and was easily forced open. By the scratches on the bolt and the marks on the door frame, forensics think it was a screwdriver or similar."

"Have you traced the van's owner?" asked Phillip.

"It belongs to a plumber who lives opposite Malaga train station. He'd been off sick for three days and only discovered his loss when our officers knocked on his door this morning. The original number plates were in the back of the van. The ones they'd used were taken from an abandoned vehicle near the station, and they stuck some black tape on the F to make it look like an E. The nearest cameras are on the station concourse, but they show nothing resembling our abductors.

"We also found the men's cordoba hats and red bandannas plus Juliet's dress in the back of the van along with her red rose and black midheight leather shoes. This suggests that they forced her to change into whatever clothing they'd taken from her apartment and that they too are now dressed entirely differently.

"We've had roadblocks out during the night and are watching all exit routes from Malaga Province, but so far we have nothing. I've released Juliet's picture to press and TV stations, who ran the story last night and today."

"Yes, I saw it," said Amanda.

"Me too," said Phillip. "What about Juliet's phone?"

"We've attempted to trace it, but they must have removed the battery and SIM card. The last signal emitted was near the abduction site. However, I do have her phone records. My office is working its way through the local calls, but there is one from England on the eve of San Isidro. Perhaps that was the one that upset her so dramatically. Phillip, would you mind calling the number please?"

Prado dug into his case, extracted a slip of paper, and gave it to Phillip along with his phone. Phillip dialed the number on the paper. It was answered on the second ring.

"Rosemary Kitson," said a woman with a faint Birmingham accent.

"I'm sorry to disturb you, madam, but I'm calling on behalf of the police in Malaga, Spain, concerning a Miss Juliet Harding," said Phillip.

"The Spanish police?" asked Kitson. "Has something happened to Juliet?"

"Before I tell you that, I need to confirm your relationship with her. Do you mind?"

"No, of course not; I'm her aunt. Her mother was my sister who died just over three years ago—suicide

I'm afraid."

"Then I'm sorry to tell you that Juliet was abducted yesterday."

"Oh no; that was her worst nightmare."

"Why?"

"I'm sorry, Mr.?"

"Armitage, Phillip Armitage."

"Your name sounds familiar; I believe Juliet may have mentioned you. Look, I'm sorry, but I'm not going to tell you anything over the phone," continued Kitson. "What I am prepared to do, though, is jump on the next plane to Malaga and tell Juliet's story directly to the police. Can I call you when my plane is due and could you pick me up from the airport?"

"Yes, but this a police phone, and they don't speak English. I'll text you my number after we hang up."

"Thank you, Mr. Armitage."

"Phillip, please."

Phillip ended the call and related the content to the others while texting his mobile number to Rosemary.

"Intriguing," said Prado.

"A new dimension to the case?" questioned Amanda.

"Let's hope we're back from Melilla by the time she lands," said Phillip.

"So, now we have two possible scenarios," said Prado. "Perhaps one of them will lead us to Juliet. Shall we go and see Hassan?"

17

An hour later, the Iberia Airways propeller powered Consorcio landed in Melilla. Amanda, Prado, and Phillip disembarked onto the apron directly in front of the airport-terminal building, which also doubles as a Spanish air-force base. The heat and humidity were noticeably more uncomfortable now they were on the African continent. The surrounding Rif Mountains looming over the city were covered in haze.

They walked quickly into the modern glass-and-concrete two-story building, through the arrivals hall, and out onto the front steps where a police patrol car was waiting to take them to the frontier.

They drove past a shabby-looking building near the golf course as they headed in the direction of the Moroccan frontier post, where dozens of poorly dressed people were milling about or cooking over open fires. Their driver informed them that it was a refugee center.

There was a long queue of traffic at the frontier, where Spanish customs officers were opening the trunks of every car heading into Morocco. Nearly all of them were Moroccans, driving an assortment of battered vehicles. They crossed into Melilla daily to purchase processed foods such as yogurt or consumer goods. On the way in, they delivered fresh meat, fruit, and vegetables. This interdependence contributed to both communities survival. There was no room in Melilla to grow anything in volume, and in Nador, no technology for processing foods.

They clambered out of the car and walked.

Prado showed his police ID to the Spanish border-control officer, who beckoned to a colleague in civilian clothes.

"Good morning, Inspector Prado," said the officer. "We've been expecting you. I'm to take you directly to the Royal Moroccan Gendarmerie post. Please have your passports ready for inspection."

They walked through the Spanish frontier and into the narrow stretch of land between the two countries. A uniformed Gendarme approached them as they neared the Moroccan side. He and the Spanish officer were apparently well acquainted and exchanged friendly greetings in Arabic. The Gendarme took a cursory look at their passports and said, in Spanish, "Follow me." They arrived outside the Gendarmerie. "Wait here," said the Gendarme, disappearing through a grubby door.

Crowds of disfigured beggars and women carrying babies with extended bellies swarmed around them, holding out their hands. Prado threw a few coins further along the potholed road, and they scrambled after them squabbling among themselves.

Minutes later, a short, thin, middle-aged policeman, dressed in a uniform of white shirt, dark-blue trousers, and a peaked baseball cap, came out. A pistol was attached to his belt, along with radio and handcuffs, and he wore a chest camera.

He introduced himself in excellent Spanish as Police Lieutenant Dahmanias and informed them that the camera was on and recording. He directed them along the street, down a narrow, filthy alley toward a battered, old Peugeot in Gendarmerie livery. The uniformed driver, sporting a broad grin of rotten teeth, climbed out, saluted, and held the door effusively for the lieutenant, who sat in the front. The others squashed into the back, and before they'd had time to fix seat belts, the Peugeot lurched off at high speed, leaving a cloud of dust behind.

The old car moved far too quickly for Beni Ansar's bumpy roads, which were teeming with Moroccans dressed in grubby white kaftans and walking in the middle of the road oblivious to the policeman's erratic driving. Phillip closed his eyes and reconsidered religion. Somehow, nobody was run over.

The differences between Beni Ansar and Melilla were notable. The sides of the road were jammed with traders and their piles of goods stacked precariously, selling everything from Heinz Ketchup to clothing, electrical products, and the ubiquitous Coca-Cola. Buyers swarmed around, hunting bargains and haggling.

The buildings were dilapidated and basic. Malnourished half-dressed children stared down at them from behind barred openings with no glass. They might only be a few meters from Europe, but this was third-world stuff at its worst.

Nador wasn't much better.

The white-painted three and four-story stucco

buildings that lined the boulevard were well maintained. They were nicely designed with an assortment of towers and Moroccan arches, decorated with ceramic tiles bearing Islamic patterns, but the streets behind were not so attractive. Rows of unmade cluttered roads were lined with unpainted buildings many unfinished. Half-built sidewalks provided access to walled houses, apartment blocks, and a variety of businesses that obviously weren't thriving.

"Hardly any work here," announced the lieutenant as they passed. "It's why more than half of our people go overseas. The money they send back keeps those who remain alive—just."

Halfway along the promenade, the driver slowed down a fraction and swerved into the car park of Hotel La Plage with a screech of tires and burning rubber. They clambered out, relieved about their survival and followed the lieutenant into the cool air-conditioned marble-clad lobby of the hotel. It was furnished with leather sofas, chrome, and glass coffee tables, wall-mounted uplighters. Giant ferns in terracotta pots completed the modern interior design.

"The hotel belongs to the Labrat family," announced the lieutenant. "They cater for the wealthy Moroccans living in northern Europe, who regularly come to visit their families. Hassan Labrat lives and works here. He's expecting us."

They went over to reception, where the lieutenant announced their arrival.

A porter dressed in a spotless white kaftan appeared and escorted them to Hassan's office. He took them over to the chrome fronted lift, where they ascended to the fourth and top floor, along a corridor, and through a full-height wooden door.

They entered a spacious square room with sliding glazed doors that opened out onto a marble-tiled terrace with panoramic views over La Mar Chica. A sofa and comfortable armchairs arranged around a glass coffee table were in the center of the room. A large rosewood desk surrounded by an assortment of office chairs stood in the far corner.

Behind the desk sat a dark-haired, olive-skinned, good-looking young man in his late twenties, dressed in a dark-charcoal-gray suit and white open-necked shirt. Phillip recognized Hassan, who stood up, came round to the front of the desk and shook hands with everyone.

Hassan indicated that they should sit around the coffee table.

They took their seats and waited patiently while the porter served mint tea.

When everyone had a full cup, Hassan said assuredly in Spanish, "A warm welcome to my family's hotel. Phillip, nice to see you again. The lieutenant informs me that Juliet is missing and you wish to eliminate me from your inquiries."

"Thank you for your friendly greetings and kind hospitality," responded Prado. "Could you tell us about your relationship with Juliet, how it ended, and where you were on the fifteenth of May?"

"With pleasure, Inspector," said Hassan, still oozing confidence. "Juliet and I were together for some two years. I met her at Don Comer on a break from my work as an assistant manager in Hotel Cavana. We hit it off, started dating, and became very fond of each other. We were two lonely people caring for and supporting each other in a foreign country.

We had common gripes about low pay and not fulfilling our potential, but we were both improving our languages and learning about another culture. We were happy."

"Did she talk about her life in England?"

"She mentioned an aunt Rosemary from Kenilworth, whom she adored. They spoke from time to time, but she never shared any news with me. When I pressed her for more detail, she would shake her head and change the subject. On its own, I wouldn't have read too much into it, but when I added the unusual physical side of our relationship, it led me to believe she had a painful childhood. She was terrified of intimacy, and we never went beyond kissing and hugging. She justified her condition by saying she was asexual, had no desire, and admitted to being a virgin. Consequently, I never once saw her naked or made love. Over time, though, I came to suspect that the asexuality was an excuse to conceal something much darker. I think that she'd been abused. I asked her about it once, and her reaction was horrendous. She sat on the floor for hours in a catatonic state, rocking back and forth. That was the last time I tried to encourage her to let all out, for which she seemed most grateful. It took a while for me to accept her as she was, but we enjoyed each other's company tremendously. Juliet is a lovely girl, and I miss her dreadfully."

"Why did you come back to Nador at such short notice?" asked Prado.

"My father had a stroke. As the eldest son, it falls upon me to take over the family responsibilities until he recovers."

"How is he?" asked Phillip.

"He's alive but unlikely to recover enough to take back the reins," answered Hassan.

"Sorry about that," said Prado. "Tell me about the argument."

"I wanted her to come with me; she didn't. That angered me, and I said some stupid things. When I arrived here, I realized that Juliet was right. She could never adjust to how we do things here. Reluctantly I accepted that and moved on with my life."

"Thank you; I'd like to see your passport."

"Certainly," answered Hassan, standing up and going to a drawer in his desk, where he extracted a green-covered document and handed it to Prado.

Prado looked at it carefully, turning the pages and checking the date stamps.

"OK, so you haven't left the country since your return from Nerja," said Prado, irritated. "But you could still have arranged Juliet's abduction, smuggled her illegally into Morocco, and have her locked up in a garage somewhere."

"Indeed I could, Inspector. However, if that were the case, I would need to feed her on a regular basis, which means that I would have to abandon the hotel three times a day to do that or have it done by trusted staff. In either case, my mother, who watches me like a hawk, would know that I am up to something. Believe me when I say that you cannot lie to my mother. Nobody can.

"Furthermore, if she suspected that I was harboring any feelings for a non-Muslim girl, my life would be hell. I would lose her love and respect, be banished from my position here, and ostracized by my siblings. Inspector, I couldn't do that to my family just for a few stolen celibate moments with a beautiful

English girl. I'd be stupid."

"Could we meet your mother and have her confirm this?" asked Prado.

"Of course, she's waiting in the next room. She's still worried about my father, so please respect that," said Hassan, picking up the telephone on his desk, punching in a few numbers, speaking in what sounded like Arabic, and hanging up.

Prado looked at Amanda with raised eyebrows.

She shook her head discretely. She hadn't understood a word.

A few seconds later, a distinguished, senior woman, dressed in traditional Moroccan clothing and a hijab, appeared at the door.

"This my mother, Fatima," said Hassan. "Between our families, we speak in Tarifit, the Northern Moroccan version of the Berber language spoken in this region. She wishes you all peace. You may ask her anything. The lieutenant will translate."

It only took a few moments for Prado to satisfy himself that Hassan's mother ruled her family with an iron rod and that Hassan was telling the truth. Aside from that, common sense persuaded him that to stash a white blond girl in a nearby secure place without someone noticing would be almost impossible. The only exception would be if a wealthy sheik had hidden Juliet in his palace harem, and that seemed too fantastic in this impoverished region.

However, he thought it politic to consult with Phillip and Amanda before making a final decision.

They withdrew to the corridor.

"What do you think?" asked Prado.

"Not guilty," said Phillip adamantly.

"With a mother like that, he'd be roasted for even

thinking of bringing Juliet here," commented Amanda.

"Agreed," said Prado. "Let's say good-bye."

They reentered the room.

"For the moment, Mr. Labrat," said Prado, "we're satisfied with your explanation, so thank you and your mother for your time and the refreshments. Lieutenant, we're ready to go now."

Just as they were about to shut the door behind them, Hassan called out, "Sorry, Inspector—wait please; there's one more thing that might help you find Juliet."

They paused and turned back to Hassan.

Prado raised his eyebrows.

"In the heat of my argument with Juliet, I said that she would regret me leaving. She would be on her own, and I knew she hated the thought of that. Surprisingly, she didn't seem bothered and said not to worry; she already had a new friend lined up to replace me."

"A new friend?" repeated Prado, eyebrows raised.

"She told me he was an estate agent and apparently looked nothing like me—whatever that meant," said Hassan.

"Did you believe her?"

"Juliet never lied. But her words enraged me, and that is why I threatened to come back for her."

"I understand. Is that all?" asked Prado.

"Yes," replied Hassan. "Except I'll pray for you to find her soon. She'll be terrified, poor thing."

"Thanks. Adios."

As the police car hurtled almost on two wheels round a sharp curve on the way back to the frontier, Phillip's phone buzzed.

It was a text from Rosemary Kitson.

She hoped to be landing in Malaga midafternoon.

Only minutes after they did.

Phillip confirmed that they would be waiting for her.

She sent a photo by return.

Oh no, thought Phillip, looking at it. She's an older version of Juliet.

He showed it to Prado, who nodded and shrugged.

Then to Amanda, who smiled at him, put her hand on his thigh, and petted it sympathetically.

18

"Phillip, you mentioned that Juliet was meeting a mystery friend at San Isidro," said Prado as they settled into their seats for the short return flight to Malaga. "Do you think said friend could also be the estate agent that Hassan referred to?"

"I've never heard her mention an estate agent," said Phillip.

"What about your regulars' table at the café. Any estate agents among them?" asked Prado.

"Come to think of it, no—not a single one. I obviously know most of the Nerja agents—they're customers of ours—but none of them ever come to the café; they're always too busy."

"It's a bit of a long shot," said Prado. "But could you make a list of possible agents in the area?"

"All of them?"

"No. Let's assume male," mooted Prado. "English speaking and under thirty-five."

"I'll work on it with Richard. It'll be a long list

though—at least two hundred."

"Well, that is better than our current status of no fucking list," said Prado.

"Good point; we'll do our best. Any other interesting numbers in Juliet's phone log?"

"Other than the English number, no. Just the typical domestic assortment and a couple of girlfriends."

They landed in Malaga on time and went straight through baggage reclaim and into the arrival hall. When they checked the display board, Kitson's plane had been delayed by an hour. Amanda couldn't hang around that long as she had an urgent appointment with the director of the Picasso Museum. They exchanged cheek kisses, and she left, walking quickly toward the short-term car park.

Phillip and Prado watched her go.

"Lovely girl," said Prado.

"Mmm," said Phillip.

"When you clear your head from this obsession with Juliet, she could be all yours," said Prado quietly.

Phillip was astonished and said, "That's damned astute of you."

"You wear your heart on your sleeve—any cop could see."

"Do you think Amanda spotted it as well?"

"Women have instincts for such matters."

"Oh, fuck. I'm a complete fool."

"I didn't sense any bad vibes about it on her part."

"Let's hope so."

After Amanda disappeared through the door, Prado and Phillip walked over to the café in the arrival hall, ordered coffees from the counter, and sat down at a table.

"Something is puzzling me," said Phillip after taking a sip of his drink.

"Tell me."

"Abducting Juliet in broad daylight. Don't you think that smacks of desperation?"

"I agree; normally abductions happen after dark or at least in a less public location."

"Some deadline maybe?"

"Possibly?"

"Could it be that Juliet knew those men?"

"To me, she looked frightened, not showing signs of familiarity."

"Girls don't willingly climb into vehicles with unknown men. If she was frightened, why didn't she scream or run?"

Prado chewed over Phillip's observation before replying, "A scream would have been wasted with all the loud music; who would hear?"

"Isn't screaming an instinctive reaction to danger, regardless of other surrounding noises?"

"Usually, yes, but Amanda's film didn't show everything that was going on. Juliet was on the far side of the van; only her head and shoulders were visible over its roof. Perhaps the men used a weapon or had threatened her in some way. Whatever the reasons for her compliance, she did climb into the van and has not been seen since. Regretfully, it's happening more and more."

"Are there many abductions?"

"A growing number of foreign girls are disappearing. We don't know if they are abducted, tricked, or go willingly. Not many are reported here in Spain, but we are receiving more and more inquiries via consulates about missing daughters last seen catching a plane to Malaga."

"What happens to them?"

"Fodder for our expanding sex industry."

"And you think that is why Juliet has been abducted?"

"It's unlikely to be for her ironing skills."

"So that's another possibility?"

"It is. Let me give you some background. It'll help you put things in context, and if we are to be working together, I think it's essential that you understand what's going on with one of the leading crime genres here on the Costa del Sol.

"For decades, our guaranteed weather and low-cost beach holidays have attracted millions of family holidaymakers during the peak seasons of Christmas, Easter, and summer. The rest of the year, it used to be relatively quiet. Over the last decade though, we've been inventing new ways to fill the low season gaps, so that we have a more even use of our resources all year round.

"I have to say that the marketing guys have done an excellent job. We are now the largest golf destination in the world and amazingly carry out more cosmetic-surgery operations than California. Apparently, they call them sun-and-sculpture breaks. We also offer walking holidays in the mountains, soccer training academies, athletics training, diving, yachting, culinary schools, cultural programs—I could go on. The one thing they have in common is that all these new activities have been successful. The outcome has been a massive increase in tourist numbers.

"While all this was happening and not spotted by most of us, there was the massive growth of Internet pornography. Lightning download speeds may well have improved the overall browsing experience, but they have also created a considerable demand for freshly made, high-quality porn clips. Previously, these were produced in studios, but with the technological advances in recording equipment, that has changed. All filmmakers need nowadays is the latest gear, a few shapely models, and an isolated villa with a pool. With those, they can churn out new footage all year round with practically zero studio or technician costs.

"Consequently, the web is jammed with porn made in Spain, and it's had a substantial effect on sex tourism. All those naughty outdoor snippets set in our gorgeous landscapes have advertised the area to porn fans. Now they're coming here for the real thing in droves. So much so that the Costa del Sol has just overtaken Amsterdam as Europe's hottest destination. Every day thousands of men arrive at Malaga airport, particularly from your country, looking for a good time. Some are in groups, such as stag parties, golfers, drinkers, soccer teams, tiddlywink players, etc. But most come in ones and twos."

"I had no idea. Where do they go?"

"Mainly, Marbella and Puerto Banus, but all the west coast towns are seeing massive increases in sex tourism."

"Local businesses must be delighted."

"There are mixed feelings about it. They like the money but not the mess and damage. As you know Brits can be pretty disgusting when tanked up with fancy cocktails or San Miguel beer, and that's just the hen parties. The stag parties are far worse. Some of the antics bridegrooms are put through by their so-called best mates' beggars' belief. For example, only last week at the comisaría in Benalmadena we had a Scottish guy in a kilt, from Glasgow I think, complaining that he'd been raped in a gay club, but he was so drunk he couldn't remember where it was."

"I dread to think what his fiancée said to him when he arrived home."

"Oh no, you've grasped the wrong end of the stick. He didn't want to go home. He enjoyed it so much he wanted to go back for more and was seeking our help locating the club."

"You're kidding?"

"Ojala. If only. No, there's certainly no shortage of punters of every persuasion. Consequently, the sex clubs are desperate for more, mainly girls, to keep pace with demand."

"Are these clubs licensed?"

"Most of them. Every town has at least one licensed *club* or *wiskeria*; they're appropriately controlled, have to meet minimum standards, and have their girls regularly inspected. It makes their use safer for all parties. But as business boomed, applications for more clubs increased. Typically, the buildings are located on the edge of town so as not to disturb the neighbors and cause minimum offense. They have high walls around them so that punters can drive in and drive out discretely. The idea is to prevent wives from discovering that his trip to the allotment meant somewhat more than just picking up a few vegetables.

"But now councils are receiving too many complaints about the number of clubs, so they have refused to issue any more permits. But that hasn't done anything to stop the demand."

"Why don't they increase the taxes? It will force prices up, which will reduce the number of punters."

"A logical British solution, but regretfully it's a tad more complicated in Spain. The hotels have become accustomed to busy bedrooms all year round. Restaurants, bars, and nightclubs prefer to be fully booked. Higher taxes on sex clubs would reduce tourist numbers and increase unemployment. Meanwhile, the sex industry has moved underground to keep pace with demand. There are now thousands of unlicensed individuals on the net offering personal services in your hotel room.

"Illegal clubs are also on the up, and they are awful, yet extremely adept at emptying wallets. They're not too difficult to find, but as fast as we close one, two more open."

"Where do the clubs find enough women?"

"That's their main problem. They lost their best girls to the porn producers who pay more for less onerous work. The clubs have replaced them with mainly Moroccans, Eastern Europeans, and more recently African migrants. But that's still not enough.

"As you can imagine, there is a high turnover of girls. The drug addicts are disposed of, some girls escape, others crack up mentally, and the prettiest ones are purchased as sex slaves. To stay in business, clubs need a continual supply of new girls. The legally constituted clubs attract the best girls and boys because they offer work contracts, health care, and pension contributions. The illegal ones, however, have to resort to ever more devious and ruthless tactics to sustain a viable number of women, and that includes abduction.

"Recently, they've started taking girls to order. One

night last week, we stopped a boat halfway between Marbella and Tangiers. In the front cabin, we found a pair of pretty blond twins from Manchester handcuffed to the bunks. They were being smuggled out to join a harem in Tunisia. Their drinks had been spiked in a Puerto Banus nightclub. Next thing they knew, they'd woken up at sea."

"So Juliet could already be in the hands of some sweaty sheik," said Phillip, shaking his head miserably. "How do you usually find out when girls have gone missing?"

"Sometimes their friends report them, but usually the next morning when they've sobered up and realized what's happened. By then it's too late for us to stand any chance of finding them. The talent scouts that take these girls are extremely clever. They have a knack for selecting women who are easy to drug or are just happy to disappear. You'll be surprised how many come here to escape from sordid relationships and lonely lives. Sadly, when they're abducted, they have nobody to report them as missing."

"And you think Juliet may have been selected?"

"To be honest, I don't know. Juliet is more beautiful than the average sex worker and may have been targeted by a wealthy individual who saw her at the café and wanted her for himself. Other than that, she could be working in an illegal club somewhere or on her way out of Spain. Irrespective of who has her, they have an eighteen-hour start on us."

"At least we know she's missing and have a range of clues. Surely they should help us find her?"

"They ought to, but as yet we have no idea, just theories."

"Then fingers crossed that your team can track them down."

"Thankfully, the legal clubs are cooperative. Otherwise, they lose their licenses. They also have a vested interest in monitoring the illegals, so they inform us about any nefarious activities. We have a specialist team that works undercover in these places. They have a photo of Juliet. Tonight they will be watching for her."

Phillip went to check the arrival board, feeling utterly depressed.

Mrs. Kitson's plane was further delayed until five thirty.

He went back to the café and updated the inspector.

"Then I'll go back to my office," said Prado. "I want to see if we've had any calls from our media campaign. Would you mind waiting?"

"Not at all. I'll bring her to you."

"I'll reserve a parking space under the comisaría."

Phillip watched Prado go and then ordered another coffee. While he waited for Mrs. Kitson, he typed up a summary of his discussion with Prado and posted it to their WhatsApp group. It would give Amanda something to think about.

19

Phillip recognized Rosemary Kitson instantly when a tall, striking, svelte, short-haired blond woman dressed in a figure-hugging black skirt, tailored jacket, and white silk blouse entered the arrival hall. Her smart appearance and stern expression seemed incongruous when compared to the hordes of casually dressed tourists with expectant smiling faces, looking forward to their week of sun, sand, and whatever.

Phillip held up his hand as her ice-blue eyes scanned the waiting crowd. She nodded to acknowledge that she'd seen him and smiled sheepishly as if relieved that someone was there to meet her. Phillip guessed she was about his age but wasn't sure. In the flesh, her resemblance to his ex-wife was even closer than Juliet. Astonishingly, it didn't bother him.

"Ms. Kitson?" he enquired as she approached, towing a small overnight black bag and carrying an elegant matching purse.

"It's Mrs., but Rosemary, please," she requested.
"Phillip Armitage. Thank you for coming."

They shook hands; her grip was firm, and her hand dry and warm.

Phillip insisted on taking her bag.

"It's quite a distance to the visitor car park. Would you prefer to wait here, and I'll come to collect you?"

"Thanks, but I'll walk," replied Rosemary. "I'd appreciate stretching my legs. Forgive me for asking, but since when have the Spanish police been employing English people?"

"I'm a voluntary translator."

"An Englishman with foreign languages—that is unusual."

"If you want to be in business here in Spain, you either speak the lingo or go bust."

Phillip led her to the back of the arrival hall and pressed the button to call the elevator. They went up to the busy departure hall. Starbucks was still packed as they went past on their way to the exit. Outside, it was a warm, balmy late afternoon.

"It was raining in Birmingham," said Rosemary, sighing enviously.

They used the walk to exchange getting-to-know-you small talk. Rosemary spoke in a matter of fact voice with a faint hint of a Birmingham accent.

As they approached the parking pay station, Phillip removed the ticket from his wallet, paid by credit card, turned to Rosemary, and said, "Let's settle you into the car. On the way to the police station, I need to update you on the investigation."

She looked at him nervously and then nodded.

Phillip extracted his validated ticket out of the machine and led her to his BMW.

He put her bag in the trunk and watched while she opened the driver's door.

She looked up, mildly embarrassed.

"Silly me. It's been a while since I've traveled."

She walked around the back of the car. Phillip opened the passenger door and, after she'd settled into her seat, closed it gently.

They drove out of the car park and headed into Malaga center along the old N-340 highway.

"Any news about Juliet?" Rosemary enquired.

"Not yet, but they have made a lot of progress. The abductors are on film, albeit with faces hidden, and the van used has been found. There's a TV campaign. Every police patrol car carries her photo, and border controls now have her passport details, but we are running some eighteen hours behind."

"Sounds good. Now I know why your name is familiar. Juliet told me about you. I can see why now?" said Rosemary.

"Hopefully, all positive."

"Certainly. Her father died when she was young. You're tall like him and were supportive of her when she first arrived. She told me that she was happy about that. She felt she could trust you as a friend, and trust is a difficult concept for her."

"That's nice to know," said Phillip, worrying whether he should share his confused feelings with Rosemary. Best not, he thought initially, but it's a relief to learn that Juliet saw me as a father figure and not an old lecher. I must have hidden my secret desires better than I thought.

"I didn't do much to deserve that," he added.

"You were always there for her. It made her feel secure in Nerja, and that helped her recover from the past and rebuild herself."

Guilt racked through Phillip's mind. He hadn't realized that his small contributions had helped Juliet so much when he'd mostly been drooling over her nubile body and pretty face.

"I've become extremely fond of your niece. Her abduction has been hard to bear, but working on the investigation makes me at least feel useful. Thankfully, I'm not sitting around, waiting for news. We were in Morocco earlier today, visiting Juliet's ex-boyfriend. Have you heard of Hassan?"

"She mentioned that he returned home to assist with his sick father or something."

"He wanted to take Juliet with him, but she wasn't interested. Apparently, they had a massive row about it. At the time, he threatened to come back and take her, but as soon as he returned to Nador, he realized the absurdity of doing so. We're satisfied now that he had no connection with the crime."

"You are fond of her?" said Rosemary, scrutinizing Phillip's animated face as he talked.

"Who wouldn't be? She's incredibly beautiful, but what confused my feelings for her is that she looks almost identical to my ex-wife. Come to that, so do you—if you don't mind me saying? Until recently, I didn't know whether to date Juliet or invite her to Disneyland."

"Well done you for keeping that from her. You said, until recently. Are you less confused now?"

"Have you heard of the Camino de Santiago?"

"Of course."

"I came back from finishing the pilgrimage earlier this week. My sole purpose for going was to sort out my confusion with Juliet."

"Did it work?"

"I learned how to control my feelings for her."

"How?"

"I realized that my problem wasn't Juliet, but my ex-wife. You guys are just triggers who remind me of her. The pilgrimage helped me come to terms with my long-held obsession for my ex. I can now accept that Juliet is a good friend and not a ghost haunting me."

"Would it help if I wore a dark wig and added some large sunglasses?"

"Ha. Sorry—bit heavy there for a moment."

"No, I respect that. You'll go the extra mile to find her."

"I would, but so far I've not achieved much. We were due to have a drink together at the San Isidro Festival, but she didn't show up. If only I'd informed the police, then we might have been further ahead with the investigation."

"Why didn't you?"

"She was meeting a new friend and said she might not make it, so I went home. When she didn't arrive at work the next day, it was me who went to her apartment and found the door open. It had been ransacked, and all her personal stuff was missing.

"Coincidently, an American journalist had filmed the abduction but didn't notice it until she was editing on her large screen at home later that night. She reported it to the police yesterday morning. The inspector handling the case and I have worked together previously, and he recognized me in the video near the place where she was abducted.

"Rosemary. The abductors drove right past me with Juliet inside the van."

"How awful? Do the police have any theories about who took her?"

"There's a booming sex industry."

"Say no more, please. I know where you're going, but believe me, there is a far-worse scenario that on first hearing sounds unbelievable. It's why I've come here to tell you personally. Do you mind if I phone my husband?"

"Not at all, do you want me to stop? Give you a bit of privacy?"

"That won't be necessary, but thank you."

Rosemary extracted her phone from her handbag, turned it on, and stabbed in the password. It took a minute for the roaming service to kick in. She spoke with her husband, confirming her safe arrival and updated him on the investigation, and then listened while he spoke briefly before exchanging tender farewells. When she'd finished, Phillip enquired.

"Have you booked any accommodation?"

"No, but my husband just confirmed that he'd reserved a room for me in the Hotel Palacio. Is that near the police station?"

"Just a short walk, but I'll drop you there when we've finished with Inspector Prado."

"Is he your boss?"

"No, I work for myself. He's the officer responsible for crimes involving foreigners and needs translators. I'm one of them."

As instructed, Phillip pulled up at the entrance to the comisaría underground car park, he announced himself on the intercom, and the steel roller shutter raised to admit him. He parked up, they clambered out, walked to the elevator door, and waited.

A couple of minutes later, a buzzer announced the

car's arrival, and the doors slid open silently to reveal Prado standing at the back. He waved them in, Phillip introduced Rosemary, and they went up to his office.

"Can we offer you a coffee or anything to drink?" asked Phillip as they arrived at Prado's office and closed the door behind them.

"A still mineral water, please," answered Rosemary.

Phillip went over to the filing cabinet and collected a plastic cup and a bottle of water and then placed them on the desk by Rosemary as Prado settled her into one of the visitor chairs.

Prado retired behind his desk, Phillip took the other chair, and they both waited expectantly for Rosemary to begin.

She burst into tears.

"Sorry," Rosemary whispered moments later after dabbing her eyes with a tissue. "I've been rehearsing what to say all the way here, but now I don't know where to start."

"Shall I ask you a couple of questions?" suggested Phillip. "They might start you off?"

Rosemary composed herself, wiped her eyes again, and nodded.

"Where do you live?"

"In…in Kenilworth," she stuttered. "It's about forty kilometers southeast of Birmingham."

"You said on the phone that Juliet's mother committed suicide. When was that, and why?"

"It was four years ago. She sat in the bath, drank a bottle of vodka, and slit her wrists. Juliet found her when she returned from school. She'd left a note on the dressing table. All it said was, 'Why me?'"

"Not particularly forthcoming?"

"She wasn't a woman of many words. But I

understood exactly why. She could never face life happily unless everything were in its place, everyone doing as expected, no dramas, and no emotions. When her husband destroyed her imagined utopia, she had nothing to cling onto. Her perfect world had been sullied by shame and perversion. Oblivion was her only solution."

"Sounds bad?"

"Yes, but she brought it all on herself with her choice of the wrong man. Graham Ferrier, her second husband, was devious and evil. She ignored his porn addiction and pretended that he never had affairs with underage girls."

"Forgive me, but your sister doesn't sound like my kind of person."

"Mine neither, but she was clinically successful as a fashion model. International catwalks, big money, and the lot. She was obsessed with her looks and appearance to the exclusion of everything else. So when her first husband Pip passed away after a short period suffering from multiple sclerosis, her first reaction was to complain about not having a man around to worship her, and that being alone was untenable. She immediately set out to replace Pip, much to Juliet's annoyance, as she'd been the one to care for him during the final stages of his illness.

"Ferrier was younger than Rachel, but more callously, she liked that he was handsome, healthy, and wealthy. He was a brilliant photographer she'd met at a shoot in London several years previously. They dated and married so quickly it was obscene. Juliet would have been thirteen or thereabouts.

"She never liked Ferrier from day one, so their relationship started with tension and grew progressively worse. Juliet was a late developer, so it wasn't until she was almost sixteen that she'd filled out into a stunningly beautiful girl. Her mother insisted that she follow her into modeling, and for that, she would need an image portfolio in a wide range of outfits. Ferrier used these sessions as an excuse to start touching her intimately, and I'm sure he was drugging her with something. Then on her seventeenth birthday, he tried to rape her.

"Somehow, Juliet managed to escape.

"She ran over to my place, which was about half a mile away. She was half-naked and in a terrible state. I called Rachel, who insisted that it had never happened. It was only a misunderstanding. His hand had slipped accidentally. Juliet was listening on the speakerphone and screamed at her mother. She accused her of aiding and abetting a rapist, and that she never wanted to see her again.

"I hung up and had a hard chat with Juliet. I warned her about the horrors of reporting a rape. Did she have the evidence to prove it? She stood, and exposed herself to me. What Ferrier had done to her sickened me.

"I called the police, who were brilliant.

"Their doctor was able to collect all the evidence needed for the Crown Prosecution Service to bring charges. It was a slam-dunk case."

"Didn't she find the trial intimidating?" asked Phillip. "I would imagine that facing her abuser across a crowded courtroom must have been more than daunting."

"She was terrified but determined that her stepfather would have his day in court. She was a sterling witness and delivered her testimony calmly.

Then handled the cross-questioning by his ruthless, uncaring barrister with a maturity beyond her years. I'm sure she'd make a great barrister herself. Anyway, Ferrier was sent down for six years."

"Good for her."

"The next day Juliet's mother killed herself."

"How did that affect Juliet?"

"She was sad that the last memory of her mother was a heated verbal exchange. At the funeral, she broke down and wept briefly, but that seemed to be it. She was withdrawn for a while, but then she opened up and told me about Ferrier's abuse and how it had put her off any interest in intimate relationships. The thought of sex made her feel sick to her stomach.

"But life goes on. I organized some counseling for her, and I was amazed how quickly she responded to it. Within a week she was back to school and buried herself in her lessons. That summer, she sailed through her exams. After the court case with her stepfather, she expressed an interest in studying law. I was anticipating a discussion about which university she preferred, but she didn't even wait for her results to come through before telling me about her plan.

"All she wanted was a new life in Spain.

"I could understand her wanting to move away from Kenilworth from the daily visual reminders of her traumatic past, but I objected strongly about Spain. I was frightened at the thought of her traveling alone, but I had to let her go and make her way in the world. She was eighteen after all.

"I gave her some money and a mobile phone and dropped her and her backpack off at St. Pancras station. We've not seen each other since."

"Why Spain?"

"She was incredibly close to her father, Pip. He was her hero and soul mate and more than made up for her mother's maternal inadequacies. They used to holiday in Nerja together when her mother was away, working. She had happy memories of the place and felt at peace. As I said in the car, Phillip, your friendship and support played a significant role helping Juliet settle down. She knew she wasn't fulfilling her potential, but you saw how she was. Mostly happy and enjoying her simple life in the sun. What could I possibly offer to tempt her back to the cold and gray of middle England? Three years of hard legal studies and a student loan of fifty grand, or a tedious admin job in my office?"

"So why did your call to her on the fourteenth upset her so?"

"I told her that Ferrier had been released from prison early and came to see me at my office."

"What on earth for?"

"He wanted to know where Juliet was. Insisted that he must apologize to her in person."

"What did you say?"

"I told him that Juliet didn't want to see him again—ever.

"He explained that his therapist had strongly advised him to make amends with Juliet. It would help put those terrible events behind him and move on with his life.

"Naturally, I didn't even believe a word, so asked him to leave it with me. He gave me his telephone number, and I promised to call him as soon as I'd taken some advice and made a decision. Then I appointed a private detective to check out his story and his circumstances."

"Did you mention any of this to Juliet?"

"Not at this stage. I wanted to be sure of the facts."

"What did your detective discover?"

"Beyond my wildest fears."

"Juliet wasn't his first victim?" guessed Phillip.

"Correct. He'd been abusing women and getting away with it for years. There'd been a couple of complaints to the police, but they were withdrawn. The girls were either grateful his images of them earned them lucrative assignments, or he paid them off. But they weren't my primary concern.

"Ferrier's probation officer revealed disturbing information about his time in prison.

"Ferrier was a pretty boy and was raped by a secession of cellmates. He complained to the governor. His rapists had their sentence extended, but Ferrier was sent back to the same cell where he was raped continually. He never complained again or showed any emotion—just accepted whatever came his way. When it came to his appraisal for an early release, Ferrier said all the right things, expressed remorse for his crime and vowed to respect women. The newly qualified psychologist believed him, and Ferrier was let out without being added to the sexual offenders' register.

"Out of prison, he no longer needed to disguise his real emotions. Ferrier's seasoned probation officer spotted immediately that Ferrier was a disturbed man. However, he was reliable and punctual for his appointments, and when he applied to leave the country, no grounds to prevent him could be found."

"Is there a restraining order preventing Ferrier from contacting Juliet?"

"No, it expired last year."

"Does Ferrier know where Juliet is?"

"He does now. He also employed a detective."

"How can he afford that?"

"With Rachel's assets and those from his photography business, he has more than enough not to work and to finance a search for Juliet."

"How did you learn about this?"

"Ferrier's detective became concerned about his intent for Juliet. He told mine in confidence. They used to be cops together."

"Did his detective find Juliet?"

"Almost immediately. When searches for Juliet's British National Insurance number didn't register any payments in the UK, they assumed she was overseas. They gained access to my telephone records and found regular calls to Spain, where she's registered with the tax authorities in Malaga. It was a simple matter to locate her address and place of work.

"Then when Ferrier's detective went to collect payment at his apartment, he saw a Ryanair boarding pass to Malaga on his coffee table. He called my detective, and I heard about it about an hour later. I contacted Juliet straightaway. That was the evening of the fourteenth May.

"That call made her sick to her stomach."

"I'm not surprised."

"Fucking families," she said.

"Can't blame her."

"Any ideas where Ferrier might be staying?"

"No, but probably not far away."

"Let me explain all this to Prado."

"In that case, I'll pop to the restroom. Where is it?"

Phillip opened the door, directed her to the far end

of the corridor, returned to his chair, and updated Prado.

"This man sounds dangerous," said Prado when Phillip had finished. "He has motive and opportunity, and although the timing is tight, he could have arranged everything from England beforehand. After four years in prison, he's bound to be plugged into a criminal network where he can purchase a wide range of illicit services. In my book, Ferrier is our most likely suspect. However, we shouldn't let him distract us from our other lines of inquiry."

"Any calls from the media campaign?"

"Yes, we're following up on a couple of them. One looks distinctly possible. A customer swore that he saw Juliet in a sex club in Marbella on the night after San Isidro."

"That sounds too quick."

"I agree, but we have to check it out. I'll contact border control to see if we have Ferrier on film entering the country. We'll also need his phone number to see if we can trace his location."

Rosemary returned and handed over Ferrier's phone number, an old photo, and a wrinkled photocopy of his passport, which was due to expire at the end of the year.

Prado went out of the office to talk to his colleagues, initiate a formal request for Ferrier's file and phone records from the Birmingham Police, and to speak with border control.

Rosemary returned, looking decidedly chirpier than earlier.

"Anything from the media campaign?" asked Rosemary.

"Nothing as yet," lied Phillip, wanting to spare her

from any pain until the sex-club facts were clear.

"What does the inspector think of my story?"

"He's confident that Ferrier is a likely candidate but we're unlikely to find out more tonight. How long do you intend to stay?"

"I'm not going to sit in my hotel room, waiting for your call; that would be pure hell. So I have a return flight in the morning. If there are any developments, I'll be back on the next plane."

"Would you care to join me for dinner?"

"Thanks, Phillip, but you don't need to entertain me, and I have a lot of work to do. I'll grab something from hotel room service."

"What work do you do?"

"My husband and I build carbon-neutral housing developments. We're growing like crazy, and it's driving me bananas."

"Did I hear you right about Ferrier inheriting your sister's estate?"

"You did."

"Why not Juliet, or at least some of it?"

"Have you seen that comedy program, *Absolutely Fabulous*?"

"Many times; love it."

"Well, Rachel was similar to Patsy, gorgeous, but stupid. Kids to her were a fun accessory so long as they were decorative, seen, and not heard. She probably just forgot."

"Sounds callous to me."

"It could have been something more sinister such as illness. The postmortem revealed that her liver was in the early stages of cirrhosis. Apparently, she was a secret drinker. You'd never have known to look at her."

The door burst open, and Prado rushed back into the office, waving a pen drive in his hand.

"I need Rosemary to look at this," he said breathlessly.

20

Amanda's meeting with the director of the Picasso Museum had gone well. She wanted to make a film about Anne Pennington, a wealthy American living in Nerja who owned several Picasso paintings. They were due to be exhibited the following January under the title, Picasso's Mistresses. The director had agreed to introduce Amanda to her and would organize a date for them to meet.

As she walked down the steps of the historic Palacio Buenavista onto Calle San Agustin, her phone rang, number unknown but from Algeciras.

"Hola. Digame," she answered.

"Hola, Sra. Amanda, soy Antonio Gutierrez," said a man's voice.

It was the captain of the Guardia Civil coast guard.

"Hi, Antonio, how's it going?"

"It's all arranged. We have an appointment at the detention center in Algeciras tomorrow at eleven o'clock in the morning. Can you be there?"

"Of course. Can you e-mail me the address?"

"On its way. See you tomorrow."

The detention center in Algeciras is a former prison. An imposing building with bars to the ground-floor doors and windows but deemed uninhabitable as far back as fifteen years ago. It's just up the hill from Algeciras harbor and is the subject of much controversy both locally and nationally. The government wants to refurbish it, but locals and several charities prefer that it closes permanently, stating that asylum seekers are not criminals and shouldn't be locked up while their asylum applications are being processed. Whereas, the government is concerned that because of free movement within the European Union, migrants may move onto other countries and cause problems elsewhere. For example, forming shanty towns outside Calais in Northern France, where they try and enter Great Britain illegally in the back of trucks.

Whilst the Spanish Ministry of the Interior has externalized much of its immigration controls to the host nations concerned, for those that do make it to Spain, the Government prefers to know where their migrants are. From detention centers, they can be deported easily and quickly when their application has been decided.

Amanda parked her car by several others at the front of the building, went up the steps and into the reception. Antonio was waiting for her. He sprang to his feet, came over, and shook hands.

"Here are the GPS coordinates I promised you," said Antonio, handing over a folded piece of paper. "They confirm that our position when the baby was born was outside of Spanish territorial waters."

"Thanks, but they're irrelevant now; the mother died, and the baby is due to be adopted by a Spanish family on the hospital's waiting list," informed Amanda.

"That will look good in your documentary."

"Just as well, the rest is a tragedy. I wonder what we'll learn here this morning?"

"Let's go and find out."

Together they walked over to the receptionist and asked him to announce their arrival.

Moments later, the door at the back of the reception opened, and a tall, bulky man with black hair and a severe dandruff problem, wearing the uniform of the National Police entered. He strode over to them, leering at Amanda, shook hands, and said brusquely, "I'm Sergeant Perez, in charge at this center. The group that came in on your ship, Captain, is assembled in the canteen. Regretfully, there are only ten remaining; the others have absconded. I'm sorry, but it's an old building and not particularly secure, plus we are underresourced. I must warn you that the migrants are bound to complain about the food and conditions. Regretfully, there's nothing we can do to improve matters until the government pull their fingers out and upgrade these premises. Meanwhile, we have some two hundred and eighty odd detainees crammed into tiny cells, sharing beds and a bucket for a toilet. No wonder the others pissed off. Follow me, please."

Perez led them down a short corridor, unlocking and locking two barred doors on the way. They ended up in a large room laid out with tables and chairs.

Amanda and the captain exchanged concerned glances.

They entered and saw the people from the boat sitting around a rectangular gray laminate table in the far corner. Amanda estimated that over a hundred people could eat here at any one time. It smelled of stale cooking fat.

"Have you any particular questions?" asked Amanda.

"If we can establish that the dead man was traveling on his own and why he was drowned," replied the captain. "That will be enough for my report."

"Will you be bringing any charges?"

"No."

"Feel free to talk with them as long as you like," said Perez, leading them over to the migrants' table. "But bear in mind that lunch is served promptly at one o'clock. When you're finished, please tell the canteen staff, and I will come and fetch you."

"Thank you, Sergeant," said Amanda.

They approached the migrants, pulled a couple of chairs from the next table, and sat down with them. There were eight men and two women still dressed in the same clothes as they wore on the boat. Their body odor competed with the kitchen smells.

"Are we all OK in French?" asked Amanda.

They nodded.

"This is the captain of the patrol boat that found you the other day. He's making inquiries about the man that was drowned. I am Amanda. My work is making films. In this case, to relate your painful stories to the world. The idea being to warn your fellow citizens of your treatment here and dissuade them from risking their lives on such a dangerous journey; only to be sent back home. Can we start with the dead guy?"

"He joined us at the last minute," said an older man at the end of the table. "He'd run all the way from the Ceuta border. Didn't give his name, though."

"He ordered us, in the name of God, to go with him to France and join his terrorist group," said the man next to him. Amanda noticed that they resembled each other.

"He was from Algeria," added another seated at the center of the table. "Offered us lots of money if we joined his battle against the French infidels."

"We didn't want him sullying our asylum applications," said one of the women.

"He was also carrying a lot of money. We stole it from him along with his passport," said the first man who spoke. "Our needs were greater than his plus we were all enraged by his behavior toward the pregnant woman; Daraja. He was initially enamored by her, but when she told him to leave her alone, he turned nasty and was disrespectful to her. When he saw her about to jump over to the Spanish police boat, I heard him shout that she should stay, but she ignored him. He was trying to prevent her going with the Spanish policeman. We couldn't permit that. Do you know how Daraja is?"

"She lost a lot of blood and died quickly," answered Amanda tearfully. "Her baby is fine, though, and is in the process of being adopted by a local family. I helped Daraja with the birth."

"You are most kind. It is sad news about Daraja," continued the same man. "Now, how may we help you?"

"Did Daraja say where she was from or anything about the child's father?"

"She was from Senegal," he continued. "It took her three years to reach Ceuta traveling with various caravans. Most treated her kindly as she was just a young girl, but the last one in the south of Morocco was a mean slave trader who raped her. When it was obvious she was pregnant, he left her for dead in the middle of the desert. Another caravan found her barely alive a day later, and brought her most of the way to Ceuta."

"Is that a typical story for most of the women?"

"Shamefully, yes," he said. The women nodded their heads in confirmation.

"Let me ask you this," said Amanda still struggling to contain her emotions. "With the benefit of hindsight, what would you say to your folks back home about taking this journey?"

The group looked at each other, eyebrows raised and deferred to the older man.

"I compare it to buying a lottery ticket," he said. "You know it is unlikely to win, but unless you participate there is no chance. We could stay at home where we know it will remain bad or," he paused. "We can chase our dreams of a new beginning somewhere nice like here in Spain. There are success stories of migrants making it big, for example, footballers, athletes, artists, and cooks. For most of us though, it would be no worse than remaining at home. However, by taking this journey, we have seen parts of the world that offer a better way of living than we are accustomed to. We have learned new skills and seen innovative things that can help us improve matters when and if we return to our loved ones. So I would say yes, the more of us that take this journey and survive, in the long term our country will benefit."

"I understand, however, you have taken enormous personal risks."

"Everything has a price. Hopefully, our great grandchildren will reap the benefit because we cannot continue as we are."

"Fair point, well made. How are they treating you here?"

"To us, it's like a luxury hotel," answered the same man. "A roof over our heads, three meals a day, plenty of water and nobody abusing us. If they called us by our names though, it could be better."

"How do they refer to you?"

"By numbers," he replied holding up a sign marked two hundred and three that had been out of sight resting on his lap. "In many ways it's good, we learn some Spanish but we have observed that the staff here do not represent the sharpest of Spanish bureaucrats or have the most retentive of memories. However, we understand that out names are difficult to pronounce and to them, we all look the same, just as they do to us. We live with it."

"Thanks, I admire your patience and tolerance. Where are you from Sir?"

"Nigeria," he answered. "I'm a farmer, but drought and warring idiots drove me and my brother here from our land."

"Why not try Lagos or one of your big cities?" asked Amanda.

"If you have ever been to Lagos, you would understand why we prefer Spain. The weather is more comfortable, water is clean, crossing the road isn't a life threatening venture, and being shot for smiling at the wrong person is unheard of."

"You're right, I've never been to Lagos. I'll make a note to scratch it from my bucket list. What about the others in your group. Are they all from Nigeria and Senegal?"

"No, from all over Africa. Do you know where they are? We haven't seen them since shortly after we arrived."

"They've absconded."

"What? All of them?"

"So the man in charge says," answered Amanda.

"Lucky them, let's hope they are safe and well. We wondered what had happened to them. We were told that they were going to another cell as ours was overcrowded; since then we have not seen them."

"Let me explain matters to the captain," said Amanda, "and then we can talk more about your journeys."

"I have enough for my report," said the captain after Amanda had finished. "As to why the other migrants were moved to another cell, I have no explanation. We'll have to ask Perez."

Amanda spent half an hour recording personal accounts of their harrowing journeys. Now she had enough to finish her video and send it off to CNN. She shook hands with everyone, wished them well with their asylum applications, went over to the canteen server and request that she inform Perez that their interviews were finished. Perez returned and escorted them back to reception.

"Were your questions answered?" Perez asked.

"Thank you, yes," said the captain. "Although, they hadn't heard about the others in their group checking out."

Perez glared angrily at the captain and said, "You

don't think we inform our detainees that others have absconded, do you? Otherwise, they'd all do a runner. All we did was try and reduce the overcrowding by moving them to another cell, although we prefer to call them dormitories; this building is not meant to be a prison. It was from their new quarters that they absconded. The window bars had rusted through and they broke out that night. We've informed the Guardia Civil, but so far there's no sign of them."

21

Prado inserted the pen drive into his laptop. Prado directed him to a video and he clicked start. Phillip and Rosemary watched a smartly dressed, handsome man with dark hair and a pencil mustache presenting his passport to the Malaga airport border guard.

"That's him. It's Ferrier," confirmed Rosemary.

Phillip didn't need to translate.

"His plane was also delayed," said Prado. "That recording was taken just before midnight on the fourteenth. Now we need to trace where Ferrier went from the airport. We're e-mailing his photo and passport details to every hotel and estate agency within thirty kilometers of Nerja. Hopefully, by the morning we'll have him in custody."

"Is there anything more we can do here tonight?" asked Phillip.

"No. But may I call you if anything urgent comes up?" replied Prado.

"Fine, Inspector. OK, Rosemary," said Phillip, "we

can go now."

"Thank you, Rosemary," said Prado in English. "Good night."

"De nada, Inspector. Hasta lluego," replied Rosemary. She shrugged as she gathered her things. "We used to go to Marbella as teenagers. That's all I can remember, other than 'vino tinto' and 'manos arriba' when the amorous Spanish boy's hands were wandering too close for comfort."

Phillip dropped Rosemary off at her hotel. On the way back home, he dictated a summary of the meeting with Rosemary onto the WhatsApp group. It would be some light listening for Amanda in the morning.

The following morning, Playa El Salon was deserted. It was a slightly cloudier day with a fresher breeze. Phillip swam as fast as he could out to the yellow buoys, thinking that there was no way Didi would be swimming this morning, even if he was in town. The Teutonic thermometer probably couldn't register such low temperatures.

While admiring the mountains, Phillip began preparing a list of estate agents in his mind, eliminating those who didn't meet Prado's criteria. It wasn't long before he acknowledged that this was something he'd have to do together with Richard.

He swam back, showered, and headed up the hill to Don Comer.

The café was quiet. Richard was on his own at the regulars' table.

They shook hands, and Phillip sat down.

"How's it going?" asked Richard.

Before he could answer, Manolo brought Richard's

breakfast and sat down with them.

"I saw the appeal for any information about Juliet on TV last night," he stated. "Any news?"

"There have been a few calls, and we have one possible sighting that's being checked out," answered Phillip. "We also have another potential suspect. Juliet's aunt flew over yesterday and told us all about her evil stepfather. We have a video of him arriving at Malaga airport on the eve of San Isidro; we're contacting hotels and rental agencies to try and locate where he is staying."

"What does Juliet's stepfather look like?" inquired Richard.

"Good-looking guy, aged about forty with dark hair and a pencil mustache. Has anyone resembling him been to the café, or been asking for Juliet?"

"Not while I was here," said Richard.

"I'll ask the other staff members," said Manolo. "Personally, I don't recall anyone of that description, but an English guy was asking for Juliet a long time ago?"

"When was that?" asked Richard.

"About a year past," answered Manolo. "When I asked who wanted to know, he shrugged and left. I saw him the next morning outside the church. He took a photo of Juliet working and then disappeared."

"Can you remember what he looked like?" inquired Phillip.

"He was a giant, obese man, blond and ugly, scar on his cheek."

"Did you tell Juliet?" asked Richard.

"No. I meant to, but we were busy."

"Brilliant. Thanks, Manolo. I'll have my usual breakfast, please." said Phillip.

Phillip's phone rang. He glanced at the screen. It was Prado.

"Dígame," Phillip answered.

"Good morning," said Prado. "I thought you'd like to know that Sr. Ferrier is currently enjoying the hospitality of my colleagues in his hotel room in Frigiliana. I'm on my way there now. Can I meet you in an hour or so at the hotel café?"

"Try and stop me," confirmed Phillip.

"I love your enthusiasm," replied Prado. "It's the Hotel Villa Frigiliana opposite the underground car park. Hasta pronto."

"They're holding the stepfather up in Frigiliana," Phillip announced. "I'm meeting the inspector there shortly."

"Awesome," said Richard.

Phillip finished his mollete as they talked over the estate agents' list and outstanding business issues including more detail about how they might work with Amanda.

"My treat," said Richard some twenty minutes later as Phillip rummaged in his pocket for some change.

"Thanks. Maybe we should add updates about Juliet's abduction to our *News* blog," suggested Phillip. "The only information about her case is currently in *Spanish Media*. Who knows it might trigger someone's memory?"

"Good idea. I'll start on it as soon as I'm home. Later."

Frigiliana is one of Spain's prettiest villages. It nestles among the foot slopes of the Sierra Almijara some seven kilometers inland from Nerja and 320 meters above sea level. Rambling, picturesque narrow streets, viewing galleries, and charming squares are linked by a labyrinth of cobbled steps and steep passageways.

Quaint whitewashed town houses garlanded with colorful plant pots complete the beautiful, tranquil setting for the population of three and half thousand residents, including many foreigners and artists.

The surrounding countryside is a patchwork of terraced allotments growing all kinds of fruits and vegetables including olives, mangoes, avocados, almonds, and grapes. The ancient olive mill continues to produce excellent oil.

Human activity dates back over twenty-five thousand years. Wandering nomads, Phoenicians, Romans, and Moors have all made their mark. An irrigation system built by the Moors over a thousand years ago still carries water down from the mountains. There are some remains of an eleventh-century fort at the top of the village, but the existing buildings are mainly of the fifteenth century.

Mounted on various walls dotted around the village are twelve ceramic tile plaques relating the gory story of the Moriscos rebellion in 1569. Moriscos were descendants of the Muslim population forced to convert to Christianity by the Catholic monarchs in 1502.

The village celebrates its diverse history with an annual Fiesta of Three Cultures. For a few days at the end of August, enchanting belly dancers undulate through the dense crowds followed by actors clad in Sephardic Jew, Moorish, or Christian costumes. Over a hundred stalls are squeezed higgledy-piggledy into the town center, offering local arts, crafts, olive oil, cheeses, honey, and the renowned fierce sweet wine.

The idea is to remind the modern-day population that the three religions lived here together in peace and harmony for over five hundred years.

Phillip parked in the underground car park and walked the short distance up to the hotel. A Guardia Civil patrol car was parked outside the front door; it was empty. He joined Prado and one of the Guardia Civil officers for coffee in the dining room.

"There are a few things we need to review before we sit down with Ferrier," said Prado.

"How did you find him?" asked Phillip.

"The hotel receptionist opened our e-mail this morning and called us straightaway," answered Prado.

"Why are you holding him in his room and not at the Guardia Civil barracks in Nerja?"

"Our main objective is to locate Juliet. If Ferrier is her abductor, it's likely that he'll be keeping her nearby. If that's the case, we can go straight there from here."

"Does he understand that?"

"Not yet. All we've said so far is that we want to ask him a few questions, and to wait in his room until the inspector arrives from Malaga. The receptionist translated for us."

"And Ferrier seemed OK with that?"

"Nervous but cooperative."

"Has his file arrived from the Birmingham Police?"

"Yes. Forensics have confirmed that his prints are all over Juliet's door and the overturned furnishings. We're assuming that he went there after the abductors had gone, saw that everything of significance had already been taken, lost the plot and trashed the place."

"What do you think made him he so angry?" asked

Phillip.

"Based on what Rosemary told us, Ferrier was obsessed with exacting his revenge on Juliet, irrespective that he was guilty of sexually abusing her. He'd spent years in prison smoldering over his stepdaughter giving evidence against him. How dare she be disloyal to a family member? He'd be seething with rage. Then, he's released, and the first thing he does is employ a detective to find her, which indicates to me that he can't wait to grab her and stash her somewhere to vent his pent-up emotions. Then the detective locates Juliet. Ferrier grabs the first plane here and goes to her home expecting her to be there or at work. But there is no sign of her, and her apartment has been ransacked. It enrages him so much, he trashes her stuff. Now he has a new problem and asks himself, 'Where is Juliet? Has somebody else taken her? If so, who?' Perhaps his rage has now been redirected toward whoever that might be."

"Sounds plausible. What do you want me to ask him?"

"At this stage, a gentle chat about why he is in Spain, and see what stems from that?"

They went to the elevator and up to the sixth floor.

A uniformed officer stood outside the room halfway along the brightly lit corridor. He opened the door and waved them in.

Ferrier was standing at the full-height window of the rustic-designed spacious room, gazing at the incredible views of the countryside to the distant hills and then down to Nerja and the Mediterranean. He was dressed elegantly in jeans, Harley-Davidson T-shirt, antique brown leather jacket, and expensive brown brogues. He was an incredibly handsome man except that his expression was miserable, eyes were bloodshot, complexion pallid, and his stomach bulged slightly over his belt. Whiskey drinker, thought Phillip.

"Good morning, Mr. Ferrier," opened Phillip. "My name is Phillip Armitage; I'm working with the Malaga police as an interpreter. This is Inspector Prado. We're sorry to keep you waiting and thank for your patience."

"What do you want?" said Ferrier curtly, taking a seat at the corner table.

"Your passport, please."

Ferrier opened a drawer, extracted the document, and held it up.

Prado went over, thumbed through the pages, and then handed it back.

"How long have you been in Spain?" asked Phillip.

"I arrived late on the evening of the fourteenth and came straight to the hotel by taxi." Phillip detected the hint of a London accent, but otherwise Ferrier spoke in a well-educated manner.

"Why are you here?"

"To talk with my stepdaughter, Juliet Harding."

"And has it been a successful visit?"

"No, I can't find her. She's disappeared."

"The word is 'abducted,' Mr. Ferrier."

Prado reached into his suit-jacket pocket, extracted a photo of the abductors, and showed it to Ferrier.

"Can you identify these men?" inquired Phillip.

Ferrier looked long and hard at the photo.

"No," he said. "Are they Juliet's abductors?"

"Yes. Did you go to Juliet's apartment on the fifteenth?"

"Yes."

"What did you find there?"

"The place had already been searched," shouted Ferrier. "That bastard has taken her." Ferrier stood quickly, walked over to Phillip, waggled his finger under Phillip's nose, and shouted, "You guys should be out there, looking for her, instead of wasting your time talking to me."

"Are you saying that you know who has taken Juliet?"

"It has to be him," said Ferrier, slumping back down in the chair.

"Are you going to enlighten us?"

"Duffy. The bastard's name is Rick Duffy."

"We suspected that you were the one that had come here to abduct your stepdaughter. Why would we believe it was this Duffy person?"

"I admit that I came here intending to take the bitch and punish her for what she did to me, but Duffy has beaten me to it."

"Why are you so sure it was Duffy?"

"It can't be anybody else. Only Duffy hates me so much to do this to me."

"And he hates you for what reason?"

"Because I reported him to the prison governor. But what else was I to do?" Ferrier was becoming more agitated by the minute but eventually pulled himself together enough to say, "Duffy was my cellmate in prison. I made the mistake of showing him a photo of my gorgeous stepdaughter. In return, he stole the photo and raped me every day. Then, when he was released well over a year ago, he vowed to find Juliet wherever she was and take her for himself."

"I see, but how did you know that Duffy was in Spain?"

"I overheard him talking with someone in the prison bathroom. They mentioned setting up a voyeur website called Peepers in La Axarquia. Something about a franchise."

"So is it just a coincidence that Juliet happened to be in the same area?"

Ferrier looked nervously about him, trembling, and then tears filled his eyes. By his facial color, his blood pressure was about to go through the roof.

Ferrier shook his head and screamed, "Yes, but somehow that bastard Duffy found her, which means that I'll never see her again. Now I'll never be able to take my revenge on her. And…and you have no idea how painful that is to me. Fuck it."

With that, Ferrier stood up, yanked open the window, and hurled himself over the balcony wall.

Prado tried to grab him but missed.

They both heard the sickening crunch followed by several metallic clashes as Ferrier smashed into the terrace furniture five floors below.

They went out onto the small balcony and looked down.

Ferrier lay unmoving, sprawled on the granite tiling, a heavily damaged round metal table lay by his side, and blood was dripping from his mouth. There was no way he could have survived such a terrible fall.

"Tell me exactly what he said before launching himself into oblivion," said Prado thoughtfully.

Phillip summarized Ferrier's last words.

Prado shook his head.

"Surely you don't feel sorry for him," said Phillip.

"No, irritated. I couldn't care less if all depraved

idiots like Ferrier killed themselves, but that one down there could have led us to this Duffy fellow and to Juliet."

Prado called his office to summon the police pathologist and then said, "You search in here; I'll go down and check his pockets."

Prado left the room and spoke with the officer outside the door. They both headed toward the elevator.

Phillip found Ferrier's laptop in the corner table drawer.

He turned it on.

The battery was flat.

He found the charger and cable, but it was a British plug. He'd have to take it home, where he had an adaptor. There was also a phone charger but no phone. There was nothing else of note in the room, just clothing and the usual travel accessories.

Prado returned with several items in his hands.

"We've covered the body with a tarpaulin," he announced. "The hotel manager was concerned for his guests. I found these in Ferrier's jacket."

Prado placed a wallet, a well-thumbed pocket notebook, gold pen, phone, and loose change on the corner table.

Phillip opened the wallet. It contained over €2,000 in €100 denominations, various credit and debit cards, and a photo. He winced as he turned it over and saw Juliet lying on a bed, naked. She appeared to be unconscious or asleep. Her hair was shorter, and she looked considerably younger. It had been taken well before Juliet came to Spain, yet the print was relatively new.

There was also a business card.

Frigiliana Area Property Services was printed in gray ink on a white background.

Underneath was written Sales—Rentals—Maintenance.

The address was on Calle Real, and the contact was Maria Martin Garcia.

The phone battery was also flat.

Phillip flicked through the notebook.

It had the number of a local taxi company and the Nerja-Frigiliana bus timetable written in blue ink on the first couple of pages. They were followed by critiques on various country villas. "Torrox outskirts: no cellar, no garage, not isolated enough. Maro village: not isolated enough. La Molineta border: perfect but over budget by €500 a month."

At the back of the notebook was a list of what appeared to be pin numbers and passwords.

Phillip explained about the notebook contents and showed Prado the business card.

"Certainly confirms that Ferrier was looking for a place near here to keep Juliet," said Prado.

"I agree, but he must have made these notes before he'd been to Juliet's apartment? Why bother after he'd learned that she'd gone?"

"Then why go to see this estate agent—what's her name?"

"Maria."

"Then we should talk with her. You fit enough for the walk up into the village or would you prefer the Tuk Tuk?"

"I'm good to walk. What about you? You're the ancient one," replied Phillip, grinning.

"I can still do hills."

They left everything in the room with one Guardia

Civil officer outside the door. The other stood by Ferrier's corpse.

It had been a while since Phillip had been in Frigiliana village. He noticed a few new shops and a bar indicating that perhaps business was picking up again.

The estate agent was based on the ground floor of an old three-story town house. The tiny entrance was through a sky-blue-painted door. A few properties were mounted on a display board in a small window next to the door. The interior lights were on, and a well-built but smartly dressed woman could be seen sitting behind a desk and working feverishly at a laptop. Only fifty years ago, this room was where the farm animals were kept. They opened the door and went in.

The woman stood as they entered, came round to the front of the desk, and said effusively in Spanish, "Good morning, gentlemen. How may I help you?"

"Police," said Prado pleasantly, showing her his ID.

"Oh, sorry. I thought you were customers," she said a tad less enthusiastically.

"Are you Maria?"

"I am."

"We're enquiring about one of your possible clients—a Mr. Ferrier; he may have visited you in the last day or two. He's English, about forty, medium height, slender build, boozer's belly, dark hair, and a pencil mustache," said Prado.

"Not surprised you guys are on his case," answered Maria. "He wanted to know if I had rented out a property to a giant-sized, fair-haired Englishman during the last eighteen months.

"I politely introduced him to the concept of client

confidentiality and asked him to leave. He stormed out in a huff, shouting what sort of fucking country did we live in?"

"When was this?" asked Prado.

"Day after San Isidro."

"Did he mention the name of this mysterious fair-haired person?"

"He did. I made a note of it, just in case I came across him," she replied, flicking through notes on her computer. "Ah, here it is. The guy's name was Duffy. Rick Duffy."

"And have you come across Duffy," asked Prado. "Or is that still confidential?"

Maria smiled and said, "No inspector, to both questions."

"Thank you. Sorry to have disturbed you," said Prado.

"Glad to have helped," she replied.

"Confirms that Ferrier thought Duffy had taken Juliet," said Phillip as they headed back down Calle Real in the direction of the hotel.

"Yes, but not that Duffy is here in Spain. We're obviously missing some pieces of the jigsaw. Maybe, there are other issues from their prison days. Listen, I have to make a report on Ferrier's suicide because it happened while in my custody. Anything you can add?"

Phillip paused for a moment, sorting out Ferrier's motivations in his mind before saying,

"I don't understand why Ferrier didn't remain in the UK. According to Rosemary, he had enough money to live comfortably without working. Instead, he chose to come here to punish Juliet for what she'd put him through. What a risk to take; no normal person would have done that. Therefore, I conclude that he was mentally disturbed in some way. Oblivion was his only road to tranquility."

"You mean he was sick?" asked Prado, astounded.

"Do you think that was normal behavior? Surely, he should have been under treatment."

"Are you saying mental sickness justifies his actions?"

"No, but it goes a long way toward explaining them. Perhaps if he'd had counseling years ago, he wouldn't have been such a wreck."

"Are you suggesting he was born with a mental condition, and we should forgive him?"

"Born no, but unpleasant events in life when added to a difficult upbringing can unbalance a normal psyche. I saw it in Afghanistan among my colleagues, and I'm sure you've noticed it in the police."

Prado went quiet, mulling over Phillip's words. Eventually, he said quietly, "Yes, I know exactly what you mean."

22

It had taken an hour and fifty minutes for the pathologist to arrive from Malaga, confirm Ferrier's demise, and cart his corpse off to the mortuary. There would be no need for a postmortem. Everyone was clear as to what had killed him and why.

There had been some more calls from the media campaign for Juliet, so Prado headed back to his office to check them out while Phillip went home to play with Ferrier's laptop and phone.

Phillip knocked up a tomato, mozzarella, and basil salad, drizzled it with some extravirgin olive oil from his sister's farm, and took it through to his study. He found his UK adaptor, plugged in Ferrier's phone, and turned it on.

He was presented with a log-in screen, so he tapped in the first password from the back of the notebook. It worked; he was in.

The log showed several short conversations with the Coventry Detective Agency. He called the number.

"I thought we told you not to contact us again, Mr. Ferrier," a man's voice answered gruffly.

"Actually, my name is Armitage. I'm working with the police in Spain and this morning witnessed Mr. Ferrier's suicide. I'm plowing through his call log, and you guys were his most frequently called number."

"Oh, I see; sorry—I assumed that Ferrier was pestering us again."

"Well, I can guarantee he won't be doing any more of that."

"Can't say that I'm disappointed. How may I help you?"

"We know he was looking for his stepdaughter in Spain. Were you the people who located her?"

"Yes, although I wish we hadn't taken the case now. We didn't discover until later that he was a sex offender and probably had evil intentions toward Juliet. We made sure to inform her aunt."

"Yes. I know that. It didn't stop Juliet from being abducted the following day, but not by Ferrier. He thinks the abduction was arranged by a man called Rick Duffy. Have you heard this name before?"

"Yes, but only from Ferrier; he wanted us to search for Duffy. Apparently, he was a former cellmate, but we declined and informed Ferrier that he was not to bother us again. We refuse to work with sex offenders."

"That I can understand. Did Ferrier say that Duffy was probably in Andalucia?"

"Oh yes, in fact, he was more specific. He said that Duffy was somewhere between Nerja and Torrox."

"How did he know that?"

"He wouldn't tell us. Just said he knew for

definite."

"Anything else you can share with me concerning Ferrier?"

"Yes. Ferrier's description of Duffy was big, blond, and ugly with a scar on his cheek."

"Then Duffy has definitely been seen here in Nerja. It was well over a year ago."

"That fits; Ferrier told us that Duffy was released around then."

"OK, thanks. Helpful stuff."

"Sorry, it's not more."

"Me too."

Phillip dialed the other numbers in Ferrier's log. One was his solicitor. Phillip informed him of Ferrier's death but wasn't surprised when they hung up, accusing him of being a hoax caller. The other numbers were his bank, stockbroker, and a Mercedes dealership.

Phillip changed the UK adaptor over to Ferrier's laptop.

The second password down on the notebook list worked. He connected it to his Wi-Fi and started browsing Ferrier's hard drive.

His e-mail app had a few junk items, a confirmation for the Frigiliana Hotel from Booking.com, a couple of things from his bank, and a spreadsheet from his financial advisor. Phillip opened the attachment and was surprised to find that Ferrier was worth slightly under £2 million. The final item was from his solicitor, confirming recent amendments to his will. Phillip skimmed through it. Ferrier was leaving everything to PACT, a prison charity helping prisoners make a fresh start. There were also a plethora of directories containing thousands of photos of attractive models in a wide variety of outfits. They were all categorized by date, location, agency, and designer. Ferrier had worked with them all—Armani, Dior, Versace, and more. He might have been a failure as a man, but he could sure wield a camera.

There were some recently completed documents, but they were only admin matters to his bank and a letter to his building society confirming the final mortgage payment for his apartment in central Birmingham.

Recent browsing history showed searches for Rick Duffy Spain but had found no results. There were hundreds of pages about Nerja and the surrounding area, the majority of which were estate-agent sites. He'd entered property details into some of their rental databases; the searches were all identical. Ferrier had been looking for a two bed, isolated inland villa with an extensive cellar. He'd also looked at About Us pages, clicking on staff photos.

His bank account was on permanent log-in giving access to a current account with a balance of some £17,000 and a monthly income of £8,000. There were the usual domestic payments, but his credit-card statement showed a subscription to a Cumulonimbus Virtual Services, costing nearly £900 a month.

He checked the drives and found a connection to CVS.

On request, he typed in the third password from Ferrier's list, and the screen opened to a listing of one directory containing one item.

He clicked on it and was again invited to enter a password.

He tried the fourth line of letters and symbols from

Ferrier's notebook, and the file opened up to an unusual URL address.

Phillip recognized the format immediately.

It was used on the deep web often referred to as dark web.

He clicked on the URL, and the familiar green-and-white backdrop and Onion logo of the TOR browser opened up.

TOR is short for The Onion Router. It's a free, legal to use, open-source software program developed for the US Navy. It provides a totally secure environment for browsers and traders. Users can operate freely and anonymously without risk of detection.

During Phillip's time in the military, he'd served with the British Intelligence Corps and had used TOR substantially to search for terrorists, their bankers, and arms suppliers. He knew his way around, and although it had expanded enormously during the thirteen years he'd been in Civvy Street, its functions had remained the same.

The page on the TOR screen was entitled Peepers. The splurge described it as live-streamed broadcasts for the discerning voyeur. This confirmed what Ferrier had overheard Duffy discussing with someone in the prison bathroom.

Why had Ferrier subscribed to Peepers? Phillip wondered. Searching for Juliet or pleasure? At least the site's existence proved Ferrier had been telling the truth.

Peepers used a room layout similar to the TV reality show—*Big Brother.*

The small rectangular room contained six beds, each with a white-painted midheight bedside cabinet between them. Three beds lined each side with low sofas back to back in the middle of the room. At the far end was a dining table and six white chairs and an archway through to the white tiled bathroom.

The beds were covered with white bottom sheets and pillows but no bedcovers. If it wasn't for six large pot plants containing bushy *Ficus benjamina* trees, it could have been a clinic or hospital ward. Yet this was no medical establishment.

Six gorgeous-looking young girls were sprawled on the couches with liter bottles of water that they sipped from regularly. Some were reading, some were chatting, and others resting.

They were a mix of skin colors and scantily dressed in skimpy underwear and revealing blouses.

One slid off the bed and headed toward the restroom.

But she moved in jerky motions. The connection was weak, and the image kept buffering as it reloaded. It often happened at properties out in the countryside where Internet speeds were intermittent. Phillip persevered.

Cameras and microphones were everywhere. They captured every sound and every movement. There was no place to hide, and nothing could be left to the imagination. Viewers could switch images from a choice of eight different screens. Some were closeup, and others less so.

Yet most of the girls seemed quite content and comfortable living in such an open space with no privacy anywhere.

He listened to the talkers.

Some voyeurs might have found the debate stimulating. Phillip yawned and closed the screen. He felt sick for those poor girls.

Were they there willingly or receiving an income for their services? Or, was this enforced labor—in effect sexual imprisonment and slavery?

Was Ferrier trying to tell him that the mastermind behind this was Duffy?

Was Juliet being groomed as the next new performer?

The salad churned violently in his stomach.

23

"I need to show you stuff; then we need to talk," said Phillip.

"Can you come to my office?" asked Prado.

"On my way. We're going to need Amanda in on this."

"Why?"

"It needs a female perspective."

"I'll take your word on it; will you call her?"

"Sure. Do you have a cybersecurity department at the comisaría?"

"Very basic. The one for major crimes is in Madrid. Why?"

"We're going to need their help."

"Sounds ominous."

"Believe me, it's worse."

"Then you better put your foot down. I'll meet you in the car-park elevator."

Phillip gulped a glass of water and headed off to Malaga.

He called Amanda on the hands-free.

"You want to cancel dinner?" she asked.

"No way—what makes you think that?"

"Happens all the time."

"You're kidding me. What is it with Malaga men? Don't they know what they have in their midst? Seriously, I'm really looking forward to our business discussions and, more importantly, getting to know you better."

"Likewise? Oh, and how did it go with Rosemary?"

Phillip brought her up to date.

"So you're looking for this Ferrier man?"

"Not anymore. He killed himself?"

"Oh dear, why?"

"It's complicated, and I suspect that he was also mentally unstable. He'd come here to vent his wrath on Juliet, only to discover that his arch enemy from prison had already taken her. Then we came along, and he decided oblivion was more appealing. Anyway, I was calling to tell you that I've found some stuff on his laptop that warrants your feminine insights. Could you meet Prado and me at the comisaría?"

"Whew, short notice. What's the hurry?

"The website could lead us to Juliet."

"Will an hour or so be OK? I have to finish this migrant documentary."

"Great. See you there."

The view of Malaga harbor from the elevated autovia was spectacular as Phillip sped by. Tall red and blue gantries towered over serried ranks of gray freight containers and the ferry terminal to Melilla.

A long concrete wall projected out to sea. It had been built to expand Malaga's cruise ship capacity and could comfortably accommodate two massive vessels simultaneously. Today it was the turn of RMS *Queen Mary Two*, recognizable by her white superstructure, black hull, and single red funnel. Thousands of foot passengers were disgorging over her gangplanks for a day's shopping and culture in Malaga old town. They strode, ambled, or hobbled as best they could past the colorful cuboid glass structure at the Centre Pompidou in the direction of Calle Larios.

Phillip turned off the highway, wound his way down through densely built residential areas, and parked underneath the comisaría.

Prado took him up in the lift.

"We'll have to issue you with a permanent pass if we carry on at this rate," commented Prado as the lift door opened onto his floor. "I'll have a word with the boss." He nodded at el jefe superior's door as they passed.

"Amanda will make it as soon as she can," said Phillip.

"Do you prefer to wait for her?" asked Prado.

"No, no, let's crack on," answered Phillip, setting up Ferrier's laptop.

He gave Prado a quick resume of Duffy and that it matched Manolo's description of the man who came to Don Comer about a year ago, asking about Juliet. He summarized his conversation with Ferrier's detective, and then showed Prado around Ferrier's personal files before moving onto the Peepers website.

Prado nodded and occasionally grunted as Phillip guided him through it. When he'd finished, Prado looked at him, shaking his head, and said, "I can't make any sense of this. Since our visit to the estate agent in Frigiliana, I've searched our records for anything about a Rick Duffy. We have nothing on file or any comments from border control. Officially, Duffy is not in Spain or in mainland Europe, yet Ferrier was adamant that Duffy was here, and now Manolo claims he saw a person matching Duffy's description.

"As for this weird website. What's the significance of it? How does it fit in with Juliet's abduction, and why did Ferrier subscribe to it? Any ideas?"

"I've been wrestling with those same questions. I don't have any answers, only some theories."

"Well, let's hear them."

"It's hard to locate Peepers or similar websites on the dark web on your own. Normally, you'd have to be told about them. The fact that Peepers exists confirms that Ferrier told us the truth. He did overhear Duffy in the prison bathroom. Perhaps this Peepers website is a franchise set up by Duffy and another cellmate from the prison. Maybe the Virtual Network Provider CVS are the owners of Peepers? Maybe Duffy has Juliet lined up as a new star?

"One more thing. Sex offenders have to seek special permission to travel outside Britain. The Spanish police should have been warned about Duffy's arrival in advance? The fact that they weren't could imply that he has dual nationality or a forged passport?"

"That makes sense, but we need some evidence to support that. Duffy's prison record and a list of all Ferrier's cellmates would help us. Normally, I'm obliged to apply through Interpol for such information, but am reluctant to do so because their involvement will delay our investigation or they may take over the case. Do you think Rosemary could assist in any way?"

"We can ask."

"Before you do can you answer this?. You showed me a monthly payment that Ferrier made to his virtual private network, —Cumulo thingamabob? Could we ascertain where this money was transferred to?"

"I'll check now."

Phillip clicked back into Ferrier's bank account, opened up the last monthly CVS payment, and then turned the screen to show Prado.

"I might have known," said Prado, sighing. "CVS Ltd. Hispanic-Commerce Bank. High St. Gibraltar. It'll take me, a Spaniard, months to obtain any information from that lot."

"Then why don't we prevail on Rosemary? Her bank could check them out as a potential supplier."

"Brilliant thinking, Phillip. Call her now. We owe her an update anyway."

Prado disappeared with Ferrier's laptop. He wanted to copy everything and set his team loose looking at every single girl's face in that awful room. He was hoping that one of them had been reported missing.

Phillip picked up his phone and dialed.

"Don't tell me you've found her?" asked Rosemary.

"Sorry, no, but we are getting warmer."

Phillip regurgitated the latest news on the case.

"Wait. You said that Ferrier is dead?" she asked.

"Saw him myself."

"Well, that's wonderful news, provided it wasn't him that stashed Juliet away. If it was, who is going to feed her and how will we find her?"

"Have some faith, Rosemary; we are confident that Ferrier had nothing to do with her abduction. He was way too late on the scene."

"Very well."

"Now, we need you to do two things to help us."

"Shoot."

"Ferrier paid a monthly subscription to a company banking in Gibraltar. If I e-mail you a copy of the payment advice, could you have your bank check them out and obtain a copy of the accounts and information about its shareholders and directors?"

"Sure. You said two things?"

"Ferrier was relatively young and had plenty of money, which, by the way, has been bequeathed to a prison charity. He'd paid the price for his crimes and was in a healthy position to spend the rest of his days doing whatever he wanted. Yet he threw such a rosy future away. So why did he chase Juliet to Spain and why kill himself?"

"Do you have a theory?"

"I can relate to his smoldering anger driving him to take revenge on Juliet for her testimony against him in court. It had kept him going through his awful times in prison and explains why the first thing he did on his release was to appoint a detective to find her. That she was in Spain came as a surprise to him, but at the same time worried him sick."

"Why was that?"

"Rick Duffy."

"The name means nothing."

"He was the cellmate who raped Ferrier in prison. We suspect that Duffy is also in Spain and may well have taken Juliet."

"Really. What do you want from me?"

"Could you find out with whom Ferrier was serving time? We know about Duffy, but need a photo of him, and there may be others who connect somehow."

"Can't Interpol help?"

"Yes, but they will slow us down, and we may lose control of the investigation, which will slow up the search for Juliet."

"I understand. I'll discuss it with my husband and revert to you in the morning."

Prado returned. Amanda accompanied him, looking stunning in a lime-green dress that hugged her figure and accentuated her silky olive skin. Her glossy raven hair cascaded over her bare shoulders, and she seemed taller than the last time Phillip saw her.

"Wow, you look special today. More elevated somehow," Phillip said, standing up and exchanging cheek kisses.

"Thank you." She blushed and flashed her high heels. "I'm meeting a producer from the British Broadcasting Company for dinner. I'll explain tomorrow night. Can we make a start? I can't stay long."

"To prepare you for any embarrassment, I have to warn you that Ferrier's leisure activities have nothing to do with playing tennis."

"I'll try and be brave."

Phillip opened up Peepers once more. The girls were all gathered around the table, eating.

"Wait," said Prado, glancing at his watch. It's just before seven o'clock, yet they are eating supper already. That's way too early for Spaniards, and look at the food, dark bread, ham, salad, Dutch style cheese, herring, smoked salmon, boiled eggs, and coffee in a Thermos flask—that's not what we eat."

"Nor English," said Phillip. "They'd be drinking tea

with milk."

"I'd say German or Scandinavian," suggested Amanda.

"Yet the milk carton is from Asturias," said Phillip.

"Look underneath the table, there, on top of the trash," said Prado. "There's a plastic supermarket bag; can anyone read what it says, my eyes…"

"Aldi, Torrox-Costa," said Amanda. "And have you seen the furniture. While it appears new, it is actually Spanish timber but painted white; you can see the ornate paneling on the doors. My mum has one just like it."

"Does that mean we can safely assume that this room is near Torrox, and not in the Philippines somewhere?" asked Prado.

"Would you go to the expense of exporting Spanish furniture and milk all that way?"

"I'll take that as a yes then?" replied Prado, smiling.

"Amanda," said Phillip. "Note that there are six girls. There are no windows or exit doors visible. Nobody is forcing them to do things against their will; there are no cameramen or film directors. Yet the girls seem obedient, happy, or at least are acting so. They're certainly not pacing about scheming or worrying. None of them bite their nails, smoke, or drink alcohol, and they appear alert and drug-free. We can see that there are two African girls, three white, and one Asian. They all speak good English and seem comfortable with one another despite the lack of privacy. There's no bitching, no complaining, and no one is crabby. It seems too good to be true. What are your thoughts?"

"Whew, where to start?" said Amanda. "My first reaction is that they are accustomed to this. They've been together for a while."

"I haven't watched long enough to see if they change shifts," commented Phillip.

"What do they talk about?" asked Prado.

"It's limited," said Phillip. "Looks, makeup, clothes, music, and films. There's no mention of global news or their previous life."

"Probably accounts for their domestic bliss," said Amanda, laughing.

"I suggest they've been brainwashed to behave like this," mooted Phillip. "Yet I'm confused by their behavior—why would they be so happy and compliant? Why aren't they tearing the place apart?"

"They're prisoners," responded Amanda. "Look at their bodies, if you can force yourself. They are all slim. Not excessively so but thinner than average, particularly for the nature of their work where you would expect more voluptuous figures. I think that food is being used as a controlling mechanism. They were probably starved initially but now are fed just enough to keep them satisfied."

"I see what you mean," said Phillip. "But why do they seem so happy about being locked up?"

"Maybe some are illegal migrants? They could even enjoy this type of work. A roof over their heads, three squares a day, and no one abusing them. That could be a considerable improvement on their previous life in Niger or Senegal."

"Interesting observations from both of you," said Prado. "And I agree with everything you've said. Clearly what we're looking at here is a sexual-slavery ring based somewhere east of Malaga. Now can we discuss some criteria for its potential location? For example, town, village, or countryside?"

"I noticed that the Internet transmission speed here in Malaga is amazing compared to mine at home," said Phillip. "There's not a trace of buffering. Do you have fiber optics here?"

"I have no idea," said Prado. "Hold on—I'll call someone."

Prado picked up his phone, dialed, asked his question, and hung up.

"Apparently we have the fastest available on the new fiber-optic network. The same as those who watch TV via the Internet."

"Good, because to deliver such a high-quality streaming experience Peepers would need the same connection speed," said Phillip. "To date in Andalucia, fiber optics has only been installed in major towns and larger urbanizations."

"So what you're saying is that we can ignore all locations without fiber optics?" asked Prado.

"Correct," answered Phillip.

"Well, that should reduce our options hugely," said Prado. "I've heard that the uptake of fiber optics has been slow as most households aren't prepared to pay the extra cost, especially for the high-speed option. We'll contact the service providers for a list of actual installations. What other search criteria should we consider?"

"I think it's in a cellar underneath a property and not in an outbuilding," said Phillip. "It's easier to soundproof, secure, and to deliver food and victims without risk of exposure. They can drive into the garage and take things directly into the house or underground out of sight. A villa with a cellar underneath on a busy urbanization would be perfect. Whereas a town house is unlikely to have a garage, and any noise would be difficult to disguise."

"I agree," said Prado. "That still means we have thousands of properties to search, but at least the list is coming down in size. Any other insights?"

"Just one," said Phillip. "Continuous streaming of high-density images uses enormous amounts of bandwidth. Most folks shut down about midnight and traffic dies off substantially. If the service providers could monitor activity for, say, three o'clock in the morning and give us a list of those areas that remain busy, it will help us refine our search zones down even further."

"There's one more refinement I can add," said Prado, clearly enjoying the brainstorming. "Cellars are a relatively recent feature in Spanish homes. Until the 1980s we couldn't afford the machinery to hew them out of our predominately rocky terrain. Consequently, most speculative builders didn't bother because it was cheaper to add another floor on top. The cellars that were built tended to be commissioned by private individuals building their own properties. The clean straight lines of the walls in the Peepers cellar indicate that it is probably under a recently built property. The lighting is modern. The taps and bathroom fittings seem new. If we check building licenses for private building projects for, say, the last twenty years and then cross-reference them with the criteria you mentioned earlier, we should be able to slash the options into a relatively short list."

"That's still a lot of information for so few people to collate and analyze," said Phillip.

"Then we'll have to find you some help," boomed a male voice behind them.

24

"Good evening, sir," said Prado, standing.

"Carry on, please," instructed el jefe superior. "Did I overhear lists that need compiling and analyzing?"

"Correct, sir. Let me introduce you to our voluntary translators," said Prado.

They all shook hands.

Prado summarized the case to date.

"Good work in such a short time scale," said el jefe. "I'll allocate two officers to your team for the list production."

"Very kind, sir," said Prado.

"I'll leave you to it. Nice to meet you both," said el jefe, closing the door behind him.

Prado waited until his boss had gone then said quietly, "Amazing, I didn't even have to ask for more resources. Something about our case must have spooked him."

"Respect for the British press moves in mysterious ways," commented Phillip.

"Of course, he's worried about those fair minded, accurate reporters from your little island?" said Prado, grinning.

"You should remember that for the future?" commented Phillip. "And resources will magically appear?"

"Sorry to interrupt guys, but I have one more thing to tell the inspector before I have to run," said Amanda, glancing at her watch.

"Go on," urged Prado.

"You recall I told you about filming migrants on a Guardia Civil patrol-boat the other day. Well, I was at the migrant detention center yesterday to translate for the boat's Captain. He needed a report from the migrants explaining why some of them had drowned one of their fellow travelers. Anyway, we resolved that, but what concerned me more is that twenty-six of the migrants had absconded. I've done some additional research and discovered that during this year alone over two thousand migrants also absconded. That's more than the actual number of asylum applications that have been processed. If you ask me, something stinks down in Algeciras."

"Mmm," said Prado, rubbing his earlobe. "Where did you find those numbers?"

"From a local journalist. There have been a lot of protests from local people about the detention center, and he has a line into one of the warden's that work there."

"I'm worried that your journalist contact may have some political leanings," replied Prado. "So I wouldn't trust those numbers without further inquiries. I'll discuss it with el jefe, and let you know what, if anything, we will do about it."

"Thanks," said Amanda. "You could be right about the journalist, but I still think there was definitely something excessively malodorous about the chief warden, Sergeant Perez."

"I hear you Amanda. We'll look into it," reassured Prado.

Amanda gathered her things and headed for the door.

"Good luck with the BBC man," said Phillip.

"Actually, it's a BBC woman," retorted Amanda. "See you tomorrow night."

By Saturday midday the lists were coming together.

This was the third day since Juliet had been taken. Prado had earlier expressed concern that they were too far behind. It was usually crucial to take immediate detecting actions during the first few hours after an abduction to stand any chance of a speedy solution. They'd started a long way behind, but slowly they were catching up.

Prado's team had been checking the faces on the Peepers website. So far they had identified one Spanish girl who had gone missing two years ago, and the two Africans had reportedly absconded from the Immigrant Detention Center in Algeciras only two months previously. They were with a third girl, but she had vanished completely.

Prado had put up a case board in his office and had pinned photos of Juliet and the new missing girl named Gabriella. He'd added all the three African girls. The two in the room were from Niger and known as Samira and Yasmina, and the missing one was from Senegal; her name was Amadou, a sour-faced ugly girl. Hassan was also there along with

Ferrier, the two abductors, and their van. For now, Duffy consisted of a written description on a yellow Post-it note.

Prado decided not to reveal the discovery of Gabriella to the Spanish media or her parents. He wanted to keep her under wraps until more detailed information about Juliet became available.

Phillip had just awoken from his siesta on the terrace when his phone announced Rosemary's call. He stretched, yawned, and swiped the screen.

"Good afternoon, Phillip," said Rosemary. "It's raining here again."

"Then why not build your special houses here in the sun?" asked Phillip.

"I'm tempted, but as you said, if you can't speak Spanish, you soon go bust. Listen I have the information you wanted. I'll start with the bank. The directors and shareholders of CVS Ltd. are Gibraltarians, probably nominees. I have their names and addresses and will e-mail them to you. It's a Gibraltar-registered company based in a firm of lawyers called Martin and Bayne located on Main Street next to the Hispanic-Commerce Bank. It has no known associations or interests with any other company either in Gibraltar or overseas. The firm has a triple-A credit rating but no physical assets. Its income derives from subscription payments from all over the globe, totaling over £2 billion annually and is expanding at a phenomenal rate. According to last year's accounts, which I have here, it pays its costs locally such as the bank, directors, and professional fees, plus a few miniscule Gibraltar taxes. The rest is transferred out to property companies based from

Austria to Zambia, so it makes little or no profit."

"Do you have a list of those companies?"

"No, for that you'd need a Gibraltar Court Order and a visit to Martin and Bayne's offices."

"Well, it's a start; we'll have to work on some grounds to submit to the court."

"My lawyers can help if you need them. Let me know if I can do anything else."

"Any news on Ferrier's cellmates?"

"That proved to be a lot easier than I thought. My husband is a member of a local lodge, where the prison governor also attends. Nudge, nudge; know what I mean?"

"Isn't the British-old-boy network wonderful?"

"Ain't it just? Anyway, I'm expecting delivery of photos, dates, and criminal records of all the prisoners on the sex-offenders' wing during Ferrier's incarceration. I'll send them on as soon as they arrive."

"Thanks, Rosemary, I'll keep you posted."

He forwarded everything to Prado with notes in Spanish then called him.

"CVS is an enormous company," opened Prado. "Do you think they have other websites of a similar nature to Peepers?"

"Possibly, but the only way we can discover that is in their lawyer's office in Gibraltar. As yet, we only have suspicions of one potential sexual slavery ring. For all we know, the girls are being paid or working voluntarily. I don't think the Gibraltar courts are likely to issue a search warrant against CVS on the strength of that, do you? Especially to the Spanish police."

"You're right, and for the moment, we need to

focus on finding Juliet. I know it's dangerous to assume anything, but Juliet has to be another candidate to join these six girls in the Peepers room. Why else would they abduct her? In theory, they should all be in the same building. After we locate them, we may find clues that lead us deeper into the bowels of CVS, but we can worry about that later."

"Fair enough. Listen, I know it's Saturday," said Phillip. "But is there any chance that someone is working in the computer room at Hacienda tax department?"

"Highly unlikely; what do you need?"

"CVS receives bills from property companies from all over the world. If there were such a property company in Spain sending any invoices to a Gibraltar business, they would have to apply for an exemption from value-added tax. There will be a record of that exemption at Hacienda. It could point us to the company managing the property near Torrox."

"I'd never of thought of that. I'll make some inquiries. Don't hold your breath, though; we'll probably have to wait until Monday."

"Annoying, but I understand. Anything else?"

"May I call, if needed?"

"Of course."

Phillip returned to his study to work on the latest translations for Nuestra España.

Just after eight o'clock, he showered, changed into a black shirt and beige pants, and then drove off to Torre del Mar, where he parked on the seafront and walked the few hundred meters to the restaurant.

Antonio, the headwaiter, welcomed him with his usual enthusiasm and took him to a table at the quieter end of the terrace.

Amanda arrived moments later.

Phillip's heart skipped a beat.

Amanda wore a short plain black sheath that clung to her curves. A small pair of diamond stud earrings added an alluring sparkle to her elfin face framed by her luxuriant silky hair. Her full lips carried a trace of lipstick, but she wore no other makeup and didn't need any.

Phillip stood up, placed a hand on each of her shoulders, and kissed both of her cheeks in the traditional Spanish fashion.

"You look lovely," he whispered in her ear.

She smiled demurely, sat in the chair being held for her by Antonio, and said, "Thank you. You too."

They were both a little shy at first, but after a glass of cava and ordering their food, the conversation began to flow.

Then Antonio arrived with a plate of fresh oysters, placed them in the center of the table, and left them to it.

They looked at each other, then the oysters, and helped themselves to one each. They added a squeeze of lemon, a dash of Tabasco, raised the shell before their mouths, and swallowed.

They nodded their satisfaction to each other, and picked up another oyster.

"I saw some of your action videos," said Phillip before gulping down another.

"Been checking up on me, have you?" said Amanda cheekily, before lifting another mollusk to her mouth, and swallowing it.

Phillip watched her spellbound; it was one of the most sensual things he'd ever seen.

He shook his head before replying, "I thought that

as this is a business meal, I should do some research."

"You like to study your subjects beforehand, huh?"

Phillip looked straight into her eyes, smiled warmly, and replied, "I generally find that good preparation leads to a more agreeable outcome. Don't you?"

Amanda grinned and cocked her head to one side.

"Seriously, though," Phillip continued, "your videos are, what you Americans say, awesome, yet the number of viewings on CNN is pathetic. Do they still have the copyright?"

"Not now; our deal was for three years only. As from about two months ago, I can show them wherever I want. It's what prompted me to think about my own website."

Over the main course of fresh turbot baked in sea salt accompanied by roasted green peppers, Phillip outlined what he and Richard had discussed earlier. "We'd be happy to make a website to do what you want and sell the footage to major broadcasters, but we would also like for Nuestra España to use your videos to animate some of our historical articles. The action videos, however, will appeal hugely to our major advertisers. They are so good they could become viral; it would mean some serious income. Is that what you are looking for?"

Amanda thought about Phillip's proposals. Then made a few false starts to reply before actually saying, "Er, wow, this really is a business discussion, and you really have prepared for it. All I can say now is that my initial reaction is positive, and I promise to think seriously about what you have offered, but this is a big step for me, so I'm not going to rush into anything. Do you mind?"

"No, of course not. I, sorry, Richard and I just

wanted to establish that we are most appreciative of your talents and would like to find a way to work with you. This offer is one solution."

"Listen it's fantastic and is just what I'm seeking, but my reticence to commit has nothing to do with that. I'm used to working on my own. It would be a new experience for me to work with a team although the thought of it is most appealing. First, I need to acquaint myself with you better. Not with your editing talents, which, having looked at your work on the Nuestra España site, are far better than mine, but you as a person. We'll be traveling long journeys around Spain together sharing ideas and arguing about them. Such a close working relationship means that I need to respect and trust you. For example, I feel that you are sorting your emotions about Juliet. But they stem from your ex-wife about whom I know very little. I'm aware that it's a painful subject, but can you tell me about her?"

"Of course, if it helps you to understand me better," said Phillip, taking a deep breath thinking where he should begin. "She was er. Valentina was Russian, and I loved her at first sight more than the world itself.

"But it wasn't enough. I failed miserably to match the strength of my feelings with the attention she was seeking. I was concentrating on my business and missed her I-want-a-family signals because I was blinded by the next deal. Eventually, she gave up on me and had an affair with a Russian neighbor.

"Nobody was more shocked than I when she served me with divorce papers. I agreed to it, thinking that if I paid some serious attention to her needs, then I could rescue her feelings for me. Because, no matter how much her affair hurt me, I carried on loving her. I even agreed to the most onerous divorce payment to stay in her good books and keep her in my life. Nevertheless, she took everything, sold up, and went back to Moscow with her new man. When my parents died, they left me their villa here in Nerja; it was just the trigger I needed. At last, I could escape the rat race and her nagging memory. Yet, as soon as I arrived here, I met Juliet, who could either have been my ex or our daughter. My behavior toward her has always been exemplary, but internally, I didn't know whether to ask her out or take her to the toy shop. The pilgrimage helped me put that in perspective by mentally burying Valentina once and for all. Something I should have done years before.

"Then Rosemary told me that Juliet's mother was a real bitch. She was a successful model but a useless parent. To compensate, Juliet had a wonderful relationship with her father, who sadly died when she was thirteen. They often came to Nerja and swam together on El Salon beach. While I don't resemble her dad, my height and ways reminded her of him. It was why she trusted me and liked having me around. It made her feel safe, especially with all these men coming onto her. I tell you Amanda, when Rosemary told me that, it shamed me. I felt like a dirty pervert. I was disgusted with myself. How dare I lust after such a loving and trusting young girl who just wanted a father figure around to turn to when she was feeling low or had a problem to share? Thankfully, my mind cleared instantly. I still love her dearly, but now I'm happy to play the role Juliet always thought I was playing. Shit, Amanda, I don't know what you've done to me, but that's the first time I've actually put these thoughts into words. Thank you."

Amanda stretched out her hand, took his, and squeezed firmly.

"Don't be so hard on yourself. You're just a man, you keep your brains between your legs just like the rest of you, and Juliet is a very sexy girl. Irrespective of your confused good intentions toward her, you can't ignore natural instincts. Any man would have felt the same, but at least you acted with decorum. Most couldn't have resisted her charms, and you should be proud of that."

Her phone rang. "I'm sorry—this might be important," she announced while groveling in her black purse, extracting her phone and looking at it blankly.

She shrugged and said. "It's an e-mail from an unknown address, but it says for Amanda." She clicked again. Phillip saw a video appear.

Amanda looked at it lovingly.

Phillip had never seen such a powerful expression of tenderness.

Amanda put her hand to her mouth.

Tears rolled down her cheeks.

25

Amanda turned the phone around and showed Phillip the video.

It was a tiny baby gurgling among some cushions, wearing a pretty pink outfit and lace booties.

"It's...it's..." she couldn't speak. Her shoulders shuddered as she tried to control her distress.

Phillip was concerned. He stood up, went round to console her, and put his arm around her shoulder. She turned, buried her head in his chest, and wept quietly.

Phillip was oblivious to the nearby diners' looks of sympathy.

He waved Antonio away as he approached.

"It's all right. I'm fine," sniffed Amanda. "Really. It's just I never expected to see her again."

Phillip returned to his chair and nodded to Antonio that all was in order.

The diners resumed their conversations.

The waiters continued their tasks.

"I'm sure you remember that I was on a Guardia

Civil coast-guard cutter last Monday," began Amanda. "Whilst I was on board, I helped a migrant give birth to this baby. The mother died later in hospital without ever seeing her child. The nurse who took the baby from me christened her Amanda. It was only meant to be a temporary name until they found adoptive parents. This video is from them. They decided to keep the name.

"It's such a surprise. I never thought that they would want to use my name let alone contact me. I'm sorry; I'm being silly, but it was the first time I've ever held a newborn baby and it drew out my repressed maternal instincts. I understand how your ex-wife felt about not having children."

"Well, aren't we both happy puppies tonight?" said Phillip quietly.

Amanda smiled wanly and then asked, "Do you regret not having children with your ex?"

"More than anything," answered Phillip, his eyes watering.

Amanda nodded, seemingly happy with the reply. She reached out, grabbed his hand, and said, "This is not quite how I imagined our evening."

"Me neither, but I don't regret a single moment."

"Knowing the baby has a proper home has lifted a heavy weight from my shoulders," said Amanda, squeezing his hand tightly and dabbing her eyes with a serviette.

"I'm happy for you, and I thought we'd be discussing BBC ladies."

Amanda looked shocked, "Shit. I forgot to tell you," she said.

Phillip's phone rang.

"Sorry, Amanda, but I set my phone so only Prado

can call me. Do you mind?"

"Of course not, I'll pop to the restroom."

Phillip watched her every move as she walked away from him into the hubbub of the restaurant interior.

"Dígame, Leon?" he answered.

"I seem to be making a habit of disturbing you at your leisure; I'm sorry, but such is the nature of police work."

"I understand."

"Amanda's not upset then?"

"Not because of your call; anyway, she's popped to the ladies. Has there been a development?"

"Not really, I just wanted to let you know that I now have all the lists and am cross-referencing them with my two new eager beavers. We'll be working all night, but I hope that by morning we will have some properties to visit. Any chance of a photo of Duffy?"

"Rosemary's still working on it. She'll send it as soon as it arrives."

"OK, then enjoy the rest of your evening, and we'll talk tomorrow. Buenos noches."

Amanda returned, looking refreshed and happier.

"Whew, I'm full," she said. "And a little tipsy."

"Stroll along the promenade? We could have coffee at one of the Chiringuito's?"

"Great idea, and I insist on going halves with this bill."

"Can't argue with you. Age of equality and all that."

Phillip caught the waiter's eye and made a writing gesture with his hand. The waiter nodded and tapped in the instruction to his digital order device. Minutes later Antonio appeared with the check in a leather wallet and offered them a liqueur on the house, which they declined. They paid half each of the ninety-odd euros in cash plus a 10 percent tip and headed out toward the promenade.

As they moved away from the glow of the orange streetlights, the heavens appeared. A mass of stars twinkling in a black sky, in the center of which glowed a full moon. It carved a mesmerizing phosphorescent path over the sea from the horizon to the beach.

They strolled next to each other, arms touching and exchanging tender glances.

Philip spotted several empty tables at a new Chiringuito. They walked over a canvas mat that protected their shoes from the sand, sat down next to each other, and ordered coffee.

At first, they were content to soak up the romantic atmosphere. They could hear the surf lapping gently against the shore. Couples strolled arm in arm, paddling in the wavelets, occasionally pausing to hug or embrace. Spanish guitar music thrummed at an acceptable volume.

"Can't find this in London," said Phillip, breaking the comfortable silence as the waiter served them.

"Coffee's not bad either," said Amanda, replacing her cup back down on the saucer. "Do you want to hear about the BBC offer?"

"Tell me."

"Basically, they want to use some of my videos to illustrate a documentary on Spanish culture."

"Would that prevent us from using them? You know just in case we do agree to work with each other?"

"Not at all. They are paying a price for non-exclusive use."

"Then that sounds like a great deal. When?"

"They will pay me in advance next week. The program won't be broadcast for another six months though."

"We could use this to launch your potential partnership with us."

"Mmm, food for thought. What did Prado have to say?"

"Nothing really, just a progress report. They should have the lists ready by the morning. Then we can start knocking on doors. We urgently need a photo of Duffy from Rosemary, but that's taking time."

"I'm sorry about the histrionics earlier."

"Amanda, it was an extremely frank exchange, and I feel privileged that you were comfortable enough with me to let rip. If you're up to it, I'd like to learn more about you?"

"I guess that's only fair," Amanda confirmed gathering her thoughts. "Well, as you probably gathered, I care enormously about children and dream of being in a loving relationship with a man who would happily contribute equally to a parental experience."

"As I said yesterday, what is it with Malaga men?"

"It's not them. I'm the problem. I've tried the online dating stuff but found that descriptions never matched expectations. I don't mind divorced, so long as there are no kids involved as I refuse to be a stepmother or deal with ex-wives. Men have to accept me as an equal in all departments, and that includes the finances and chores. Hard to find in Spain, where macho still rules and mothers do everything, especially for their sons. What about you? Do you have a girlfriend?"

"No, despite my sister's best intentions. She keeps

inviting Spanish girls to dinner to tempt me, but I can't adjust to the large family thing. As Prado said, all those celebrations to attend, pretending that you enjoy the same old faces, jokes, and conversations. I prefer my own space."

"Me too but not all the time."

"Go with that."

They finished their coffee. Phillip insisted on paying the grand sum of three euros. He then escorted Amanda back to her car.

As they kissed each other's cheeks, Amanda whispered, "Thank you for a perfect evening. I can't wait to do it again."

"Me too," he whispered back, heart thumping.

She clambered into her Prius, slipped off her heels, and drove away, waving her hand out of the window. Phillip watched her go, relishing the memory of her lips on his face and her soft breath in his ear.

He walked to his car and drove home, feeling more content than he had for years.

26

Prado hadn't called or left a message overnight, so Phillip opted for his usual swim. The roads were quiet for Sunday morning, and the underground car park only half-full. Manolo was laying out tables at Don Comer, ready for another day's alfresco business. Phillip waved as he passed by in the direction of Playa El Salon, but Manolo was too preoccupied to notice.

As he bobbed up and down, clinging to his usual yellow buoy, he pondered on the previous evening with Amanda. Half of him didn't care if she decided to work with him and Richard or not. It would be brilliant if she did, as then he'd have an excuse to see her regularly. If she didn't, he'd find another way to be with her. Tonight, he'd call to see how she was and bring her up to date with the search for Juliet.

After his swim, Phillip found himself still too early to meet Richard for coffee, so he went for a walk on the freshly high-pressure jet-sprayed Balcon. There weren't many people around, the cigarette butts and chewing gum had disappeared temporarily, and a few street cleaners in their high-visibility lime-green and blue uniforms were busy emptying the bins.

He stopped by the statue of King Alfonso, exchanged good mornings with some keen photographers snapping away at the diminutive monarch, and looked down at the stunningly beautiful Calahonda beach.

It was less than half the size of El Salon and completely protected by limestone cliffs. Perched on top was a hotel next to an apartment block. Underneath was Puerta del Mar, Nerja's finest fresh-fish restaurant.

Short rows of sun beds and reed-covered parasols filled the central beach area. A small cottage was built into the foot of the cliff. The ruins of a dilapidated, disused bar nestled at the bottom of the steps, awaiting a council decision on its future. In the meantime, it had become a haven for the homeless, addicted, and feral cats.

A colorful fishing vessel was undulating gently as it rounded the headland of the Balcon. Two stocky, deeply tanned fishermen—presumably father and son by their close resemblances—sat abreast on the central thwart, rowing effortlessly and harmoniously and thrusting their tiny craft steadily toward the shore. In the prow, a grubby white plastic container brimming with seawater was balanced precariously on top of damp folded nets. It was teeming with sardines, sea bass, and king prawns, some still wriggling.

A squabble of aggressive seagulls swooped daringly close to the container, risking all for a fishy breakfast.

The son stood and swung an oar at the airborne marauders in a futile attempt to protect the meager fruits of their long night's labor. Needless to say, he missed, caused the boat to rock alarmingly and almost tottered overboard. At the last minute, the father grabbed a leg and steadied him. The lad sat down clumsily, cursing. Dad laughed out loud and shook his head at such youthful folly before both resumed their metronomic rhythm.

Approaching the shore, the two heaved vigorously in unison. The tiny craft surged forward and landed with a jolt in the shallows. The men shipped oars, stowed them in the bilges, scrambled out, and hauled their boat further up onto the deserted beach.

A black kitten prowled impatiently near the water's edge, keenly monitoring the men's progress through luminous green eyes. It tiptoed back, meowing plaintively when the wavelets splashed too close. The father twisted the head off a sardine and hurled it onto the nearby rocks. The young cat scampered frenetically after it, pounced, successfully pinned it to the rock, and began nibbling tentatively.

Phillip laughed at the young cat's antics and headed for Don Comer. It wasn't busy at all, and he sat down at an empty regulars' table. Manolo served him personally and hovered, assumedly curious about the investigation.

"If you have time, sit down a minute," said Phillip.

"I don't, but how's it going?"

"I believe we might be making some progress. We haven't found Juliet yet, but we have some real possibilities that might take us nearer to her."

"Great. I'll fetch your breakfast."

Phillip's phone rang.

It was Didi.

"WhatsApp is cheaper," answered Phillip.

"I can't be bothered with all that," replied Didi. "A phone's a phone."

"How's Bremen?"

"Cold and gray as usual, but I'm not calling to complain about the weather. I've just seen your news blog about Juliet's abduction. Have you found her yet?"

"No. Why?"

"I may have been the last person to see her. She was watching the San Isidro dressage with a young man. They seemed enamored, you know, holding hands and kissing stuff."

"What time was this?"

"Not long after the dressage started, so just after three o'clock."

"Did you recognize the man?"

"I'm sure I've seen him before in an estate agent's office. We were looking in the window at a penthouse they had just sold. It was the sort of property we're after in town. Anyway, I saw him sitting at a sales desk inside showing brochures to an elderly couple."

"Which agency, Didi?"

"The one on Calle San Miguel; I think they're Scandinavian. I have a photo of Juliet and him if that helps?"

"Are you able to send it to me?"

"I can only cope with e-mail. Will that do?"

"Of course. Thanks, Didi."

"Auf wiedersehen."

Manolo delivered Phillip's breakfast just as the e-mail arrived from Didi.

"Do you know this young, good-looking blond

guy with Juliet?" asked Phillip, holding the photo up for Manolo.

"Yeh. He's been here a few times—drinks a large latte," said Manolo. "Seemed to be hitting it off with Juliet. His first name is Lars, but that's all I know about him."

"Thanks." Phillip picked up his mollete and took a bite.

While he was chewing, he brought up the Swedish agency website mentioned by Didi, and browsed the contacts.

He found a photo of Lars Eriksson, a brief CV, and a mobile number.

He dialed it.

The call was forwarded to the estate agency. A guy called Steen answered.

"Lars quit on the eve of San Isidro," said Steen. "He wasn't doing well in Nerja, said he was going to try his luck in Marbella, nothing about a girlfriend though. Sorry, but I have no other number for him."

"Thanks," said Phillip. He ended the call then forwarded the photo of Lars and Juliet with an explanation to Prado.

Prado called him back fifteen minutes later.

"They seem a happy couple," opened Prado. "And Eriksson doesn't resemble any of our abductors. I've checked him out, and we have no records other than that he's self-employed and uses an address in Stella Maris down on Calle Antonio Ferrandiz Chanquete. I've sent a local Nerja cop to check it out."

"How's it going with the lists?" asked Phillip.

"We've finished cross-referencing and managed to reduce it down to some six hundred probables," he said. "These are properties that meet all the criteria;

that is, with late-night Internet usage, high-grade fiber-optic connection, town or busy-urbanization location, garage access to the house, and have building licenses for a substantial cellar. Our patrol car is on its way to begin searching, but I estimate they will need at least ten days to visit them all.

"We're also building a list of possibles, whereby they meet nearly all the criteria. I'm worried that we are relying too much on honest citizens building legal cellars. Twenty years ago, many just built the damn thing without permission. I propose to contact former builders to see if we can locate a few more, but as most of them went bankrupt during the crash, that won't be easy. Hold on; a colleague is just handing me a note."

Phillip heard a thud and paper rustling.

Then Prado saying in the background, "What the fuck is this?"

27

Juliet shivered and opened her eyes.

She reached for a bedsheet to cover herself but then recalled there wasn't one.

She was cold, and the long pink T-shirt they had given her did nothing to protect her from the chill of the air conditioning. It ran continually and had done ever since she'd first woken in this hospital-like room, however many days ago it must have been. She thought four, but it could have been five; without daylight it was impossible to be sure.

Her stomach grumbled.

She glanced at her food cage, but there was nothing in it.

She'd seen the cameras all over the place, so she knew that someone was watching, but the room must have been soundproofed because she could hear no external noises. Other than the quiet hum of the air conditioner, there was not a peep.

She'd read the printed notes placed in her food

cage.

A hand was all she could see, inserting them through a sliding door at the back of the cage. There were three different hands. One was massive, matted with blond hair and dirty fingernails, another male, which was slender, delicate, and exquisitely manicured. The third was dark skinned with chewed nails and chubby fingers, probably an African girl, thought Juliet.

The notes contained printed instructions. No touching. No talking. Food—only when you remove your T-shirt, meanwhile drink as often as you can.

At first, the others had shared their meals with her, but that soon came to a halt when nothing was served for hours and hours. Eventually, the others received a note saying they would only be fed if they were not sharing with Juliet.

She looked over at the others.

Lars was flat on his back. Angelika lay in a fetal position.

Both were naked and asleep.

What a mess I'm in, thought Juliet. As soon as Aunt Rosemary told me that my stepfather had been released early, I knew he would come for me. I may have destroyed him in the courtroom, but his parting words, swearing revenge, I will never forget. And that look in his eyes, so full of hate. He would find me wherever I was hiding. I had to disappear mysteriously and quick.

Lars assured me that his scheme was foolproof, although I still don't know why I believed him? I suppose I was grasping at straws. I should have told Phillip, but I didn't want to expose him to any danger.

Lars had these customers: Rikard Olsson and

Malcolm Crown. He said they were two gay guys who owned several properties in the countryside in and around Nerja. Lars had never met Rikard but had become friends with Malcolm, with whom he liaised to arrange rentals. Malcolm employed a couple of Syrian men who maintained the pools and gardens; their wives cleaned and changed the linen. The men would find a van, meet me near the dressage at San Isidro, pretend to abduct me, and take me to one of their isolated properties in the countryside between Frigiliana and Torrox. I'd be safe there for a week or two. That should be long enough. I was confident that Auntie would soon find a way to send my stepfather back to prison.

As arranged, I left Lars at the dressage and walked down the track to where the van would be parked. Yet as soon as I met my abductors, despite the fact that I couldn't see their faces, I could sense something wasn't right. I stood by their van and could feel the tension between them. They seemed more nervous than I was. Why I didn't scream and run then, I'll never understand.

They told me that I would have to change into some of my other clothes that they had collected from my apartment. I was cross; Lars didn't tell me they were going there, and I refused point-blank to strip in front of them.

Then I felt a prick on my upper arm, and one of them shoved me into the van.

The last thing I remember was banging my shin on the doorframe.

When I awoke, the first thing I noticed was that there was a girl on the fourth bed, the furthest from me. She beckoned me not to talk. "Talk means no food," she'd whispered in perfect English. "I am Angelika from Denmark. I've been here for about three weeks. Two men bundled me into a van on my way home from school. I assumed that I'd been kidnapped, but all this time here, and nothing has happened. They never say anything, so I don't know if my father has paid the ransom or not." With that she burst into tears.

I noticed how beautiful she was. Long blond hair like me, blue eyes, slender but curvy figure, but she was barely sixteen, perhaps younger.

It must have been the second time I surfaced when I saw Lars on the nearest bed to me. He was wide awake and looking straight at me nervously.

"Sorry," he mouthed. "I fucked up. I thought Malcolm was my friend. When I showed him your photo and told him about your stepfather problem, he was eager to help. Yet when I arrived at the villa as we planned later that evening and parked my car in the garage, I went into the kitchen and found no sign of you or him anywhere. I had no phone and didn't know if I should wait or go. Then I heard a car. I rushed outside, expecting Malcolm, but instead, there was this mean, ugly, massive, hirsute man. He plucked me from the ground like a toy doll and injected me with something. When I came round, I was here. Wherever that is?"

"What do they want from us?" whispered Juliet.

"What do you think?" said Lars.

"You mean?"

"Well, it's sure not naked Monopoly."

"Thanks for nothing, asshole," Juliet said, glaring at him viciously. "What a fool I've been to trust you?"

The food cages were opened.

The delicious aromas of fried chicken wafted through the room. Angelika and Lars rushed to grab theirs, stuffing it into their mouths by hand as fast as they could.

Juliet felt faint.

She desperately needed to eat. Her determination not to expose herself was fading progressively with each passing mealtime.

Her confusion was heightened further when a plate of the same food was placed in her cage, this time by the huge hairy hand. He then stuck a note in front of the food, leaning it against the metal bars of the cage door.

"T-shirt off now, and this is all yours," it stated.

Juliet was indecisive—her mind said no, but her stomach disagreed. She'd had practically no food since the second day.

"Eat, Juliet," whispered Lars. "You'll need your strength to find a way out of here."

Juliet stood by the cage, rocking back and forth.

Her stomach rumbled.

She reached down, took off her top, and stood there defiantly.

The massive hand extracted the note and unlocked the cage. The fingernails were disgusting.

She reached in and took out the plate.

The hand beckoned.

She wondered what he wanted.

"Give him your top," whispered Angelika.

She threw it in the cage and then slammed the door.

Juliet carried the plastic plate to the small table by the archway into the bathroom and joined the others. She picked up the chicken and nibbled at it delicately.

There were no knives and forks. It tasted divine.

She noticed Lars blatantly admiring her.

She judged that by the excessive squirming going on below the table that he was more than pleased to see her naked.

At that moment, given an appropriate weapon, she could quite happily have sliced off his offending appendage then killed him. However, at that moment, Lars wasn't Juliet's primary worry. Where was she? Who were these depraved monsters? What were they going to do with her? She imagined the worse yet somehow forced herself to eat some chicken but she couldn't prevent the tears from streaming down her cheeks.

"I don't know if this will comfort you, Juliet," whispered Angelika concerned at Juliet's distress. "But in all the time I have been here, nobody has touched me or asked me to do anything untoward. Also, I've been sitting naked for so long now—it feels normal. What I find worst of all is that it's so boring; there's no entertainment, nothing to do except listen to my thoughts and the fears that haunt me. My biggest concern is, how do I leave this dungeon? All I want is to feel the warmth of the sun, breathe fresh, clean air, and be with my family?"

They wept together, terrified for their immediate future.

28

Amanda hadn't slept a wink after her night out with Phillip. She'd tossed and turned as her head refused to stop churning over the emotional roller coaster of an evening. The video of little Amanda had been a lovely, unexpected surprise, but man, it had shredded her heartstrings.

In the morning, she planned to tap out an e-mail, thanking the baby's adoptive parents for keeping her in the loop and offering any help or support that they might need for her as she grew up.

The offer from Phillip to work with the Nuestra España team was perfect for her. It didn't interfere with the BBC thing and it would mean that she could concentrate more on her filming. Technically, Phillip was a far better editor than she could ever be. There would be less administration, she wouldn't have to worry about finding customers, she could earn substantially more money, and would not have to work so hard. However, the element of the deal that appealed to her most was that she could bounce her ideas off intelligent people who shared a common interest, and that would enhance her creative juices.

Also, she was extremely pleased that Phillip had really opened up to her, which, in her experience with men, was rare. She was beginning to bond with him and would feel perfectly safe traveling together. His feelings for Juliet were still a tad concerning. He had explained himself well, but did he really mean what he said? She believed so. As dawn approached, she mentally agreed to work with him and Richard.

But could she sleep?

No.

This case with Juliet worries me sick, she thought, as her mind whirled aimlessly around what they had learned so far. She struggled to summarize the evidence. An Englishman in Spain, abducting English-speaking girls to pose on a voyeur website. It seems an unlikely scenario, more like something from a movie plot. Real life can't be like that, can it? Is Prado guilty of assuming too much? Does Duffy really have Juliet? Was Juliet's naked photo enough stimulus to tempt Duffy to Spain, or is Juliet's abduction just a sideline? And why set up Peepers in Spain? Why not in his own country, where there are no language problems, and he understands how to work the system, and then he wouldn't need permission to travel abroad.

On the other hand, why not? In the United Kingdom, Duffy would have to report regularly to his probation officer. Assuming he's a registered sex offender, any neighborhood he moves to would know that and watch out for him. It would be impossible to set up a room and keep those girls prisoner without a suspicious neighbor reporting him. Whereas in Spain, nobody knows who he is, and he can move about without impunity. So perhaps Prado is right? Duffy does have Juliet.

If that's so, I wonder if Duffy cares that Juliet is Ferrier's daughter. Has he taken her for revenge against his former cellmate? Or, because she is a, beautiful, young female, and men like him only have one end game in mind for such delicate creatures. To exploit her sex appeal to make money. The persons behind the abduction had it well planned professionally from the outset. Amateurs would have left a trail a mile wide for the police to follow, otherwise why, after nearly four days since the abduction, is there still no sign of Juliet?

What if something like this happened to me? How would I feel imprisoned and abused at will? Could I mentally survive such inhuman treatment? Then there are the spectators. Millions of men, and it would be men, skulking illicitly in front of their computers, lusting after me, all for a few seconds of pleasure.

She shuddered.

How could I face myself afterward? I couldn't walk the streets, worrying that someone passing by had seen me on screen.

Don't be a daft woman. I wouldn't stand a chance to walk anywhere.

After Duffy has finished with me, what then? I couldn't be released—I knew too much. I couldn't be kept—I cost too much, and my novelty value would soon reach its sell-by date. There is only one possible outcome for Juliet.

Death.

When Duffy, or whoever, has done with her, she

will be killed and disposed of like a piece of unwanted trash where nobody will ever find her. How will Phillip handle that?

He may well have sorted his head about his confused feelings for Juliet. But to me, whether he loves Juliet as a father or a woman is irrelevant. Either way, her death will upset him, and I don't want him to suffer any more pain. He's been through enough over that girl for the last three years.

It's about time he had some peace.

"All right," she mumbled out loud. "Admit it. You want him for yourself."

The alarm went off.

Amanda reached for her phone and dictated a summary of her overnight thoughts about Juliet's case onto the WhatsApp group. It would give the guys some food for thought. She struggled out of bed and headed for the shower. Next week was Romeria El Rocio over near Sevilla. She was due to make the whole pilgrimage on a traditional gypsy horse-drawn caravan. She had to buy the right clothing and prepare her screenplay for the video.

29

Phillip sipped his coffee with his phone jammed to his ear, straining to hear what was going on at Prado's end.

There was only a faint mumbling in the background.

"Sorry to keep you waiting," said Prado after a few minutes. "My colleagues have been monitoring the Peepers website on Ferrier's laptop. The girls continue to sleep, talk, and eat. It's been about as interesting as watching paint dry until a few minutes ago when a pop-up window announced a forthcoming event. I'm forwarding a screenshot to you by e-mail. If I've translated the headline correctly, I promise you won't think much of it. Call me back when you've read the small print."

Phillip waited nervously, his mind running riot. It had to be something bad concerning Juliet; why else would Prado send it?

He imagined what possible kind of event could be

broadcast from such a dull setting. Naked knitting? He shook his head.

Then his phone beeped, announcing the message from Prado.

He opened up the attached image.

His heart leaped into his mouth.

It was far worse than his flippant musings.

It was a close-up of Juliet's face. She looked terrified.

The headline read,

Two Reluctant Virgins—One Night Only

Starring the Danish Siren—celebrating her sixteenth birthday—and the beautiful English rose.

On Monday at 2200 hours, CEST, two beautiful, pure, young, and tender virgins will be deflowered against their will. Member's viewing fee is US$1,200.

Warning: Adult entertainment, including scenes of sexual violence. Satisfaction not guaranteed. No refunds.

Gold members qualify for double Onanios, which can be spent in the Peepers' online adult store. This month's special offer is golden handcuffs, for an enhanced bondage experience.

Phillip's eyes filled with tears. He picked up a serviette from the dispenser and dabbed them away.

His anguish at Juliet's fate was worsened by the knowledge from Hassan that she was an actual virgin. Not because of the free choices she'd made as a woman on her path through life, but because of the mental damage her stepfather had imposed on her. This ordeal might not kill her physically, but it would finish her psychologically.

He could not let that happen.

He phoned Prado back.

"Was I right?" Prado asked.

"Regretfully, yes; it's devastating," answered Phillip and then explained in full what was about to happen to Juliet.

"That means we only have thirty-six hours to find her and prevent this depravity," said Prado.

"Is there any possible way we can increase the resources? One car with two officers just ain't going to cut it in time."

"I'll speak to el jefe and see what we can do," replied Prado. "Tell me again. What was the text saying about the Danish girl?"

"It's her sixteenth birthday."

"Inhuman bastards—I hope I can control my team when we do find them."

"Frankly, Inspector, I don't give a damn what your guys do to them. I just want to find Juliet and save her from these animals. Can you send me part of the list so I can help search for her?"

"Phillip, I understand how you feel, and in your position, I would want the same. However, I won't insult your intelligence by boring you with all the reasons why I cannot send the list to you. Other than to say that this is dangerous police work, I cannot risk a civilian in the front line."

"I would remind you that I am ex-military and can take care of myself. Also, many of the properties will be occupied by foreigners; they will need a friendly translator around to calm them down and ask for their permission to look in their cellar. Can't you deputize me or similar?"

"I see what you mean. I'll have to discuss that with el jefe also. Later."

Phillip's phone beeped again.

It was a message from Rosemary:
> *Photos of Duffy attached, along with fellow inmates and criminal records. There are a lot of images, so I'll send a few at a time. Good luck. R.*

Phillip opened the first image.

It was a full frontal of a man's head and shoulders holding a sign showing his prisoner details.

R. Duffy was the name.

Even though prison photos aren't in the least flattering, Duffy's appearance was worse than everyone's nightmare. Cropped blond hair. Ugly face with a mean-looking expression, blue but cold eyes, and a deep scar on the left cheek. He was huge, and although he looked as strong as a horse, he was obese with flaccid, bulbous jowls, shoulders as wide as a house, sticky out ears, and a crooked nose.

"Not the sort you would care to bump into on the way back from the pub," mumbled Phillip out loud. "Especially after what he did to Ferrier."

Wait—I've seen this guy, thought Phillip, racking his brain. Where? Come on, man.

Of course.

Didi's photo.

He flicked through his gallery and brought up the image of Juliet and Lars at San Isidro.

Standing directly behind—towering over them, wearing a black cordoba hat that was way too small for him—was Rick Duffy. He was staring at Lars with a lecherous grin.

Phillip paid up and drove home. He didn't tell Manolo about the latest developments but called Richard and updated him. He and Ingrid were on their way to Granada; they were having lunch with their advertising agent at the Parador Hotel in the Alhambra Palace.

Phillip booted up his computer and took a closer look at Duffy and his cellmates. What a motley crew? he thought. Just ordinary-looking guys except for Duffy. You could pass them on the street and not even notice them, but they were all sex offenders. Dirty, grubby, evil animals, and one or more of them were intent on using Juliet to satisfy their depraved urges and earn a shit load of cash.

After scrutinizing the rogues' gallery, he started reading their records.

Duffy had served eight years for abusing young boys at a private school near Leamington Spa, where he had worked as a janitor. Although it was his first offense, early release had been not been allowed due to his bad behavior in prison. Now, this was interesting, thought Phillip. Duffy's father was from Northern Ireland, but his mother was Swedish with the surname of Olsson. Duffy's first name wasn't Rick; it's Rikard.

It seems likely then that Duffy does have dual nationality, which would account for him slipping out of England unnoticed on a Swedish passport.

Previous cellmates of Duffy and Ferrier were also included. Phillip glanced quickly through them. One innocuous looking man caught his attention.

Malcolm Crown.

He was serving three years for minor offenses against young men. Crown, although born in the United Kingdom of British parents, was actually brought up in Marbella and attended one of the international schools. He was fluent in Spanish and had been employed as an IT consultant with a major computer company based in Warwick. He and Duffy had both been released on the same day thirteen months and twenty days previously. "That must be him," Phillip said out loud, "Crown is the other man Ferrier overheard talking with Duffy in the prison bathroom. He's IT competent, knows the language and his way around Malaga province while Duffy provides the muscle. This really increases the likelihood that the Axarquia Peepers franchise is their website. Is the one on Ferrier's laptop the only one or are there more?"

He packaged up the critical elements of this new information into a Word document, added his comments, and sent it off to Prado.

At least they knew whom they were looking for.

Now it was just a question of where.

30

"Come," said el jefe's voice faintly through the door after Prado's tentative knock.

Prado entered, sat down and updated his boss on the latest developments. When he'd finished, el jefe nodded and said, "Thanks, I'd like to see a photo of Duffy and Crown, but before we start on that I want to share with you my thoughts on the migrant detention center in Algeciras. I've been rooting around in the Ministry of the Interior in Madrid trying to find out who really pulls the strings on immigration. Not just for the detention center in Algeciras, but the other five centers around the country.

"I have to tell you that I'm being passed from pillar to post. No one person is claiming responsibility for making decisions on deportation or allowing migrants' asylum. This concerns me greatly.

"In my experience, when nobody in Government will talk to me, I suspect a cover-up. Something is rotten up in our Capital city.

"I'm having words with my counterparts in the other regions to learn if they are having similar problems, and will revert to you in due course."

"Thank you, Sir," answered Prado.

Prado's phone beeped; he glanced at it. It was a message from Phillip.

He indicated to the boss that he needed to read it.

The boss shrugged.

It was the photos of Duffy.

"Most timely," said Prado, showing el jefe.

"So that's Duffy. Ye gods, he resembles a monster from outer space," quipped el jefe. "What was it between Ferrier and Duffy?"

"Monster is a fair description, boss. Duffy is a convicted sex offender who shared a prison cell with Ferrier. Although Duffy is a British citizen his mother was Swedish. He may well have dual nationality under the name of Rikard Olsson.

"Ferrier made the mistake of bragging about his gorgeous stepdaughter and showed Duffy a photo. When Duffy raped him relentlessly, Ferrier reported him to the prison governor. This was why Duffy had to serve his full sentence. By way of a thank you, Duffy took the photo of Juliet, vowed to find her and involve her in his grubby videos. Naturally, Ferrier was incensed.

"Duffy was released much earlier than Ferrier some thirteen months ago on the same day as Crown. Crown is computer savvy and speaks fluent Spanish, having grown up in Marbella. Phillip suspects that's why they came to Spain to work together."

"Why the fuck couldn't they stay at home?" said el jefe, raising his voice.

"The Brits have clamped down on released sex offenders so hard that they can't fart without a copper on their tail. Regretfully, that policy only shifts the problem elsewhere—in this case, to the Costa del Sol. Did you know that Malaga Province has recently superseded Amsterdam as the hottest European adult-tourism destination?"

"Regretfully, I do. I expect the Dutch will be delighted. Window-shopping will grind to a halt, and they can concentrate on growing more tulips. Does this mean all their whores have sold up and bought a place in the sun?"

"Apparently not. Eastern European ladies of leisure have proven substantially cheaper and are happy to work without health care or pension contributions. When we add the illegal migrants arriving from Africa, Duffy and Co. have access to a steady stream of fresh attractions. It's an ideal supply chain to fuel their business model."

"That is gross. We have to stop this downward spiral, Leon. Soon, our daughters won't be safe on the streets. Trouble is our politicians aren't so morally inclined, they're too obsessed with the tax revenues. If we're to avoid their wrath, we must adhere to the letter of the law and be discreet as we close these places down. People such as Duffy and Crown need to learn that Andalucia is not a good place to run this kind of business, although I don't think that they are our biggest problem. Didn't you say that these CVS people in Gibraltar have a multibillion euro turnover?"

"According to their last year's accounts."

"I find it difficult to believe that a couple of seedy ex-cons from the UK arrived here only thirteen months ago and have built such a giant concern from La Axarquia. They sound to me more like bit players in something much bigger."

"I agree, and we should pass the file over to Interpol. However, for the moment, we need to keep control of this case here."

"Why? Our lives would be much easier if we handed it all over to them."

"Normally, you would be right, but as of a few minutes ago, we have a more pressing deadline in the case. Look at this recent publicity that popped up on Ferrier's laptop."

Prado flipped to the Peepers' invitation.

El jefe read it out loud in accent-free English, "Tomorrow night at twenty-two hundred hours, they will rape two virgins and broadcast it live on this website." He switched back to Spanish, shaking his head, "How degenerate can people be? Right, what evidence do we have that the activities shown on Peepers are based in La Axarquia?"

"Spanish furniture, Spanish milk on the dining table, and a plastic supermarket bag from Aldi in Torrox-Costa."

"And your lists define possible properties around the area where this could be taking place?"

"Yes, boss."

"Leon, we must do everything we can to prevent this event going ahead. I have no objection to consenting adults doing whatever horizontal preferences they may have in our licensed clubs, but this perversity goes beyond anything I've experienced. It must be stopped."

El jefe banged the table with his fist. Prado had never seen him so angry.

El jefe looked once again at the reluctant-virgin invitation, shaking his head.

"The English rose I understand is Juliet," he said quietly. "But who is this sixteen-year-old Danish girl?"

"I don't know," answered Prado.

"Wasn't your kidnapped girl Danish?"

"Of course. Angelika? Why didn't I spot that?"

"I understand why not Leon. Your failure with the case disturbed you. Your solution was to wash it completely from your mind."

"That's still no excuse, but now that you mention it, her sixteenth birthday should be about now."

"Nice of them to consider her age."

"I'll dig out Angelika's file."

"Perhaps you'll be lucky and kill two birds with one stone," mooted el jefe.

"If I did, would you reinstate me?"

"Is that what you want?"

"Not bloody likely. This job has the perfect pace for a grumpy old git, and I'm actually enjoying it."

"That's a relief because your successor is doing extremely well."

"Pleased to hear it."

"That's settled then. Lists at the ready?"

"They are, but there are way too many properties for the eager beavers and me to check on our own. It'll take us twenty-four days not hours."

"Can the translators help?"

"Phillip is desperate to—Juliet is a close friend—but I don't know about Amanda."

"Tell me about this search. How do you propose to inspect these cellars? You'll be relying on the goodwill of the owners to let you check the inside of their home."

"If we could request the local police to visit the listed properties on their patch, we might stand a chance of completing the lists by the deadline. They have the neighborhood knowledge and may even be acquainted with some of the owners. But that request will need to come from you, sir."

"How many towns and villages are we talking?"

"Thankfully, only the main areas. The fiber-optic cables needed for these broadcasts have only been installed there."

"Right, give me the list. I'll start now."

"Thank you, sir? Just one more thing. I'd like to send the list to Phillip. Many of the property owners are foreigners; some are owned by companies. The names might convey something to him."

"It's against protocol, but send it. We'll sign them both up later as consultants. That way we'll be covered for this and any future work; expenses only mind."

"I'll begin immediately. Will you let me know how cooperative the local police are being?"

"I will, now scoot," said el jefe, picking up his phone.

Prado went immediately down to the records office in the basement and submitted a request for the Angelika-kidnap file. The admin officer was an old hand and remembered the file and Prado's troubles. He gave Prado a strange look but handed it over, refraining from any sarcastic remarks.

Prado should have recalled every detail of the file's contents—he'd poured over them so often. But mentally, he really had left the case behind and was ready to study it afresh, calmly and objectively.

He went back up to his office, sat down, and opened up the file.

Angelika Jensen would indeed be sixteen years old tomorrow. She was the daughter of a wealthy Danish car-hire-company owner. They lived in a luxury penthouse in the eastern Malaga district of Pedregalejo. Angelika attended a private international school in Rincon de la Victoria. On April 28, at around 1800 hours, after she finished her Spanish-dance lesson at school, she'd disappeared. Since then nobody had seen or heard anything about her.

The distraught parents were at home when they received a typed ransom note with delivery instructions for the cash. It had been placed in their mailbox between eleven o'clock the same night and seven o'clock the following morning.

Prado had been called in just after eight o'clock and had gone directly to see them. Their apartment was in an enormous complex consisting of several buildings with many entrances and exits but with no cameras or guards. In that safe area of Malaga, they weren't necessary. All occupiers had their own key fob, but they were handed around to family members and tradesmen with no thought to security. Anybody could have entered at will.

The ransom note demanded €100,000 and warned of severe consequences for Angelika should the police be involved or the cash interfered with.

The father withdrew the money from his bank later that day. Prado, however, secretly had the notes marked by the bank with what he was assured was an undetectable liquid that enabled its location to be monitored remotely.

The drop instructions were simple. The cash was

to be placed in a knotted SuperSol shopping bag and left in the foyer of their branch in Avenida Principal del Candado at the busiest time of day, which was 1900 hours that evening. If the money were not there, their daughter would be gang-raped and then killed slowly and painfully. No negotiations would be permitted.

This was where Prado had made a false assumption. The one that had caused him so much anguish.

He was concerned that if the money was handed over in one drop, the criminals would take it and kill the girl anyway. He argued forcefully with the father to hold half the money back. The abductors would then need more contact to negotiate collection of the remainder, and that would give them a better chance of locating them.

The parents agreed. Happily, they thought it most sensible.

However, none had considered the extraordinary action taken by the kidnappers.

Prado arranged with the Supermarket for their security camera to be left on permanently.

It filmed the back of a small, slender man dressed as a tramp rummaging through the money bag in the supermarket foyer only seconds after Angelika's father had placed it there. The tramp departed almost immediately, leaving the bag and money behind intact.

There had been no further demands, no contact, and not a sign of Angelika or the tramp. Despite a massive media campaign, no additional clues were forthcoming.

Prado returned the cash to the parents, who were

naturally as distraught and mystified by the kidnappers' behavior as he was. The parents placed no blame on Prado or the police. But Prado couldn't live with his error. If he hadn't interfered, Angelika may well have been back home with her parents.

His actions had deprived them of a loving and beautiful daughter. Prado imagined how he would have felt if one of his sons had been taken.

It couldn't bear thinking about.

"The wonders of therapy," he announced to himself, shaking himself back to the present.

Prado looked through the ransom note once again.

The only comment that he could add, after his fresh appraisal, was that the Spanish language in the note was not quite how a Spaniard would write it. It was technically acceptable, but the word order was not perfect, and the style too personal. The kidnappers had used "tu" instead of the more formal "usted." Prado wondered what his translators would make of it.

He picked up his phone and called Phillip.

"Thanks for the Duffy photo—mean-looking son of a bitch?" said Prado.

"If we find him scary, imagine how Juliet will feel? How did it go with el jefe?"

"Surprisingly well. He's personally speaking with the chiefs of local police in all the areas involved, requesting that they drop everything and direct all their officers to the properties involved. I'm also going to send you the list and would appreciate your thoughts on any anomalies you may spot."

"Anomalies?"

"As you said, many of the properties are owned by foreigners or companies. The names might give you some cryptic clues."

"I hate crosswords, but I'll happily check out the lists. With regard to those properties owned by companies. Does your list include the names of directors and shareholders?"

"No, but you could search for them yourself; just pay a membership fee to one of the online directories. We'll refund it, of course."

Phillip absorbed this suggestion from Prado. It wasn't quite what he'd set his mind on, but he had to agree that using the local police was a much faster way to check the cellars than he and Prado's small team rushing frantically from property to property."

"I'll make a start," said Phillip.

"Perhaps Amanda could help?"

"I'll call her."

"Just one more thing. You'll never guess whose sixteenth birthday it is tomorrow?"

"Tell me."

"Angelika Jensen."

"Who is?"

"She was kidnapped nearly three weeks ago and has never been seen since."

"Kidnapped?"

Prado explained the story and admitted the emotional damage the case had done to him personally.

"I wondered how such a seasoned professional came to be stuck with us foreigners," quipped Phillip.

"I can also laugh now, but initially it was humiliating and depressing."

"I hope that Amanda and I have made a contribution toward your recovery?"

"Ha. I wouldn't go as far as that but perhaps a tiny

slice."

"But if the Danish girl, is Angelika? Won't that go some way to rescue your reputation?"

"I believe so. Listen, I'm going to send you Angelika's ransom note and would appreciate any comments about the language. I suspect that it was not written by a Spaniard. You and Amanda may be able to shed some new light on it."

"Send it over, hasta lluego."

Phillip called Amanda.

"Hi," she said. "Any news?"

Phillip explained.

"Sounds like you're getting closer," she said.

"True, but we're running out of time, and there's so much ground to cover, so many cellars to see. Look, I don't know how busy you are, but I could really do with you here to help me with some online searches. Many of the properties on Prado's list are owned by companies. We need to check the names of their directors and shareholders to see if Duffy, Crown or CVS are involved. Would you mind?"

"Be delighted. What's your address?"

"Casa Las Rocas on Camino Viejo de Malaga. Turn left at the letterboxes just before La Molineta on the Frigiliana Road up from the motorway. You can't miss it. There's a farm immediately before it called Los Conejos."

"Sounds like a long and tedious job. I'll bring a thermos and some sandwiches."

31

It's incredible what ordinary people keep in their cellars, thought Prado, as he departed yet another unsuccessful cellar inspection. He'd spent the afternoon and evening flitting from one local police team to another, hoping that he'd be in the right place at the right time when they discovered Juliet and Angelika.

One family occupying three separate consecutive villas in Torre del Mar had built their own fully equipped health club. Under one dwelling was a gym fitted with all the latest machines. Under another, a luxury spa with marble tiling, whirlpool, sauna, and swimming pool. Last but not least was a fantastic children's playground full of climbing frames, ball baths, and a full-size tennis table. They were all linked together by a series of brightly illuminated passageways.

Under a town house in Algarrobo was a discotheque with impressive soundproofing, lighting systems, and high-end acoustic installations accompanied by a full-size statue of the owner attired in his diamond-studded Elvis Presley gear. In Caleta de Velez was a substantial aquarium with a basking shark, squid, and many varieties of tropical fish. He lost count of workshops and photographic studios, one with racy prints of a voluptuous wife on the wall—not a pretty sight.

Two hundred cellars later, there was still no sign of Juliet, and it was nearing midnight. The officers were hungry, grumpy, knackered, and most householders had retired for the night. Prado called it a day.

Prado headed back to his lonely apartment in Malaga, reflecting on the day's lessons to try and find a way to speed things up.

They often had to return several times to some villas as the owners were out. Several cannabis plantations had been found, which had to be passed onto the Guardia Civil. It took the local officers away from their primary task.

Prado concluded that they might be quicker tomorrow, but estimated that by the deadline they would still be over two hundred properties short. They could only hope that Juliet was in the first batch or that Phillip could glean some more precise intelligence from his searches.

Prado pulled into the comisaría garage just before one o'clock. On the walk home, he called Phillip.

"We're making progress but not finding anything as yet," answered Phillip. "We've solved the riddle of the ransom note, though. We're both agreed that it was written by a mother-tongue English speaker with an excellent knowledge of Spanish. Someone like Crown for example. How was your day?"

Prado related his guide to Andalusian cellar activities.

"How many more to go?" asked Phillip.

"Too many. We'll be lucky to check half by the deadline."

"Any chance of more resources?"

"There aren't anymore. What we need is better intelligence. Let's hope your searches can find something, otherwise…"

"I know. It's going to be a long night. I'll wake you up if we find anything."

"I've been thinking. Perhaps Crown's parents might still be around in Marbella. They could have a property registered in their name."

"Mmm. Hadn't thought of that. Perhaps Duffy's mother is also around somewhere. Can we ask the Swedish Consul to confirm a dual nationality for Duffy and the whereabouts of his mother, Mrs. Olsson?"

"Too late now, but first thing, I'll be onto their consulate."

"OK, buenos noches, Leon."

"Buenos noches, Phillip."

32

The food cages opened consecutively. It was the smaller male hand this time delivering the usual breakfast items of orange juice, croissant, butter and marmalade, coffee thermos, and milk carton.

Inside Angelika's cage, the hand also placed a card.

"Look," she said, showing the others.

Happy Sixteenth Birthday was written on the front. Inside it read,

> *Tonight we are having a special party for you with some friends next door.*
> *Cake and gifts for everyone.*

"That means it's the twentieth of May," said Angelika, bursting into tears again. "I've been here for three weeks."

"My fifth day," said Juliet, trembling, knowing instinctively that the reason for her abduction and captivity here was about to be revealed sometime during the next twenty-four hours. She drank the juice but couldn't touch the croissant.

Lars said nothing.

When he'd finished his own breakfast, he indicated that he wanted Juliet's.

She nodded her consent.

She'd already worked out that whatever ordeal faced her tonight would be followed quickly by death. This was going to be her final day on earth. Food was the last thing on her mind.

Inside the larger room next door, the six girls had been treated to a bumper breakfast. The extra food usually heralded another special event.

They were used to this routine. Most weeks there was something going down that required their participation. Tonight there would be more ABBA music and a glass of wine with a gourmet dinner.

After breakfast, they gathered on the sofas, looking at the blank wall opposite the archway to the bathroom.

Meanwhile, in the Malaga comisaría, Prado's team watched as the Peepers webpage on Ferrier's laptop was replaced by a maintenance screen.

"Sorry," it read, "preparing for tonight's show. We'll return at 2130 hours for the buildup."

Next door to Juliet, the six girls watched as a screen descended from a slot in the ceiling.

Its quiet whirring came to a halt just as the white plasticized canvas touched the floor. The girls stopped talking and paid attention.

The presentation began.

The first image was of Juliet, Angelika, and Lars weeping round their breakfast table.

That was followed by text scrolling slowly down

the screen, outlining their instructions.

The last line read, "Confirm that you understand your duties by raising your hand."

They obeyed in unison.

The screen rolled back up into the ceiling.

The slot guard-flap slid back into place with an ominous click.

33

Amanda and Phillip weren't making any progress.

None of the property-owners' names on the probable or possible list matched any of their suspects, relatives, or Ferrier's cellmates. Many of the properties had names, not numbers, but nothing hinted at some hidden cryptic meaning linking it to their case.

For the properties owned by companies, each search was taking hours. Most properties were owned by a Spanish company, but many of those were owned by another international firm that they also had to search. Some of those databases were in languages they could not understand, such as Hungarian or Finnish. Others were owned by offshore companies, and they were impossible to penetrate deeper into the actual ownership.

The only names they did find were those of the local administrators. They would contact them in the morning.

It was tedious work, and they took to taking a walk around the garden every hour to sustain their concentration.

There was no sign of property owned by Crown or his parents, either today or when they must have been living in Marbella. Searches for Duffy or Olsson also yielded zilch.

Around three o'clock in the morning, they were exhausted and agreed to nap.

Phillip showed Amanda to the guest room.

She cleaned her teeth, washed her face, and collapsed without bothering to undress.

Four hours later, Phillip knocked on her door.

"Come," she mumbled.

"Breakfast is served Madam," he said placing a tray on the bedside table containing a glass of orange juice, some fruit salad and a yogurt.

Amanda struggled to a seating position, yawned and stretched.

"Thanks," she said. "I need to shower."

"Clean towels already there. I'll see you in the study."

Phillip was sitting at the computer when she joined him twenty minutes later.

"How's it going?" asked Amanda.

"I've e-mailed the inquiries to the company administrators and have reconvened the searches," he announced. "But, I'm worried that we're in danger of being too organized. If we carry on plodding through the properties in alphabetical order, it could take all day, and what if the actual one begins with Z? I propose that one of us works more randomly, while the other plows on alphabetically."

"OK, you start, and we'll swap over every hour or

so."

"Great. It might not improve results, but it should make us feel more motivated."

Prado called at eight o'clock.

Phillip put him on speakerphone.

"We've resumed searching properties," said Prado. "I'm currently in El Morche but I've just heard back from the Nerja police. They've been to Lars Eriksson's apartment at Stella Maris. It's a small rental unit where he lived alone.

"According to a neighbor, Lars hasn't been seen since San Isidro, neither has his red car. When the concierge let them in, they found all his things had been cleared out. However, there was a printed property-information sheet hidden on top of the wardrobe, which they sent me a photo of.

"It's for a rental villa between Frigiliana and Torrox. The contact details imply that Lars was renting it out under his own name, and not the Swedish agency with which he was working.

"There's a website link under Lars's telephone number, and an e-mail directing potential tenants to the Owners Abroad site. There they can see more photos, and make reservations online. Can you check Owners Abroad to see if Lars is renting out any other properties?"

"Will do," answered Phillip. "Sounds a bit fishy? Do you think Lars is part of Duffy and Crown's team?"

"Or he's been set up by them," suggested Prado. "We'll worry about that later. What I need now are the ownership details of this villa. I'm being dropped back at my car in Algarrobo then I'll drive up there and take a look.

"Meanwhile, with regard to checking with Hacienda for tax exemption certificates for sending money to Gibraltar. The Hacienda office opens at eight thirty; my officers are likely to receive a more rapid response than you, so they'll call them."

"Makes sense."

"Any news at your end?"

"So far nothing, but we're soldiering on."

"Can you look to see who owns this villa while I drive up there. I'll send you this map, however, I do realize that it might not provide enough information to identify it in the land registry. If not, let me know, and I'll pop up to the Ayuntamiento in Frigiliana."

When the villa map arrived from Prado, Phillip knew instantly that it would be a problem to locate it in the land registry. He needed a plot number or a more detailed address. He called the Frigiliana town hall, but they refused to give him the information over the phone. Prado would have to go there himself.

He texted Prado with the news.

Just after nine, Phillip and Amanda took a turn round the garden. The fresh air and warmth of the morning sun sharpened their concentration. Amanda stretched languidly and said. "Did you read my thoughts on what is likely to happen to Juliet, after they have finished with her?"

"Yes, but I'd rather not dwell on it."

"I understand, but in the event of a negative outcome, I'm worried how you might handle it."

Phillip reached out and rested his hand lightly on her shoulder.

"Thanks for your concern. I'll be sad, and it will take me some time to repair the damage, but I'll bounce back."

Amanda put her arms around him and hugged him hard.

Phillip hugged her back, his eyes watering.

"Come," he whispered in her ear. "We're in danger of turning all gushy again. Let's go and renew our searching. There must be some kind of clue buried among all these company names and shareholders.

They returned indoors, holding hands, and dived back into their task with a hardened resolve.

34

The name Torrox has evolved from the Arabic, Turrux, meaning tower. The small town is split into two parts. The original village, located some five kilometers inland from the coast, perches on top of the western ridge of a steep gorge overlooking the Torrox River.

The more recent part of town, known as Torrox-Costa, was developed in the early 1970s as a beach tourist destination and marketed intensely to Germans. Consequently, it has one of the largest German communities outside of Germany.

The tower blocks spread rapidly along the coast as far as El Morche. During the 1990s, the tower block builder moved inland about half a kilometer and built some nine hundred mixed properties in a rambling new urbanization called Torrox Park.

Original marketing materials referred to it as the German village by the sea, but when the Germans stopped buying after the euro was established, it changed to the English Garden. Today, owners come from all over Europe, but few Spaniards live there.

The history of the village follows the pattern of most of Andalucia. Phoenicians, Romans—there are many Roman remains of housing and a ceramic oven. Then came the Visigoths, followed by the Moors, who were finally overwhelmed by the Catholic monarchs by 1487.

During Roman times Torrox was famous for the production of *garum*—canned fish, which was exported to Rome. Silk production and hand painting dominated the fourteenth and fifteenth centuries along with nuts and sugarcane.

The assistant to Columbus on his voyage of discovery came from the village; his house is still in use.

Nowadays, Torrox is renowned for having the best climate in Europe, its rambling narrow streets of whitewashed houses and a comprehensive cultural program.

Prado parked outside the town hall and admired the artistic display of colorful umbrellas suspended from a lattice of cables. They provided shade to the bustling central square.

He strolled across to one of the many tapas bars and bought a *bocadillo* filled with *jamón serrano* and coffee to go. He chewed it on the way up to Frigiliana as he sped faster than he should around the dangerous hairpin bends on the pothole-riddled mountain road. His coffee stood firm in the cup holder, making a sloshing noise—thankfully, the tight-fitting lid did its job.

Prado found the villa two kilometers before Frigiliana and a short way down an unmade track. He parked outside the main entrance, a whitewashed archway closed by a white steel gate. He took his coffee with him, and rang the bell.

He waited a minute or so and tried again while finishing his drink.

There was nobody home. He returned his empty cup to the car, clambered onto its roof, and heaved himself over the high wall next to the arch. He sat astride it, planning his descent, and then eased himself down onto a green trash container and onto the ground.

He peered through the glazed kitchen door and tried the handle; it was locked. He smashed the glass with his elbow, reached through carefully avoiding the glass shards, unbolted the door, turned the handle, and pushed it open.

There were no signs of occupation. The fridge was turned off, ajar and empty. Prado assumed that he would, therefore, not be disturbed by current tenants returning unexpectedly. He scouted all the rooms quickly without noticing anything out of the ordinary and then checked the garage.

Inside was a chili-pepper-red Nissan Qashqai.

It was unlocked.

In the glove compartment, Prado found a phone and a laptop. Both batteries were flat. In the trunk were several suitcases. One of them was labeled Lars Eriksson.

Prado opened the cases and quickly established that they contained only clothing and personal items. Prado assumed that Lars must have been heading somewhere that wasn't Marbella, as he'd told his former boss. Had he come here to hook up with Juliet? Was this where they would stay hidden together while Ferrier was found and sent home? If so, it hadn't happened. There wasn't a sign of anyone, and the place was spotless as if it had been cleaned recently. Perhaps Duffy has taken Lars to wherever he had stashed Juliet. Maybe Lars is also due to participate in the event this evening?

Prado pondered over these options, trying to make sense of them, as he opened the french windows and went out onto the spacious terrace. At the far end, steps led down into a ten-meter swimming pool full of gleaming blue water. The garden was lovingly maintained. The view was of a beautiful inland valley dotted with olive and almond trees and a few isolated properties. Prado concluded that this was a perfect location for the Peepers' broadcasts, except that there was no cellar or fiber optics, and it wasn't on his probable or possible list.

Then he panicked as a thought flashed through his mind.

Are Peepers using satellite instead of fiber optics? Because if they are, the telephone service providers won't know their location, and our lists would be wrong. We could be wasting our time. Phillip would know.

Prado went back inside and locked the french windows behind him.

This place is fabulous and well cared for, thought Prado as he headed into the hallway. I wonder if Phillip has traced the owner yet.

He then went through all the rooms, looking in drawers and cupboards for any utility bills, rental contracts, and emergency contact numbers, but found nothing.

He let himself out the front door, closing it behind

him, went out through the gate in the low wall that fronted the villa, and headed back to his car.

He called for forensics to come and see what they could find at the villa and then sat in his car and thought about anything else he should look for.

There hadn't been a letterbox.

Back at the front door, he saw no sign of anything to receive post and then realized that as this was a rental villa, the owners would have mail sent directly to them. Otherwise, how might bills be paid? The village post office will have that address, he thought.

He returned to his car, drove into the more modern quarter of Frigiliana, parked on Avenida de Andalucia, and walked across the road to the post office.

It was open mornings only.

Prado cursed under his breath. Now, he would have to make a fuss to locate someone to answer his question. This was all biting into their deadline. It was already three thirty, and they had just over six hours to find Juliet.

He walked along the avenue, past Las Chinas hotel then El Boquetilla restaurant to the local police kiosk opposite the old Guardia Civil building. As he approached the circular booth, which was also the tourist information center, he glanced across at the former barracks. They were now a pharmacy and a bank. He wondered how many more cuts to law-and-order services the province could sustain before anarchy prevailed.

Thankfully, the local police knew the woman responsible for the post, called her, and arranged to meet Prado there.

Half an hour later, he had what he needed.

All mail to the villa was addressed to a property-management company called Inmobiliaria Rustical Andaluza SL. It was forwarded to Abogados Sanchez and Sanchez, a firm of lawyers based in Calle Larios, in Malaga center.

Prado called Phillip.

"We're not having much luck here," answered Phillip, "and I'm conscious that it's now after four o'clock. Anything back from Hacienda?"

"Not yet, but I have the name of the company that owns the villa and the firm of lawyers who administrate it. Make a note of the name Inmobiliaria Rustical Andaluza SL.

Take a look at the land registry for a complete list of properties owned by them. One of them has to be where they are holding Juliet.

"Also, Lars Eriksson's car is in the villa garage with his phone and laptop. I'm going back to the villa now to meet up with forensics, and then I'll bring his devices down to you. Perhaps you'll have something for me by then."

"Let's hope so. By the way," said Phillip, "Lars has two other properties advertised on Owners Abroad, but neither of them is on any of our lists nor matches any of our search criteria."

"Fine, so we can forget him for the moment. One more question. What if Peepers are using satellite to broadcast their signals?"

"They won't be. Satellite only streams up to thirty megabytes a second. For buffer-free streaming of TV quality images, they need five hundred, and that is only achievable using fiber optics."

"That's a relief; I was beginning to fear that our lists might all be wrong."

"No, the lists are good," said Phillip.

"Let's hope so; this case is becoming more stressful by the minute."

"OK. Later."

Amanda wheeled her chair around next to Phillip and watched carefully as he logged back into the Malaga property registry and typed in Inmobiliaria Rustical Andaluza SL.

Bingo.

They owned thirty-five properties scattered from Malaga to Nerja.

He printed out the list.

Then compared it to their probables.

There were six matches and four more among the possibles.

Phillip switched to the commercial register to check the ownership of the company.

Ignacio Mereno Sanchez was the administrator, and the other director and single shareholder was Sergio Mereno Sanchez. So the lawyers were both administrators and owners of all these properties, thought Phillip. I wonder if they are just frontmen or the masterminds behind CVS?

Phillip called Prado.

"Forensics will be another half an hour—any progress?" asked Prado.

"The Malaga lawyers are not only the administrators, but also the registered owners of that villa and thirty-four other properties scattered around the La Axarquia."

"Wow, then we'll need to raid their offices. However, if we do that now they may warn Duffy and Crown. We'll hold off that for now. E-mail me the list of all their properties, highlighting those that match our lists. I'll direct our search teams to those first. Instead of coming to you, as soon as forensics arrive. I'll join them."

Juliet's deadline was ticking away like a terrorist's bomb waiting to wreak havoc and death. Now that they had no more database searching to do, Phillip's nerves were running ragged. He hated not being able to do anything except worry about Juliet. His coffee consumption went through the roof.

Amanda worried about him.

An hour and forty minutes later, Prado called back.

"Hola, Leon," answered Phillip.

"We've searched all thirty-four properties," said Prado. "Juliet wasn't in any of them, but two villas outside Velez-Malaga have identical cellars as shown on Peepers."

"Fantastic—then we're on the right lines?"

"It would seem so. The voyeuristic offerings vary from Ferrier's laptop. It seems that CVS offers a wide range of tastes for discerning perverts. One cellar contains all pretty African boys speaking French. The other a mix of African boys and white girls speaking Spanish. Both villas also have a second room next door to the live-streaming room. We found four distressed underage Moroccan girls being starved into compliance in one villa. In the other were four young African mothers and their babies from Mali. Each person has a food cage, which is only unlocked when they comply with instructions, such as removing clothing. We've taken them all to the hospital in Velez-Malaga for a checkup."

"I hope they'll be OK. What will you do with them next?"

"The migrants will have to go to a detention center

and apply for asylum, and the remainder will depend on their circumstances, but our objective is to help them not punish them. They've been through enough."

"Have any of the boys or girls seen or heard of Juliet?"

"No, but I believe our other discovery at Baviera Golf will lead us to her."

"Other discovery?"

"A fingerprint match with those in the van and at her apartment," said Prado. "Phillip we've found Juliet's abductors."

35

Amanda scrutinized Phillip's face carefully as he listened to Prado on the speakerphone. She could see the tension tighten in his eyes as he heard about the abductors.

"We found them with their wives and children in a terraced house overlooking the fifth fairway," said Prado. "They speak little Spanish but can manage some English. Between the two, my officers established that they are from Syria. They came via Morocco over a year ago on a smuggler's boat but were picked up by the Guardia Civil cutter just off Algeciras. They were locked up in the detention center for about a week until two English-speaking foreigners came to collect them. One was a giant, ugly, blond man, and the other smaller and more elegant. They offered them a free home and a little money in return for maintaining their properties and any other business they wanted without asking any questions.

"Potentially, Phillip, what that implies is that staff at the detention center, my fellow Spanish civil servants, are selling migrants as cheap labor. No paperwork, no asylum application, and a quick reduction in outstanding case numbers. I'll be starting an inquiry into that later. Meanwhile, we need to encourage the Syrians to tell us where they delivered Juliet, and for that, I'm prepared to offer them a deal.

"If they identify those at the detention center who handed them over to Duffy and Crown, the police will do everything we can to facilitate their asylum application and make sure that they are protected. Their kids can then go to school, and eventually, they will receive Spanish citizenship with passports and official work permits."

"That's generous," commented Phillip.

"I can't guarantee anything. These decisions are out of my pay grade, but we've done it before, and we can do it again. The important thing for me, at this stage, is that I don't want to alarm them unduly by splitting the parents from the children. They've already been through enough trauma back home and on their journey here. Could you and Amanda meet me at the entrance to Baviera Golf, and we'll go talk to them together?"

Fifteen minutes later, Phillip pulled up at the entrance to Baviera Golf.

Prado was already there. They followed him a short distance up into the urbanization, parked, and went into a terraced house.

The Syrians were sitting around a kitchen table.

Their petrified expressions were painful to look at. They'd come so far to escape the horrors of war back home, only to find themselves in the clutches of the

Spanish police.

Phillip leaned against the kitchen worktop, feeling sorry for them, but they were his only route to Juliet.

Amanda stood next to him.

Prado was by the door.

An armed officer, with a holstered weapon, stood in the narrow hallway.

"Do they have passports?" said Prado.

Phillip tried in English.

"No," said the elder man. He could have been a Spaniard from his Mediterranean coloring, which is probably why they had survived unmolested to date. He was below average height, with unkempt black hair, bushy mustache, wild eyebrows, brown eyes, and a couple of days' stubble. He was dressed in jeans and a T-shirt as were his similar-looking friend and the wives. The four children, aged between four and eight, clung to their mothers' legs, weeping quietly not daring to look at the intruders.

"We'll talk about your paperwork and how you come to be here later," started Phillip. "At the moment we only have one question that needs answering and urgently. Five days ago you abducted a blond girl from the San Isidro Festival in Nerja. We need to know where you took her. If you cooperate, the Spanish authorities will do everything they can to organize passports, jobs, Spanish residency, and schools for your children."

The Syrians looked at one another hesitantly, unsure whether to believe this shaggy-haired Englishman. The women seemed hopeful; the men skeptical.

"Our employers threatened to kill us all if we tell you anything," said the elder haltingly, unsure of his words. "Your offer of papers etc sounds attractive, but frankly, we've heard all this before, and nothing ever materializes. Why should we believe you?"

"I can understand your cynicism," replied Phillip. "However, this time you are not dealing with corrupt officials but the criminal police. The downside of not being cooperative is that you will be arrested for abduction, aiding and abetting rape, and possibly murder. The consequences of that are not pleasant. You men will be sent to Spanish jail for many years, and your wives and children will be deported. You may never see one another again."

"I understand," said the elder. "We need to talk about this among ourselves in Arabic, so everyone is clear on our position."

"Fine; go ahead, but we remain here," said Phillip, glancing at his watch.

It was nine thirty.

Half an hour to go.

36

The food cages were opened by the African person.

A white silk robe was inserted into each accompanied by a typed note, which read, "A celebration dinner for Angelika's birthday will be served shortly in the next room. Put these robes on and stand by the door. When it opens, turn left and wait for further instructions."

Juliet trembled as she slipped into the robe.

Usually, she would have enjoyed the sensuous caress of the soft material, but she knew that this was the beginning of her journey to oblivion. However, with it on, she was no longer exposed to the relentless intrusion of the camera lens and that helped somehow.

All three stood by the door in their robes.

They hugged one another briefly.

The door slid open.

They walked through into the brightly lit corridor and turned as directed.

Another door slid open at the far end.

They walked one behind the other. Lars in front. Juliet bringing up the rear.

They entered an identical but larger room.

Juliet noticed the food cages to the left of the door.

Six girls of various ethnic backgrounds welcomed them with warm smiles and cheek kisses. They escorted them to the dining table at the opposite end of the room, where they were seated and served with a glass of champagne. The girls sang "Happy Birthday" to Angelika.

After the last line, the six girls turned to face the door.

A screen was lowered from the ceiling.

A video of the Swedish music group ABBA appeared, singing "Chiquitita" in Spanish. The volume was excessively loud and prevented anything other than rudimentary conversation.

The six girls served smoked salmon and caviar, but Juliet couldn't touch it. Lars pigged hers as well as his, stuffing the excellent tasting fish in his mouth with his fingers like a pig in a trough. Juliet frowned. Angelika picked at her salmon.

Then came a cold roast beef platter and cherry tomatoes with rocket leaves sprinkled with parmesan, black pepper, and olive oil. This was served with a glass of red wine.

Juliet was already feeling woozy from the champagne, but she happily drank the wine. Anything that might soften the blow of whatever was to come. She prayed that there would be no pain. Anything else she could probably cope with.

The music changed to another ABBA number.

"The Winner Takes It All."

Juliet watched the video of Agnetha singing and couldn't help but feel sad at the beautiful blond singer's pain as she wrestled with the highly charged emotional lyrics.

She drank another glass of red wine, much too quickly.

Her head spun; she felt nauseous.

The music changed to another Swedish group.

Europe.

The opening refrains of "The Final Countdown" registered somewhere distant in Juliet's head. Halfway through the music, the screen disappeared back up into the ceiling. The door slid open and closed quickly.

A giant man wearing a white plastic face mask and covered in an identical white silk robe entered and stood there motionless as the music pulsed.

The six girls moved sensuously toward Lars and began caressing him. They teased him out of his chair and over to the middle bed on one side of the room. They tempted him up onto the bed and encouraged him to turn onto his hands and knees, so he was kneeling down just on the end of the mattress. Then they held him by his arms and legs and tied him to the bed using leather straps that they pulled up from the metal bed frame under the mattress.

Then they started the same with Juliet and Angelika.

When the two realized what was going on, they screamed deafeningly and fought to prevent their restraint. But the six girls were well accustomed to their task.

Within seconds they too were kneeling just as Lars was.

The music neared the end.

The giant moved behind Lars and grabbed his sides.

The music cut out.

The room turned black.

Lars screamed.

Seconds later, the lights came on.

Two armed policemen stood by the door, weapons drawn. They indicated that nobody should move.

The giant had disappeared.

The only sign of his former presence was a broken facemask on the floor.

A noise came from the bathroom.

One policeman dashed in there weapon raised in front of him only to discover an opening in the wall over the bath.

"There's an escape hatch, he's gone," said the armed officer, coming back from the bathroom.

Phillip and Prado entered the room only to hear that the giant had escaped. Phillip sighed with relief when he saw Juliet alive. He dashed into the bathroom, spotted the opening, clambered into the bath, and through the hole in the wall onto some concrete steps. He sprinted upwards, through an open metal hatch in the lawn that brought him out at the far end of the garden. In the faint glow of a distant street lamp, he spotted Duffy, his white robes billowing as he waddled at an incredible speed toward a sleek black Porsche Cayenne parked on the street at the back of the house.

Phillip had parked behind it before joining Prado and his officers to force entry to the villa. He'd left Amanda in the passenger seat talking to Richard on her phone.

Duffy spotted her. Amanda was concentrating on her screen with her headphones on and didn't see him coming. Phillip shouted, but she didn't hear. Duffy yanked open the BMW door, and plucked Amanda out with one hand as if she was a rag doll. He lumbered to the Porsche, opened the rear door, heaved Amanda onto the back seat, and slammed the door. He squeezed into the front, and took off with a squeal of burning rubber.

Phillip ran to his car and followed.

The Porsche headed out of Torrox Park at phenomenal speed, Phillip several hundred meters behind. He could see Duffy reaching back to thump Amanda as she fought to open her door. She fell back out of sight. Duffy turned to concentrate on his driving as he raced over the bridge crossing the Torrox River and up toward Torrox Town.

Duffy was driving way too quickly for the dark and narrow road.

Somehow, he negotiated the speed humps and hairpin bends, drove through the town, and out onto the Competa Road, renowned for its dangerous curves bordering on almost vertical ravines.

Phillip lost sight of the Porsche. Duffy was leaving him behind, but the bright glow from the headlights of the big SUV remained in view. He wasn't that far ahead.

Phillip pressed his accelerator to the floor. The powerful BMW surged forward. He looked across a ravine and observed the back door of the Porsche swing open as it slowed almost to a stop for an exceptionally sharp hairpin.

Phillip had to concentrate on his driving, so saw nothing more. He pressed his foot to the floor and sped along a short straight. His lighter, more nimble vehicle was slowly gaining on the Porsche.

He was only a hundred meters behind. He slowed because he knew the road well, and there was a terrible hairpin coming imminently. The Porsche failed to notice in time, jammed on its brakes too late, and smashed through the crash bar and sailed out into the darkness, headlights illuminating the olive trees and grapevines as it descended into the valley.

Phillip stopped his car by the damaged railing and looked down just in time to see an enormous explosion some two hundred meters below.

He called Prado.

Prado told him to stay where he was and warn other drivers until a patrol car could reach him.

Phillip opened his trunk. Put on his high-visibility vest and placed his luminous warning triangles on both approaches to the crash site. He left his car locked with warning lights flashing and sprinted back down the hill toward Torrox.

Half a mile down, a car was stopped on the hairpin around where he'd seen the Porsche door open.

He ran as fast as he could.

A man was helping someone up from the grass verge into his passenger seat.

They were moaning.

It was Amanda.

She was bruised but OK.

They hugged. Amanda wept.

37

It was Thursday, May 23. Just over a week since Juliet's abduction.

As with all Phillip's invitations, Ingrid and Richard arrived bang on the hour for the two-o'clock grill luncheon at his villa. Richard handed over his entry fee of two bottles of Arzuaga Crianza, their favorite *vino tinto* from Ribera del Duero.

Rosemary Kitson, her husband Martin, and Juliet arrived marginally behind them. They brought Belgian chocolates.

Prado came next with a bottle of Malaga wine, followed by Manolo and Pepa with a plate of recently cut *jamón ibérico/pata negra* and sliced Manchego cheese.

Amanda was last. She limped slightly and had a bruised cheek but smiled happily as she handed over half a dozen chilled bottles of Reserva de la Familia by Juves y Camps, Spain's most prestigious cava.

Glenda, Jose, and Phillip's three nieces had been

there most of the morning, helping prepare.

Phillip loved cooking on the BBQ. His father had taught him the basics years ago. Since he'd been in Spain, he'd experimented further and developed his own recipes and spicy marinades.

In his kitchen, he simmered the ribs in water. When cooled, he marinated them in olive oil, crushed garlic, a touch of chili, molasses, and tomato paste. For the fish, he melted brown sugar with butter, added soy sauce, freshly grated ginger, dijon mustard, and olive oil. He smeared the mixture over the salmon fillets and left them in the fridge on dampened cedar planks while he cleaned his Weber charcoal grills. One was for fish, and the other for meat and vegetables. For him, gas barbecues were a no-no.

The wine flowed steadily, the conversation volume grew louder, the delicious grilled food devoured, and the kids released with an ice-cream each to run around the garden.

Leaving the adults sitting around the table and nibbling cheese.

Rosemary cleared her throat.

Everyone went quiet.

"I just wanted to say thanks to all of you for your contributions in rescuing Juliet," said Rosemary.

"Auntie, please, you don't," said Juliet.

"I know," interrupted Rosemary. "It's not every day that your niece is brought back to you from the clutches of the grim reaper. I know it was bad for you, Juliet, but it was pretty dreadful for us too, not knowing where you were and imagining the worst. Anyway, I propose a toast to say thanks."

"Salud," said everyone, clinking glasses.

"Inspector," said Amanda in Spanish. "I've been out of sorts since my sudden desire to be stunt woman of the year. Can you recap what happened in Torrox Park?"

"Of course. First, though, I want to thank Phillip and you for your input to this puzzling case. Without your language skills and insight, we would still be thrashing around Andalucia like headless chickens. Overall, I think we have evolved into an effective team. My boss is more than happy, and believe me, that is a rare condition with him. Phillip and I have been interviewing all those involved, and I believe that we have now reached the point where we understand what Crown and Duffy were up to and what Perez and his cohorts were doing with the migrants in Algeciras.

"The Syrians finally admitted to abducting Angelika on instructions from Crown. Crown explained what happened. One weekend, he and Duffy had hired a car from Angelika's father. They spotted Angelika working in his office at the airport and decided that she would be perfect for an event. They tracked her for a week and made their plans to take her. It was Crown dressed in a tramp's old coat who had checked the cash bag outside the supermarket, discovered that they'd been shortchanged, and left the cash where it was, assuming that it had been marked in some way. If he had taken the money then, this case would have been resolved weeks ago, and I'd still be running our serious crime squad. So in some ways, I'm glad he didn't, because what we are doing together is far less stressful for me.

"The Syrians had been a little vague in describing which property in Torrox Park they had delivered

Juliet to. It could have been one of two. Thankfully, the builder of Torrox Park confirmed that only one villa had a full cellar underneath so we were able to hit the right one straight off. Our team didn't bother knocking politely, just burst in through the front door, where we found Crown and a sour-faced African girl in the dining room operating the cameras and computers. She was the third girl who absconded from Algeciras and had been so grateful to be purchased by Duffy and Crown that she happily managed the household for them without any thought of escape.

"She dived under the table when we arrived, but the quick thinking Crown hit an emergency switch, which opened the bathroom escape panel in the cellar and turned off the lights. It took us but a few moments to persuade him to turn them back on again, and show us downstairs.

"When we entered the cellar, I assumed some sort of satanic ritual was taking place, what with those ghostly robes, the clinical decor, and the loud music. Then Phillip heard the officer mention a bathroom escape panel and hurtled after Duffy like a man possessed, before screeching off to do his Lewis Hamilton bit."

Everyone applauded.

Juliet came over with tears in her eyes, sat on Phillip's lap, and hugged him.

"Thank you," she said. "You saved my life."

"It was a combined effort," said Phillip meekly, stroking her hair. "But, you, young lady, what are your plans now?"

Juliet stood up and returned to her seat.

"I'm going back home to study law," she replied.

"I'll never forget you guys, though, and you'll be pleased to hear that, now my stepfather is dead, my inner demons are fading already, and my stolen life has begun its journey back to normal."

Amanda translated for Prado.

He nodded approvingly.

"What have you done with Crown?" asked Amanda.

"He's languishing in our guest quarters underneath the comisaría, pending the outcome of our inquiries in Algeciras," answered Prado. "He's not being particularly revealing.

"Whoever is in charge of CVS uses fear extremely effectively. No matter what consequences I throw at Crown, he tells me nothing, just shakes like a terrified rabbit.

"Despite Crown's lack of cooperation, our technical people have discovered hundreds of Peepers' websites all over the planet. Wherever there is a flood of illegal migrants, CVS are there to exploit them.

"From what I've gathered so far, criminals such as Crown and Duffy purchase a Peepers' concession from CVS, which includes an exclusive territory. In their case, La Axarquia. CVS then acquire properties in the area through Sanchez and Sanchez, their lawyers in Malaga. Most of the buildings are for legitimate rentals to launder their dirty money. However, when they come across one with a suitable cellar they offer it as a Peepers concession. The concessionaire is obliged to decorate the set to fit the CVS corporate design and then identify and acquire sex slaves locally. They either purchase them from traffickers such as Perez, or abduct those whom they like the looks of.

"What staggers me most is the scale of the business. The volume of properties purchased by the Sanchez brothers just in Spain alone on behalf of CVS is phenomenal. Worldwide their property empire must be incalculable. I'd give anything to identify this mastermind behind CVS but they could be anywhere. Tracing whoever it is will be a laborious investigation well beyond the reach of the Spanish police, so we're handing the case over to Interpol. They can deal with Gibraltar and our Hacienda tax department directly. Good luck to them."

"That's a shame," said Amanda. "It must be fascinating to work on such a massive case."

"Only if you're anally retentive," quipped Prado. "Its mostly laborious list analysis just like you and Phillip were doing on the property searches. Can you imagine doing that day in day out?"

"Not so fascinating then," replied Amanda. "What was happening at the Algeciras detention center?"

"That is a lot easier than the CVS investigation," informed Prado. "We've arrested Sergeant Perez and three senior civil servants from the Ministry of the Interior in Madrid. They've been charged with human trafficking and corruption and face up to twenty years each behind bars.

"They'd built an impressive operation. When new migrants were delivered from the coast guard, they filtered out the unsuitable ones and processed their asylum applications diligently. We uncovered a special room in the basement where they cleaned up the pretty ones, dressed them smartly, and filmed them. Perez uploaded the clips to a CVS website, where they were auctioned to the highest bidder. Crown and

Duffy bought the majority of their sex slaves through this network."

"Perez told me that most of the group on the boat I was on had absconded," said Amanda. "Was that the case?"

"When Perez used the word 'absconded,'" continued Prado, "it usually meant that he had sold the migrants to people such as Crown and Duffy. He conveniently justified their disappearance on the age of the building and its inadequate security. Apparently, he boldly requested funds from his bosses to upgrade the premises, but they ignored him. It was a brilliant ruse to divert attention from his trafficking activities. According to the highly detailed records he stored on his laptop, your particular group was sold to a farmer in Castilla La Mancha for two thousand euros per person. Plus an optional thousand each should the buyers want work permits and Spanish passports for them."

"That is despicable, " cried Amanda. "Effectively, stealing their lives for two grand each. Have you been to the farm?"

"No, but I have read the report from our colleagues in Valdepeñas. The farmer provides them with accommodation and food in return for free labor. If you consider that one legal worker would cost him at least fifteen thousand euros annually, the farmer is making substantial long-term savings on his labor costs. At first, I couldn't understand why the migrants all needed Spanish passports, but then I realized that farm workers were highly visible. Passersby can see them working in the fields. It wouldn't take long for someone in authority to notice that a farmer who previously employed wandering

Rumanians or light-skinned Moroccans suddenly had fields full of Africans. The Ministry of Labor would crack down on them and put them out of business.

"This is where the civil servants in the Ministry of the Interior earned their thousand euros, by making sure the farmer had legal paperwork for all his migrant workers. By the way, Perez had over two million euros in a Gibraltar bank account."

"How many of Duffy and Crown's sex slaves were migrants?" asked Richard.

"In all three of their cellars, it came to sixteen," informed Prado.

"Did they have Spanish passports?" asked Amanda.

"No Crown deemed official papers for them as unnecessary," answered Prado.

"What will happen to them?" inquired Amanda.

"They've been released on supervised bail and are being accommodated in a Torre del Mar hostel. We're providing them with counseling and Spanish lessons. In the meantime, we're rushing through their Spanish-citizenship papers. Eventually, they will all be released and should be able to find some kind of work. Hopefully, their torrid journeys here won't have been in vain."

"Can you trace previous migrants who were auctioned off?" asked Amanda.

"We found detailed records of transactions going back four years on Perez's laptop. Now we have to trace them, which won't be easy as they are spread all over Spain. We've handed everything over to the National Crime Squad in Madrid. It's way beyond our resources."

Amanda summarized for the English speakers.

"What did Lars have to say?" asked Juliet in

Spanish.

Prado smiled at her, acknowledging her linguistic effort, and then went on to answer her question.

"Lars explained that he was utterly taken in by Crown. I suspect that his judgment might have been somewhat clouded by the high commission they paid him for finding rental clients. Lars assumed that they were generous property magnates. In reality, Crown needed someone to be an acceptable independent front man for the rental side of their business. It was why they were most supportive when Lars asked to borrow a villa to hide himself and Juliet. They'd also bought him his car and paid for the rental of his apartment in Stella Maris.

"However, when Lars showed Crown a photo of his girlfriend, and it turned out to be Juliet, he and Duffy thought, why not. Both of them hated Ferrier because he'd reported Duffy to the prison governor for raping him. As a result, Duffy had to serve his full sentence. This had been a way to punish Ferrier. Crown was ecstatic when I told him that Ferrier was in Spain and had recently killed himself."

"I saw Duffy a year earlier at the café," said Manolo. "Why hadn't he taken Juliet then?"

"Duffy was desperate to, but Crown prevented him," answered Phillip. "Crown was adamant that taking Juliet for their own pleasure was too personal, and Nerja was too close to home. As Crown delicately put it, they did not shit on their own doorstep and were in business to make money, not sample the goods. But when Juliet fell inadvertently into their lap via Lars, it stirred their warped creative juices, and they came up with the reluctant-virgin show. For the first time, Crown let Duffy participate. Thankfully, we arrived in the nick of time."

Glenda served coffee.

Rosemary passed the Belgian chocolates around.

They chatted a while longer and watched the beginnings of another stunning sunset.

Then Ingrid and Richard said their thanks and farewells, which prompted a mass exodus.

Juliet was reluctant to leave. She clung to Phillip, weeping and thanking him repeatedly for saving her. Eventually, after more hugs, cheek kisses, and tears she departed holding her uncle's hand.

Phillip heaved a sigh of relief. He was sad to see her go but relieved that, finally, he was free from the daily torment of her pretty face and the ghost of Valentina.

Prado shook hands with everyone and departed, promising to keep them up to date with the ongoing investigations into CVS.

Glenda and Jose took their daughters home to bed.

Manolo and Pepa were the last to leave.

Phillip and Amanda stood together, arms touching, waving good-bye.

When the gate had closed, and the final set of car taillights disappeared into the darkness, they turned face-to-face and gazed lovingly into each other's eyes.

Then they wrapped their arms around each other and kissed deeply.

The Author

Paul S. Bradley, originally from London, England, lives in Nerja, situated on the Mediterranean coast of southern Spain.

He has traveled extensively throughout the Iberian Peninsula for over twenty-five years. His popular Spanish property guides, lifestyle magazines, and travelogues have been published in English, Spanish, and German.

Darkness in Malaga is the first volume of the Andalusian Mystery Series and his debut novel.

Made in the USA
Columbia, SC
05 March 2018